THE HORSEMEN'S SHADOW

THE SEPTEM CYCLE
BOOK 2

JOE NATHAN PAUL

LEGAL DISCLAIMER

EPIGRAPH

And behold—a white horse.
Its rider held a bow, was given a crown,
and rode out as a conqueror, bent on conquest.

Then came a second—a red horse.
Its rider was granted the power to take peace from the earth,
so that men would slay one another.
A great sword was placed in his hand.

I looked again and saw a black horse.
Its rider held a pair of scales—
measuring survival in grain and coin.
'Two pounds of wheat for a day's wages,
and six of barley...
but do not touch the oil and the wine.'

And then—I saw a pale horse.
Its rider was named Death,
and Hades followed close behind.
They were given power over a fourth of the earth—
to kill by sword, by famine, by plague...
and by the beasts of the earth.

(Revelation 6:1–8)

PROLOGUE

Power is an illusion—until you find yourself standing in its shadow.

It moves in silence, shifting the world long before you realise it has changed. Wars, economic crashes, revolutions—none of them happen by chance.

Every crisis serves a purpose. Every collapse is a step forward.

History is not written. It is engineered.

For centuries, the architects of power have dictated the course of civilisation. They decide who rises, who falls, who lives, and who is erased.

They do not govern from palaces or podiums. Their power is not granted. It is cultivated, concealed, and wielded without restraint.

Most people will never know their names.

Until now.

Because something has shifted—a fracture in the design, a single error threatens to unravel everything.

They have planned for every outcome. Every contingency. Every failure. Except this.

And when those who shape the world feel it slipping beyond their grasp, they do not hesitate.

They burn it all to the ground.

The signs are already here. The tipping point is close.

And by the time you see it, it will be too late.

Because the end of the world isn't coming.

It has already begun.

ONE

Dr. Nathaniel Voss was out of time.

The research station groaned beneath the storm's assault. Rain hammered the glass in a machine gun rhythm. Wind shrieked through fractured seams, rattling the walls with every gust.

A hurricane—engineered, not born. Not a freak of nature. A weapon. A message.

Nathaniel staggered to his desk, each step wrung from a body already failing. The first explosion had torn through the east wing, killing the lights, the backups, and any hope of escape; the second had sealed his fate.

They weren't just shutting him down. They were erasing him —off the grid, out of memory, gone from history.

His hands trembled as he shoved aside papers, field notes, weather models, and encrypted logs. Two years of tracking anomalies—hurricanes forming in dead-air zones, flash floods targeting infrastructure, droughts choking breadbaskets.

He hadn't just found a pattern. He'd uncovered a design.

He activated the secure terminal. His breath came ragged,

3

each inhale like a blade between his ribs. Sweat-slick fingers flew across the keys.

Recipient: d.ross@cryptmail.com
Attachment: FINAL-Proof.xdf
Status: Uploading…

The progress bar crawled. Too slow.

A crash echoed down the corridor—metal on metal. Then footsteps. Heavy. Measured. Close.

They'd found him faster than they should have.

Nathaniel ripped open a drawer. The pistol lay there. Cold. Ready.

He wasn't a soldier. But he wouldn't die on his knees.

78%.

A shadow slid across the frosted glass. The door handle turned.

He pulled the trigger.

Click.

Silence.

No recoil. No shot. The gun was dead—disabled.

The figure stepped through. Tactical gear. Suppressed weapon. No insignia. No hesitation.

Nathaniel met the assassin's gaze—and exhaled.

No time. No way out.

His eyes flicked to the screen.

Upload failed.

The shot was a whisper—two taps, quick and final. Precise. Unavoidable.

Voss collapsed over the keyboard, blood seeping into the keys.

The assassin tapped his earpiece. 'Target neutralised. No leaks.'

A voice replied, flat and calm. 'Good. Erase everything.'

Methodically, the killer wiped drives, smashed terminals, and set the charges.

By dawn, the station—and everything Voss had discovered— would be ash and silence.

But beneath the desk, something blinked.

A red light.

A backup transmitter.

Missed. Overlooked. Still alive.

It blinked once.

And in its final breath, *it reached another recipient.*

TWO

The world was burning. And they held the match.

Viktor Tarlen. Silas Vega. Jeremiah Solis. Julian Thorne.

Not elected. Not crowned. Not born into power.

They were drawn together by something older—a deeper pattern.

Not belief.

Gravity.

They moved like celestial bodies, pulled by inevitability.

They didn't rule from thrones or speak from podiums.

Their kingdoms were built on infrastructure, information, perception, and fear.

No one named them.

But history had.

The Horsemen.

* * *

Tarlen was force, veiled as strategy.

He shifted economies like fault lines under pressure—silent, inevitable, devastating. Governments fell in his wake, not because he demanded it, but because he allowed it.

He never sought attention.

Only impact.

To him, civilisation wasn't built on consensus. It was hammered into shape beneath the weight of sustained coercion.

He believed pressure could fracture anything—
bones, borders, and ideologies.

Tarlen didn't light matches.

He supplied the fuel. And the bullets.

Solis held the arteries of the modern age—
ports, pipelines, supply corridors, and black sites.

He didn't need an army.

He let scarcity run its course.

Power, he understood, wasn't measured in stockpiles.

It was measured in access.

Deny it long enough,
and the world would collapse on cue—
desperate, divided, already halfway broken.

He never raised his voice.

He never had to.

He kept a photo of his daughter and grandchildren,
tucked inside a hidden drawer.

Not for comfort.

For remembrance.

Thorne ruled perception.

Not with charisma, but saturation.

He built the filters.

Focused the lens.

Taught the world what to see.

Truth wasn't something you destroyed.

It was something you **drowned** beneath signal, spin, and silence.

He didn't need to lie.

He only needed to flood the system until no one could remember what had been real.

Most never saw him coming.

Most never saw him at all.

And Vega—

Whilst the others engineered collapse, he was planning what came next.

To the world, Silas Vega was the messianic mind behind Stellarion, promising salvation through science, climate control, and orbital cities.

But he wasn't saving humanity.

He was curating it.

He had seen the pattern—not in data, but in inheritance. The cycle was not forecast. It was remembered. It echoed through forgotten manuscripts and unexplained signals.

The convergence was coming.

The exact sequence that had turned Mars to dust.

He knew it not through science alone, but through memory.

An inheritance.

Older than Earth.

The others didn't know.

They couldn't.

They believed they were shaping the future.

Vega alone understood: *they were repeating the past.*

* * *

They sat now in a compound carved into the side of a mountain.

Storm winds clawed at the glass.

Rain lashed the walls like static.

Inside, a curved projection wall spilled light across the room, displaying global indices, energy grids, orbital telemetry, and timelines that blinked red.

The countdown was no longer theoretical.

It had started.

'Currency fractures in twelve sectors,'

Tarlen said, raising his glass. Brazil and Turkey won't last the quarter. Europe's grid is buckling. Just as expected.'

'Supply thresholds are slipping,'

Solis added. Port lockouts in Africa. Diesel panic in the Midwest. Give it another month—then they'll beg.'

Vega didn't speak.

His eyes were fixed on a spiral of planetary vectors—orbital alignments blinking with rhythmic precision.

Not fear.

Recognition.

They had estimated five years.

Maybe they still had that.

Maybe not.

Thorne rotated in his chair, tapping the console.

'Riots in Jakarta. Protests in Madrid. Conspiracy spikes across the West.'

He smiled faintly.

'Eyes exactly where we want them—looking away.'

'People don't want the truth,' he said.

'They want coherence.'

'Then give them fire,' Tarlen muttered.

'No,' Thorne replied.

'Give them noise to distract from the fire.'

* * *

Outside, the storm stitched lightning across the sky.

Inside, the data danced like omens.

To Tarlen, it was a campaign.

To Solis, a calculation.

To Thorne, a performance.

To Vega—a warning.

They thought they were steering collapse.

They didn't realise they were fulfilling it.

Vega had never told them the whole truth.

Their alliance. Their emergence. Even their names were echoes.

Echoes of a world already lost.

Earth wasn't falling apart.

It was repeating.

Phase Zero had begun.

The world didn't know it yet.

Soon—it would.

THREE

The Vatican Library's inner sanctum was a vault within a vault, where time bent under the weight of secrets.

Dim light flickered across polished marble, casting long shadows between sealed chambers. The air was dense with the scent of ink, parchment, and slow decay. History didn't sleep here. It watched.

Few ever crossed its threshold. Fewer still left with what was secured inside.

Among relics exiled from daylight, one manuscript had consumed Jeremiah Solis for years. It was not a prophecy. It was a pattern.

Visions of the Stars.

Entombed beneath Vatican stone for centuries, it had defied time and dogma. A document so precise it should not have existed—detailing a cycle of celestial alignments that triggered collapse, convergence, and rebirth.

It didn't foretell the end.

It charted its return.

Its pages, bound in weathered calfskin, formed a labyrinth of biblical iconography and astronomical precision. The Four

Horsemen rode through its illustrations, each entwined with planetary glyphs and strange equations. Between the symbols were fragments—references to the Seven Seals, not as divine judgements, but as planetary alignments influencing gravitational fields, solar harmonics, and resonance thresholds.

One image showed four planets spiralling inward, each crowned by an ornate rider's helm. Their designs were alien, brutal, and carved with a purpose lost to time.

For decades, Hendrik Vega had kept it buried. His influence within the Church was absolute—his access unchallenged, his silence unbroken.

'This knowledge is not yours to share, Silas,' he once told his son. 'Some truths are anchors. Some are weapons. And some are both.'

But to Solis, it was neither relic nor warning.

It was a blueprint.

The manuscript didn't speak of fate.

It spoke of recurrence.

The Four had risen before, under different stars, bearing different names. The symbols weren't metaphors. They were instruction.

The Horsemen weren't chosen.

They were encoded.

'The scribes buried the truth in scripture,' Solis once whispered. 'The Seals were never signs from God. They were planetary events—markers of collapse.'

He had already identified two of them: Venus aligned with Conquest, and Mars with War.

The others—Saturn and Jupiter—remained elusive, their alignments scattered across cycles lost to time.

Tonight, at last, he was closer than he had ever been.

* * *

In the silence of the vault, Father Ludovico's hands trembled as he entered the access code. A hiss escaped the pressure seal. The case opened with a whisper, revealing the manuscript—unfaded, untouched by time.

A man of faith might have wept at the sight.

Ludovico saw only failure.

For decades, he had watched over the manuscript, sworn to protect it.

Not out of reverence, but out of necessity.

If its knowledge spread—if the cycle was understood—it would shatter the illusion of order.

Nations would fracture.

Religion would falter.

Fear would ignite.

He had told himself that duty outweighed temptation.

Then Solis came—soft-voiced and surgical, promising anonymity, protection, and wealth far beyond the reach of Rome.

He prayed for forgiveness.

The silence was answer enough.

* * *

In Geneva, Solis studied the images.

Encrypted photos lit the walls of his penthouse—a digital mosaic of scripture, symbols, and sin.

Each image had cost a fortune. Every frame, a betrayal.

His fingers moved across the screen, tracing ancient ink with quiet reverence. He paused on one passage, letting the Latin form on his lips:

'Quando pulvis deglutit flumina et aer fit ignis, magna exodus incipit.'

When the dust swallows the rivers and the air turns to fire, the great exodus begins.

He had assumed it was a metaphor. Now he wasn't so sure.

He flipped to the next page. Another line, more ominous than the last, ran through the manuscript like a warning:

'Cum Mars incendit caelum et Saturnus aperit portas, signacula frangentur et equites descendent.'

When Mars ignites the heavens and Saturn opens the gate, the Seals shall break and the Riders shall descend.

It was a cycle. A cosmic code. A planetary countdown dressed as scripture.

He turned to the final image. The words were sharper now:

'Clavis numquam destinata est regibus. Nec diis qui se servatores vocant. Filii amissi stellas vindicabunt, sed Terra eos vindicabit primum.'

The key was never meant for kings. Nor for gods who call themselves saviours. The lost sons will claim the stars. But the Earth will claim them first.

He exhaled.

This wasn't religion. It wasn't science.

It was a reckoning.

And he wasn't ready.

He leaned back, pressure tightening across his chest. Some glyphs still defied translation—composites of mathematics, obsolete dialects, and something older. Something that felt remembered.

Despite all his resources, Solis knew: the manuscript was beyond him.

And he was no longer the only one chasing it.

Vega had buried it for decades, but cracks were forming. Tarlen had begun asking questions. And Thorne, as always, watched from the shadows.

The images weren't enough.

He needed the original.

And he needed help.

His gaze drifted to a photo beneath the glow of his tablet. Sofia, laughing. Holding little Gabriel. The boy's curls were wild in the summer light, unaware of the machinery built beneath his name.

He had built Nexa for them.

For their safety. Their legacy.

But they had walked away.

Sofia had seen Nexa for what it truly was:

an invisible cage.

A controlled burn disguised as progress.

She hadn't shouted. Hadn't cried.

She had just looked at him.

With disappointment.

She changed her name to Castellano—

a name with roots.

With integrity.

Things he had sacrificed for power and position.

And now, she was gone.

But the pattern remained.

The alignments were real.

The clock was still ticking.

What if Vega was right?

What if there was nothing left to save?

Solis pushed the doubt aside.

He couldn't afford it. Not now.

He turned back to the screen.

Somewhere in those lines—

in the cold dance of planets and prophecy—was an answer.

He would find it before the cycle ended.

For that, he needed an expert.

And the Smithsonian had her.

FOUR

The first thing Adam Hayes remembered was the smell of the sea. Salt thick in the air. Waves erasing his footprints faster than he could make them. It was 1977—the Queen's Silver Jubilee. He was seven, chasing seagulls along a windswept English beach while Union Jacks snapped and cracked in the distance. The water crashed endlessly, pulling the shore back into itself, wiping away every trace.

That memory was the last remnant of a childhood untouched by violence.

By age ten, the laughter had vanished. The beach gave way to a war zone. His mother's bipolar disorder turned the home into a battlefield. The kitchen. The hallway. The garden. All held scars—physical and invisible.

When the rage came, it came without warning. Her hands in his hair, yanking him to the sink. Ice-cold water blasted his face. Nose flooded, lungs panicking. She didn't stop. Not until he went limp. Only then did she release him, breathless and shaking, knuckles white against the porcelain basin.

He didn't learn defiance. He learned precision.

Endure. Observe. Anticipate. Survive.

And somewhere between the bruises and the silences, he found the way out.

In the attic, beneath mould-stained boxes and forgotten memories, he found an old electronics kit. A maze of wires and dusty manuals. It started as a distraction. Became obsession. Escape through circuitry. He didn't yet know it, but he was already learning how systems broke—and how to bend them.

By twelve, he was rebuilding radios, and by thirteen, he was designing his own circuits. At fifteen, he hacked the school's primitive network during a detention. Left no trace. Not even a whisper.

Teachers called him gifted. His classmates called him something else.

'Geek.'

'Freak.'

'Knobhead.'

He didn't care. He was lean—faster than he looked. The playground was just another battlefield. Pain, he understood. Tactics, he mastered.

When a group of older boys cornered him behind the science block, fists clenched and teeth bared, he didn't brace.

He calculated.

They swung. He stepped in. Disrupted balance. Used angles. Impact. Collapse.

It wasn't just a fight. It was geometry. Momentum. Pattern.

The same rules applied, whether in a hallway, a hard drive, or a battlefield. Every system had a flaw. Every rhythm could be broken.

It wasn't long before someone noticed. Not a teacher. Not a friend.

A man in a tailored coat, shoes too clean for a stormy day. Watching from a distance. Making notes. Noticing things others missed.

By seventeen, Adam Hayes would be gone, pulled into something larger.

He enlisted straight out of school—quiet, focused, already a weapon forged in silence.

Basic training sharpened what life had already carved: endurance, discipline, and compartmentalisation.

By nineteen, he was marked for selection. Not for brute strength, but for his mind. For how he saw the field as a system. Not chaos. Just code.

The boy with circuits and bruises would become the man who broke codes, bent systems, and never ran from storms.

But all that would come later.

For now, the sea was gone. The water was cold. And survival was the only language he spoke.

Rescue was a myth. *Escape was a plan.*

FIVE

The SAS selection process was brutal. Relentless. Only a handful made it through.

The first phase was designed to break men—sort the wheat from the chaff. Endless marches across the Brecon Beacons, every step dragging through sodden mud, boots heavy, blisters raw and bleeding.

Food was scarce. Dry rations crumbled to dust in the mouth.

The cold wasn't just discomfort—it was a weapon. It seeped into bones, gnawed at focus, and turned every breath into labour. Sleep became a myth. The wind howled through the hills, slicing through thin layers and freezing from the inside out.

Sometimes, they were blindfolded and dumped in the wilderness, left with nothing but instinct and memory to find their way back.

Adam didn't just survive. He thrived.

The instructors noticed it early—his stamina, tactical mind, and ability to think under pressure rather than react. Where others hesitated in the dark, Adam moved forward. There was no other option, no obstacle too great.

Pain was nothing new. He'd learned to endure it long before he even understood the word.

His mother's rage was unpredictable. His father's silence was worse. Adam was eight when he realised the truth: no one was coming to save him.

The house was a battlefield. He adapted.

He learned to keep quiet. To take a hit without flinching. When the bruises were fresh, his father would stare past him like he wasn't even there.

That truth settled deep: no one would fight for him.

So he made a promise—he would never be powerless again.

That defiance made him perfect for what came next.

In combat simulations, he was relentless—his mind always two steps ahead. Calculating, scanning for weakness.

Where others saw obstacles, Adam saw design.

A line of razor wire? A kill zone.

An abandoned rifle in a trench? Bait for the desperate.

He read opponents like battlefield maps—tracing movements before they were made. No hesitation. No second-guessing.

Survival wasn't about strength. It was about being the last one standing.

He learned to fight. Learned to kill. But survival always came first.

His first kill came easily. Too easily. A twist. A burst of blood. Silence.

No hesitation. No emotion—until afterwards.

The face never left him.

Killing wasn't just a skill. It was a residue—a weight.

Then came Belize.

Jungle drills under full load, the heat like wet cement pressing against his lungs.

The instructors whispered his name now. Not in fear. In respect.

Others broke. Adam didn't.

He could go longer without food. Endure more pain. Sleep less. Move farther.

Nothing the SAS threw at him rivalled what he'd already survived.

By the time deployment orders arrived, the weak had already left.

On paper, his first mission wasn't extraordinary—a hostage rescue in Northern Africa.

But it would shape everything that followed.

It was there he met Tony.

Loud, magnetic, brashly confident—Tony was everything Adam wasn't. They clashed immediately. Tony moved on instinct and impulse—fists before plans. Adam studied, calculated, and adjusted. But under fire, differences didn't matter.

The op went sideways fast. Under moonlight, they breached the compound expecting light resistance. Instead, they walked into an ambush.

The walls inside were tagged with strange symbols—circles intersected by vertical strokes, etched deep in ash and soot. Tony waved them off as local superstition. But Adam paused. Something about them gnawed at him, like a pattern he'd seen before but couldn't place.

Gunfire tore the silence. Bullets kicked up sand. Shadows surged from alleyways.

Tony went in first, controlled bursts, two down before they fired back. Adam flanked, every round precise, each movement calculated.

Then came the explosion.

A rocket-propelled grenade slammed into the convoy's lead vehicle. The blast flipped the Land Rover, cutting off their escape. Smoke and sand swallowed the night. Radios spat static.

No signal. No backup. They were cut off.

Adam hit the ground beside the wreckage, heart hammering.

Their comms unit was wrecked—shattered circuits, scorched housing—but not beyond repair.

Tony crouched beside him, slapped a fresh mag into his rifle.

'Well, we're proper fucked now.'

Adam's eyes locked onto the twisted comms box.

'Cover me,' he said.

Tony didn't hesitate. He swung out, laying down suppressing fire as Adam moved in. Fingers tore into the damaged tech. He stripped wires, rerouted power, and bypassed blown circuitry. Bullets hissed overhead.

Tony barked over the chaos.

'Any time now would be fucking great!'

Adam's hands moved faster. Then—static. A flicker of signal. He latched onto an enemy frequency and tapped out a distress call in tight Morse.

Minutes later, cavalry arrived.

Gunships roared in. Ordnance lit the night. The battle ended in minutes.

Tony dropped onto a rock, exhaling hard. He looked at Adam for a long moment, then offered him a flask.

'That,' he said, 'was bloody close.'

That night, a bond was forged—one built on fire and silence. It would be tested, tempered, and reforged again through the years.

They operated across the world's harshest fronts—from Middle Eastern deserts to Belfast alleyways.

Adam was the quiet strategist, decoding enemy chatter, intercepting signals, always watching. Tony was the spark, the kinetic force, the glue that held the chaos together.

Together, they embodied the creed they'd earned.

Who Dares Wins.

SIX
2025

Twenty years ago, Dave Ross was just another CIA analyst, buried in classified reports and drowning in the inertia of bureaucracy. He hadn't set out to see what others missed. He hadn't planned on becoming the man who couldn't look away.

But obsession doesn't ask for permission.

It started with something small—an anomaly in satellite data, a climate variance no one could explain. Then came another. And another. Before long, the puzzle consumed him. And obsessions come with a cost.

He paid with sleepless nights, a crumbling marriage, and a body beginning to betray him. He had uncovered a black budget operation that didn't officially exist—and knew too much to forget.

* * *

WASHINGTON, D.C. - 2002

Dave wasn't a field agent. He wasn't chasing targets through alleyways or breaking into compounds. He was a pattern-hunter, connecting dots buried in metadata and intelligence summaries. His battlefield was data.

Then he ran into Adam Hayes.

A chance meeting, overlapping contacts, drinks at Old Ebbitt Grill. Two men from different corners of the machine—both disillusioned, both circling the same truths.

Dave had been watching a cluster of names—contractors, power brokers, shadow figures who never appeared on official manifests yet always surfaced near global crises.

'Ever hear of a group that doesn't exist?'

He'd muttered, more out of irritation than belief.

Adam had smirked. 'Plenty.'

Dave shrugged. 'Vega. Solis. Tarlen. Thorne. *The Horsemen*.'

The names meant little to Adam. But one stuck. A whisper in a jungle op. A name over an encrypted line. It came and went like static. That night, it was just noise. But years later, it would start to echo.

* * *

LONDON - 2002

A liaison post. A new start, or so Dave believed. But the ghosts followed.

Simon Arkwright was the spark. A ghost in the machine, slipping into systems no one could touch—Nexa, SphereNet, Stellarion. Not for money. Not even ideology. Just because locked doors begged to be opened.

Washington wanted him silenced. London wanted him controlled. Dave wanted to know what he had found.

Arkwright hacked a cache buried so deep it was never meant to be found. But he hadn't unlocked it—just glimpsed it. Patterns emerged. Not just noise—design. Something Dave had seen before.

A dataset. Beyond decryption. The best minds stalled on it. A key to something no one dared open—its fragments whispered of planetary harmonics, predictive collapse, and memory-encoded architecture.

There were references—buried deep—equations written in a language physics didn't recognise. Phrases like 'resonant intelligence' and 'Helion anomaly.' Fragments. Noise. But they hadn't been random.

That discovery made Arkwright a liability. If he fell into U.S. custody, he wouldn't be interrogated. He'd be erased.

Dave understood the game. So did MI6.

Adam and Dave were given one instruction: disappear him. Not officially. Quietly.

The operation was surgical. One day, Arkwright awaited extradition. The next, he was gone.

He wasn't free. He was hidden. Contained. Not to protect him, but to keep him close. MI6 hoped one day he would break the code.

He never did.

He remained in a safehouse—a prisoner of knowledge no one could unlock. The fact that he remained alive proved one thing:

Whatever he found had the power to burn the world down.

That decision—Dave's decision—cost him everything.

No orders disobeyed. No official backlash. Just silence. Clearance revoked. Trust evaporated. Slowly, systematically, the machine erased him.

He became radioactive.

Lisa had tried. She fought to hold him in the present, to remind him there was more than data and secrets.

'You're not here, Dave.'

'I'm doing this for us. For the world.'

'No. You're doing it for you.'

She was right.

He should've stood up. Should've fought for her. But he stayed, staring at the cursor, convinced one more connection would make it worth it.

By the time he looked up, she was already gone.

The sound of her suitcase wheels on hardwood was louder than any alarm he'd ever triggered.

Then the tremors began.

First, a flicker. Then a twitch. By the third dropped mug, he stopped lying to himself. The diagnosis confirmed what he already knew.

Parkinson's.

Not a death sentence—but a slow erosion. The worst part wasn't pain or even fear. It was vulnerability. For a man who had survived on his sharpness, the betrayal of his own body was intolerable.

He worked anyway. Clumsier fingers, slower keys. The meds dulled his mind, but the fire still burned.

He hadn't just uncovered the truth.

He had enabled it.

There had been one moment—just one—when he could've let it all go. Let Arkwright vanish. Let the file stay buried.

But he didn't.

And maybe that was when the world started to end.

The systems he trusted—his marriage, his agency, his body —had all broken down. Not in explosions, but in tremors. Quiet failures. Irreversible shifts no one wanted to name.

Now he scrolled through declassified logs. A name surfaced —Adam Hayes.

Buried in a report. Central America. An intercepted transmission.

Then it hit him:

Horsemen will not be compromised.

The jungle. The op. The name Adam couldn't place.

This hadn't started recently.

It had started long before.

Dave exhaled. Rubbing at the ache in his temple. A tremor in his hand.

The past wasn't buried. It was waiting.

If Adam had heard the signal once, he might still be willing to help. That's if the world hadn't swallowed him whole.

There wasn't much time left.

Dave had already paid the price—marriage, clearance, health. But if the world let the Horsemen define the truth, then what the hell had it all been for?

Maybe it wasn't too late.

Maybe Adam still remembered what they were fighting for.

SEVEN

LATE 1990S

Belize, near the Guatemalan border—Forgotten by maps. Remembered by predators.

The jungle was alive—a breathing, pulsing thing. Insects droned in an endless, buzzing chorus. A howler monkey's cry rolled through the jungle like distant thunder.

Sweat pooled under Adam's gear, his body tense as he scanned the tangled foliage. Something felt off.

Beside him, Tony hunched over a battered radio scavenged from a cartel outpost they had raided hours earlier. His fingers adjusted the cracked dial, and the dim glow of a flickering lantern illuminated his face.

'I'm getting something,' Tony muttered.

Adam crouched beside him.

'Cartel traffic?'

'No. This is different.'

Tony's usual cocky demeanour slipped, replaced by something sharper; focus, maybe even unease.

The transmission was garbled, layers of encryption distorting the message, but fragments still bled through. Adam heard them, too. The radio crackled, spitting out bursts of static before the words came through.

'Directive confirmed—expansion phase initiated.'

'Final timeline is secure.'

'Horsemen will not be compromised.'

Adam blinked. 'Horsemen?'

He glanced at Tony, who was already looking back. No smirk, no flippant remark. Just listening. Processing.

Tony exhaled, shaking his head.

'Fantastic. Bible-thumpers with machine guns. Exactly what we need.' Adam dryly said,

'At least cartels have a business model. These bastards sound like they offer blood sacrifices at shareholder meetings.'

He frowned. The voice on the radio hadn't just delivered orders. It had preached to them like doctrine.

'Doesn't sit right. Cartels don't talk about expansion phases.'

Tony hesitated. His cocky grin twitched at the edges, but it didn't land.

'Doesn't sound like your average smuggling op, does it?'

Adam replayed the words in his head. The way they'd said the name Horsemen, reverent, absolute, like a reference to the gods.

This wasn't about drugs. This wasn't about weapons. This was something else, and Adam suspected he wouldn't like finding out what it was.

Tony adjusted the frequency, trying to lock in a clearer signal. The radio crackled violently, then went dead.

'Shit,' Tony cursed. 'They cut the line.'

Adam's instincts flared. 'Not just the line.'

He gestured toward the undergrowth.

'Listen.'

The jungle had gone silent. No birds. No insects. No distant howls. Just breathing.

Theirs.

Then, a low growl.

Tony moved first, slowly, hand hovering over his rifle. Adam followed his line of sight. A pair of amber eyes gleamed between the trees, fixed on them with predatory intent.

Jaguar.

The massive cat was barely visible, a shadow among shadows. Its muscles coiled like steel cables, ready to strike. Too close for a rifle shot. Too fast for a knife.

For the first time in a long time, Tony didn't move. Didn't breathe. Adam flicked his gaze toward his sidearm, measuring the odds.

But before he could act, a shot rang out. Not theirs.

The jaguar vanished into the trees, spooked by gunfire from somewhere beyond their position. Adam didn't hesitate. He snatched the lantern and crushed the flame between his fingers, plunging them into absolute blackness. The jungle swallowed them whole.

Tony froze—no quip, no cocky remark. His rifle was already up, his knuckles white around the grip—a single breath, barely audible.

Then another. Not theirs.

'Not cartel,' Adam whispered. 'Too controlled.'

Tony exhaled slowly. Yeah. And too close.'

Their extraction was still two clicks out.

They weren't alone in the jungle, and whoever was here wasn't supposed to be.

Another shot. Closer this time. Suppressed.

'Time to move.' Adam signalled.

They moved fast and low, weaving through the dense undergrowth, every sound amplified in the silence. The jungle was no longer a battlefield but a hunting ground, and they weren't the hunters.

Fifteen minutes of hard movement. Branches clawed at their

gear, sweat stung their eyes, and every breath felt louder than it should've been.

No more shots. No more voices. Just the hum of insects slowly returning.

Only then did Tony finally exhale.

'We were never meant to hear that, mate.'

Adam nodded. He already knew that.

'We need to log that frequency.' Adam muttered.

'Someone back home needs to hear it.'

They reached the extraction point, an open clearing where their contact was supposed to meet them. But the moment they stepped into the moonlight, Adam's gut twisted. The landing zone was empty. No chopper. No backup.

Just a corpse.

Tony crouched beside the body, his fingers brushing the blood-soaked earth. His voice was low, measured.

'Whoever did this left in a hurry.'

Adam didn't answer. His gaze swept the jungle, its tangled depths shifting with unseen movement.

'No,' he murmured.

'They're still here.'

The jungle held its breath.

Then, from deep in the green abyss, the jungle whispered back.

Not an animal. Not a man

Something older.

Listening.

EIGHT
2002

For years, Adam Hayes and Tony Shaw had fought a shadow war across Central America—disrupting cartel networks, dismantling smuggling routes, and eliminating high-value targets with clinical precision. Their missions were shrouded in secrecy, unmarked victories in a war few knew existed.

When the last op closed, they were granted a rare indulgence: three months of leave. For soldiers trained never to stop, it felt like falling without a parachute.

Ever hungry for movement, Tony disappeared into South America on a motorcycle—chasing dust trails, dive bars, and women who didn't ask questions. Adam went the other way. He drifted north, crossing Mexico and the American Southwest, pulled by something quieter. Something he couldn't name.

He didn't plan on ending up in a Washington, D.C. gallery. But there he was, standing before a towering painting of the Four Horsemen of the Apocalypse—and listening to Claire Armitage.

The exhibit was her creation: a curated reflection on humanity's obsession with endings. Adam had wandered in on impulse. He expected pretension or boredom, but he didn't expect her.

Claire stood beneath the Horsemen, rendered in vivid, violent brushstrokes— war, famine, conquest, death—and her voice carried through the hush with clarity and force.

'This piece,' she said, gesturing to the canvas,

'Was inspired by the Book of Revelation. The Four Horsemen represent more than chaos. They're archetypes— symbols of the cycles humanity repeats. Over and over. The question is: are these divine judgments... or reflections of our nature?'

The crowd leaned in. Adam stayed at the back, arms folded, gaze steady.

'Civilisations don't collapse by accident,' she continued.

'They fall because they ignore the warning signs. The Mayans, the Romans, and the Mesopotamians overreached, depleted their resources, and failed to acknowledge the stresses they imposed on their people and their systems. They believed they were untouchable. Until they weren't.'

She took a step closer to the audience.

'But history whispers something else, too. Something quieter. Redemption. Cultures that choose to change—societies that face their mistakes—can survive. That's what I hope this exhibit evokes: not just fear of the end, but recognition of the chance for renewal.'

She let the silence hold for a beat. Then, with a calm edge to her voice:

'Because if we don't learn—if we keep repeating the same patterns—then the next collapse won't be a single empire. It'll be the world.'

Adam shifted his weight. Her words landed harder than he wanted to admit. He had seen what collapse looked like—up close and personal. In warzones. In villages torn apart by greed and fear. Not in prophecy, but in flesh.

Still, something about her certainty caught him. ***Irritated him.***

After the crowd thinned, Adam lingered, pretending to study

another canvas. Claire approached, her steps measured but unhesitant.

'What did you think?' She asked. Her tone was warm. Direct.

Adam hesitated. 'It was... interesting.'

She raised an eyebrow. 'That's usually code for not impressed.'

He half-smiled.

'You said humanity can learn that we can change course. I'm not sure I buy that.'

'No?'

He nodded at the Horsemen.

'People don't learn from history. They dress the same mistakes in new uniforms, give them better PR—but it's always the same in the end.'

Claire studied him for a moment. Her eyes—sharp, blue, probing—seemed to see more than she should.

'You've seen it firsthand,' she said quietly.

Adam shrugged.

'Enough to know redemption's a nice idea. But when things fall apart? People don't reach for meaning. They reach for survival.'

Claire didn't blink.

'Maybe. But what if the two aren't mutually exclusive? What if survival can include change?'

He looked at her. No smugness. No performance. Just conviction.

And that made it harder to argue.

'I just don't see how you get people to care about the future,' he said, 'when they're drowning in the present.'

'That's why we have to try,'

Claire replied. 'Because if we don't, who will?'

Adam didn't answer. He wasn't sure what unsettled him more—that she believed it... or that a part of him wanted to.

He had always believed history was a loop, not a line. But

this—her voice, her conviction—made him wonder if loops could be broken from inside.

For the first time in a long while, he felt something stir. Not adrenaline. Not a threat.

Possibility.

NINE

The city was built on power.

Here, men in tailored suits carved borders, signed wars into existence, and whispered the futures of entire nations across mahogany tables. As Adam walked the National Mall, the past seemed to press in from all sides—Lincoln's solemn gaze, Jefferson's cold stare, and echoes of battles fought behind closed doors.

Washington didn't just remember history.

It wrote it.

Drawn by instinct more than intention, Adam stepped into the Old Ebbitt Grill—a relic steeped in oak and brass, where politicians, journalists, and intelligence operatives drank under dim lighting and shared secrets in murmurs. Information flowed freely here for those who knew how to listen.

Adam hadn't planned to listen to anything until he heard a voice he recognised.

Dave Ross.

He'd never met Ross in person, but the voice was familiar. Tony had once played him a debrief recording—a clipped conversation from a jungle op where Ross predicted a cartel ambush days before it happened. Calm. Measured. Dangerous in its certainty.

Now, that voice cut through the low din.

'Washington's a mess,' Ross was saying.

'Since 9/11, it's all leaks and lockdowns. But the real threats? They're already inside.'

It wasn't just what he said—it was how he said it. Not theory. Experience.

The man across from Ross—a former State Department type —checked his watch, muttered an excuse, and vanished. Ross sighed, swirling the remains of his drink.

'Didn't mean to bore you,' he muttered.

'You didn't.'

Adam slid into the vacant seat. 'I know who you are.'

Ross glanced up, eyes narrowing slightly. He studied Adam for a beat, reading him.

'So, what's your angle?'

Adam flagged the bartender. 'I'll tell you over a drink.'

What followed was quiet but charged. Hours slipped by in the low hum of conversation, until—

'You boys look like you're about to solve the world's problems.'

Claire Armitage.

Adam turned, caught off guard. She was the last person he expected, and somehow the only one who made sense.

They'd met just days earlier—her gallery lecture on Renaissance depictions of the Apocalypse still echoed in his mind. She wasn't just articulate. She was awake. And now, here she was again. Coincidence?

Or something else?

Ross, ever the opportunist, gestured to the empty chair.

'Join us, then. Maybe you can explain why religious iconography keeps appearing in classified intelligence reports.'

Claire slid into the seat, raising an eyebrow.

'Is this an ambush or a seminar?'

The banter faded as the conversation deepened.

Ross took a long sip of whiskey and exhaled, as if it hurt.

'Ever heard of the Four Horsemen?'

Adam tilted his head.

'Biblical stuff? Plagues, famine, the end of days?'

Ross smirked.

'Something like that.'

Adam half-laughed.

'Christ. What's next—the Illuminati?'

But Ross didn't smile.

'Vega. Solis. Tarlen. Thorne. The Horsemen.

He said the names like gunshots.

Adam's smirk vanished.

'They don't just predict history,' Ross said.

'They write it.'

The weight of it landed heavily. Ross's voice wasn't theatrical. It was resigned—like a man who'd stared too long into something he wasn't meant to see.

Adam leaned forward.

'And you're telling me this because...?'

'Because I don't think they're writing a future we want to be part of.'

Adam didn't flinch, but the air shifted around him. The names weren't new. He'd heard them, scattered like static across past missions. But now, the pattern was forming. Fast.

He looked at Claire.

She didn't speak, but something in her eyes had changed—recognition, maybe. A thread pulled tight.

'You've come across this before,' Adam said.

Claire hesitated. Then:

'I've studied ancient texts for years—patterns in myth, prophecy, and apocalyptic symbolism. One theme keeps surfacing—civilisations don't fall by accident. They're guided toward destruction.'

Ross leaned in.

'Exactly. These men—Vega, Solis, the others—they're not just amassing power. They're engineering collapse. On a scale we've never seen.'

The words hung in the air, leaden.

Then Ross's phone buzzed. One glance at the screen, and his expression darkened.

'We need to wrap this up.'

Adam's instincts kicked in.'Something wrong?'

Ross slipped the phone into his jacket.

'Let's just say someone's paying attention.'

Claire's brow furrowed.

'You sound like one of those tin-foil types. Next, you'll tell me the moon landing was staged.'

Ross cracked a dry smile.

'Oh, it was. Great camera work. Kubrick, I think.'

Then, more seriously:

'I don't do fairy tales. I do patterns. And every war starts with people ignoring the obvious.'

'So what's 'obvious' this time?' Adam asked.

Ross downed the last of his whiskey.

'That governments don't run the world. It's run by the people you never see coming.'

Claire stood, gathering her things. Before leaving, she brushed Adam's arm lightly.

'I've got an early start tomorrow. But maybe we'll run into each other again—before you disappear.'

It wasn't a question. It wasn't quite a promise. But it stayed with him as she walked away.

Adam watched her go, then turned back. Ross raised his glass, half-smirking.

'She's something else, isn't she?'

Adam let out a slow breath.

'Aye. Proper trouble, that one.'

Ross chuckled.

'Trouble's where the truth usually hides. Come on—let's call it a night. Pretend none of this ever happened.'

He stood and disappeared into the Washington night.

Adam lingered, the wind rattling the windowpanes. Ross's words echoed, digging deeper with each passing second. This wasn't paranoia. It wasn't theory. It was infrastructure. Invisible scaffolding, holding up everything—and now, beginning to crack.

He'd spent his life following orders in places where right and wrong had uniforms. But this? This was different.

And then there was Claire.

A complication he hadn't planned for. A question he wasn't ready to answer. But the thought of her stayed with him, unshakable.

That night, he walked the empty streets of Washington, caught between duty and something far more dangerous.

Hope.

TEN

He found her at the gallery the next morning, standing in front of the Four Horsemen. Sunlight slanted through high windows, casting shadows long enough to feel symbolic.

'You're back,' Claire said, her voice quiet, smile forming.

Adam nodded. 'Didn't tell you what I thought of your lecture.'

She raised an eyebrow. 'And?'

'It was the best apocalypse exhibit I've ever attended.'

Claire laughed. 'And how many have you been to?'

'Just the one. But I'm confident.'

She flushed slightly. 'Confident enough to come back for seconds?'

There was a pause—not awkward, just weighted.

Then she asked, more softly, 'Do you think we shape the future, or just relive the past with better lighting?'

Adam held her gaze. He didn't know. But she made him want to.

'Maybe we don't get to choose,' he said. 'But some things are still worth the fight.'

Claire studied him. 'Is the future one of them?'

And for the first time in years, he thought: maybe.

* * *

They slipped into something unexpected over the next few days —walking tours through the Smithsonian, late-night bars tucked behind shuttered jazz clubs, conversations that lasted too long and not long enough.

Claire saw through things. Through him.

In a quiet café after midnight, she leaned forward, fire in her eyes.

'You talk like the world's already over.'

Adam stirred his drink. 'Maybe it is.'

She didn't flinch. 'You don't believe that.'

'I believe in staying alive. That's enough for me.'

Claire held his stare. 'And what about making a difference?'

'That's your department.'

'Or maybe you're just scared to try.'

He didn't respond. Just let the silence settle between them.

'Fear keeps you alive,' he said eventually.

'No,' Claire said. 'It just keeps you running.'

That was Claire—unafraid to break open the things people buried.

And somehow, he didn't mind.

* * *

Claire had spent years keeping admirers at arm's length. Not from fear—fatigue. Most wanted the shape of her, not the substance. But Adam didn't try to impress. He didn't chase. He just stayed—and left a mark anyway.

When his leave ended, he returned to Hereford, expecting the spark to fade. It didn't.

Their conversations moved from calls to letters. Not updates —truths. The kind that only survive in ink.

One night, Claire sat at her desk, his latest letter open beneath the lamplight.

You said I see the world as broken. You're right. But I'd still like to see it once—just once—through your eyes.

Claire made a decision. She took a post at the Warburg Institute in London. Around the same time, Adam finally accepted the MI6 offer.

They had a window before the machinery of duty consumed them. They didn't rush. They wandered.

* * *

Cornish cliffs. Edinburgh alleys. Places steeped in history and salt.

On a windswept beach, Claire leaned into him, her hair a mess of defiance.

'You ever think about what comes next?'

'You mean after today?'

She smiled. 'Yes, Adam. After today.'

He hesitated. 'I don't know.'

'That's alright. We've got time.'

And for the first time, he believed her.

He started to feel like the days might add up to something. That this wasn't just another cycle waiting to repeat—not another circle of silence and loss. For once, it felt like a break in the pattern. A pause in the rhythm. The moment you trace the spiral long enough and realise you've begun to shift its shape.

* * *

In a Yorkshire pub, Claire introduced him to her father. The handshake wasn't new, but the context was. William Armitage's eyes said more than his words ever would.

They sat in a quiet corner.

'Claire doesn't need protection,' William said. 'But if you hurt her, you'll answer to me.'

Adam's reply was calm. 'Understood.'

William studied him longer now. 'You were sharp, even then. But there's a difference between battlefield instincts and life.'

Adam nodded. 'I know.'

William gave a final nod. 'Good.'

Nothing more was needed. Men like them didn't waste breath on ceremony.

* * *

Later, walking village lanes, Adam spoke without thinking.

'I don't think I've ever believed in the kind of future you talk about. For me, it's always been about getting through the day.'

Claire slowed. Waited.

'Leaving something behind,' he said. 'Making things better— it feels… distant.'

'But isn't that what you already do?' she said. 'Protecting people—that's a legacy. Just a different kind.'

Adam looked at the hills. The dark horizon.

'Maybe. But it doesn't feel like building anything. It feels like holding back a tide that never stops.'

Claire stepped closer. Her voice was steady.

'That's why you and I work. You hold the tide. I remind people what's worth saving on the other side.'

He didn't believe in fate. But he felt the gravity of something larger—something old. Not prophecy. Pattern.

He looked at her. At the fire in her eyes.

'You make it sound simple.'

'It's not,' she said. 'That's why it matters.'

* * *

Their time together was short, but sharp-edged and clear. Hope stitched into shadow. Love carved from a world breaking at the seams.

Underneath, their truths remained: Claire believed in legacy. Adam believed in survival.

But when he joined MI6, he didn't just carry a weapon.

He carried her conviction. Her clarity.

The voice that reminded him not just who he was—but who he could become.

And for the first time, he wasn't just fighting to survive.

He was fighting for something.

A circle, maybe. But not closed. Still turning. Still changing. And this time, maybe not repeating.

ELEVEN

The hills rolled like a memory. Broad-backed and wind-scoured, they cradled the village of Hawes in their ancient, green hands. Dry-stone walls stitched the land into history. A narrow river cut through the valley, glinting in the light and murmuring softly, like a sleeping giant.

It was here that Sergeant William Armitage had chosen to disappear.

Once, his name had been whispered through barracks and briefing rooms, spoken in the silences before doors were kicked in. A legend in black kit. The kind of man others followed into the fire because he never flinched.

In the early 1980s, the world saw a glimpse of that man.

A hostage crisis in London. Cameras rolling. Politicians holding their breath. The black-clad silhouettes of the SAS stormed the building—ruthless, silent, precise. William was first through the breach. Rifle steady. Nerves honed to surgical steel.

The men inside were prepared to die.

William made sure they did.

The operation lasted minutes.

The legend lasted decades.

He earned the Queen's Gallantry Medal for that night. But medals didn't matter when the nightmares followed you home.

In the late '80s, it ended. A covert op overseas. An ambush. Bullets in the dark. The stink of burning fuel. The sound of your blood leaving you.

When he woke in a hospital bed weeks later, bandaged and broken, they told him the truth.

The leg was gone. The Regiment was over.

The SAS had been his world.

Without it, he was a ghost in his own body.

Margaret pulled him back.

She found the cottage in Hawes. A place untouched by war, where the rain still smelled like stone and the air moved without fear. Their stone home overlooked the river. The world here was smaller, slower. Not softer—but survivable.

Margaret was his anchor. Sharp-minded, unsentimental, warm when it mattered. A historian who believed words could shape futures. She taught him that not all battles were fought with bullets. And that survival meant more than walking away.

She gave him Claire.

From the start, Claire was relentless, curious, incisive, and always questioning. Margaret nurtured her mind with books and conversations that ranged from the Crusades to Cold War coups—history, philosophy, and consequence.

But it was William who gave her the edge.

It began as small lessons. How to move through a forest without breaking a twig. How to tell if someone was watching you. By twelve, she could strip and clean a rifle. By thirteen, she could land a clean shot centre mass from fifty metres. Before she could legally drive, she knew how to disappear and survive if the world turned black.

He never forced it, and he never called it training. But Claire understood because she saw how the world really worked.

Her mother shaped her mind.

Her father shaped her will.

And when she was thirteen, the stories she'd overheard began to look different.

It was late afternoon when the man came—eyes too sharp, hands too still. He claimed to be lost, but his questions were exacting. His gaze kept flicking to the house. To William.

Claire felt it before it happened. A shift in the room. A current pulling taut.

From the kitchen, she watched her father cross the threshold. No threats. No weapon. Just a single step—placing himself between her and the door. Shoulders square. Voice quiet but final.

The man left without incident. But Claire never forgot.

That night, William sat her down.

'There are men in this world,' he said, 'who won't fight fair.

They won't come with flags. They won't come with warnings.

And I don't want you to be afraid when they do come.

I want you ready.'

* * *

In 1995, tragedy came again.

Margaret fought, but cancer fought harder.

William sat at her bedside as her laughter faded from the home, as Claire whispered stories back to the woman who had once taught her how powerful stories could be.

When Margaret was gone, the house became quieter. Not broken. Just... emptied. A silence too complete to be healed.

Claire—barely out of university—threw herself into the pursuit of history. But not the curated kind. She chased what lay beneath it. Patterns of control. Power. Echoes of conspiracy. The architecture of truth beneath the lies.

She wasn't trying to save the world.

She just wanted to understand who already owned it.

* * *

Years passed. And then—unexpectedly—he came.
Adam Hayes.

Claire had spoken of him. In letters. In late-night phone calls. A British soldier she'd met in Washington. Unusual. Controlled. Too sharp around the edges for someone so young.

But William had met him before.

Years earlier. A knock at the door. No context. Just a man who looked like he'd walked out of a war and hadn't yet decided if he'd left it behind.

'You don't know me,' Adam had said.

'But I think I'm becoming you.'

William hadn't answered. Just poured two glasses and let the fire do the talking.

They didn't speak of it again.

So when Adam returned, this time with Claire, William said nothing. He watched.

And what he saw was different.

From that day on, Adam was part of the family.

* * *

In 2003, Claire and Adam married.

A year later, Olivia Hayes was born.

For William, Olivia was something he hadn't known he needed.

A second chance.

A spark.

A reason.

She had Claire's fire and Adam's quiet focus. She filled the house again—not just with sound, but with presence. With life.

He often sat her on his knee, pointing to the hills beyond the cottage.

'This is your heritage,' he told her.

'And one day, you'll understand just how special it is.'

And for the first time in decades, William Armitage felt something he hadn't dared to believe was still waiting for him.

Peace.

TWELVE

Silas Vega was ten years old when he first glimpsed the world as it truly was—a place where power moved in shadows, where destinies were shaped not by votes or laws, but by nods behind closed doors.

The Vega estate, perched in the hills outside Barcelona, was both palace and prison. Its marble floors and curated art masked Hendrik Vega's suffocating presence.

To the public, Hendrik was a visionary industrialist—a man who built schools, donated to hospitals, and maintained devout ties to the Vatican. But inside those stone walls, he was a tyrant. His love was conditional, awarded only when Silas met his impossible standards. Failure was not corrected—it was condemned.

But it was his voice that left the deepest scars.

'Your mother had a soft heart. It made her weak. Don't let it make you weak too.'

The words lingered long after Hendrik left the room.

'This world has no place for the soft. If you want to survive, you must be ruthless.'

That night, Silas lay awake, the ceiling lost in shadow. His mother's gentle and fading voice rose from memory like a lullaby from a forgotten life.

'Your father thinks the world belongs to those who take. But real power, Silas... real power is in knowing what to let go.'

He hadn't understood her then.

By the time he did, she was gone.

* * *

One evening, Silas wandered into his father's study after a tense, wordless dinner. The air was thick with cigar smoke, and the silence was heavier still. His fists ached from clenching through another meal of passive-aggressive remarks and veiled commands. He had grown up in that room, watching men in tailored suits discuss markets, weapons, and war like chess pieces on a board. He had memorised the scent of control long before he understood its shape.

That was when he noticed it—a drawer, slightly ajar. A misstep. Rare, in a man like Hendrik.

Inside: documents, old photographs, and a journal bound in black leather, secured by a silver clasp. Silas hesitated, then opened it.

At first, it read like a business ledger—dates, numbers, transactions. But the deeper he went, the darker the entries grew. Unnamed operatives. Offshore accounts. Arms deals coded in Latin phrases. Then one line arrested his eye:

'The Vatican dossier—final payment received. The manuscript has been secured off-site, as instructed. If Solis attempts to interfere, he must be reminded of the consequences.'

The Vatican?

His heart kicked into his ribs.

Even at ten, Silas remembered the name. Solis had once dined at their estate—quiet, calculating, always watching.

Why would a man who flaunted his faith in public hide dealings with a manuscript?

And what did Solis have to do with it?

He kept reading. Names appeared—some he'd heard in the hallways of the estate. Others he'd seen shaking hands with Hendrik, whispering over brandy and deals. Generals. Senators. Cardinals. Men who never appeared on television but who made history from the shadows.

Then the entries stopped. A page had been torn out—neatly, deliberately. Whatever followed, Hendrik had made sure it couldn't be read.

Silas paced the halls that night, restlessness growing like static in his chest. From his father's private office, voices rose. The door was cracked open.

'The manuscript's significance cannot be underestimated,' said a deep, unfamiliar voice.

'If it falls into the wrong hands, you understand the stakes.'

Hendrik's reply was measured steel.

'You forget who you're speaking to. My Vatican contacts ensure its security. If anyone interferes, they'll regret it.'

Silas's breath hitched.

He pressed closer to the wall as the conversation shifted— global acquisitions, covert operations, and the burying of inconvenient truths. Then came the final exchange.

'And the boy?'

A pause. Then Hendrik's laugh—dry and dismissive.

'Silas? He's naïve. Unformed. But he'll learn. I'll make sure of it.'

Something in Silas cracked.

* * *

Hendrik found him in the study the next day, poring over a textbook on orbital mechanics.

Hendrik snatched it from his hands with a sneer and tossed it onto the desk.

'Dreams won't protect you,' he said. 'If you want to survive, learn power. Learn to wield it. Start with me.'

Silas hesitated. His fists clenched. A spark of rebellion flared —but he extinguished it with a nod.

Resistance would come. *But not yet.*

That night, the dream returned.

Planetary cycles, constellations, strange numerical harmonics —the kind that hummed in the back of the mind like a forgotten melody. Among the shifting images, a page—real, remembered —etched in symbols he could not yet decipher. Resonance fields. Recurring prime sequences. Planetary harmonics that felt more like memory than math.

And beyond it, a red horizon—barren, endless, waiting.

The manuscript. He had held it once, fleetingly, years ago when his father was distracted. Its pages pulsed with something ancient. Something alive.

It wasn't a book.

It was a blueprint.

And Hendrik feared it.

* * *

Years passed. Silas listened more than he spoke. He learned which voices held power, and which merely echoed it.

By sixteen, he was outpacing his instructors. Physics, mathematics, systems theory—his mind sliced through them like light through glass. His inventions drew discreet attention from military contractors.

But his gaze was elsewhere.

Upward.

Astronomy became his sanctuary. The stars, ungoverned and

distant, offered freedom. A canvas untouched by men like Hendrik.

But the more he learned, the more Earth repulsed him. Greed. War. Collapse. Endless cycles of failure.

His father had tried to bend the world to his will. Silas saw futility in that.

He didn't want to control Earth.

He wanted to escape it.

Mars—raw, untouched, unscripted—became his North Star. A place where society could be reborn from first principles. A world unburdened by the ghosts of history.

That belief crystallised into purpose.

Yet one question remained, buried beneath layers of equations and ambition:

What truth had Hendrik tried so hard to hide?

He returned to the journal. To the torn pages. Cross-referenced dates, traced gaps in financial records and shipping manifests. There were references to an order older than any church or crown. A single line remained etched in his thoughts:

The cycle does not begin. It does not end. It only continues. And we, the lost sons, will inherit its burden.'

Silas read the words again—this time, as prophecy.

Hendrik Vega had never feared losing control.

He had feared the past—and what it revealed.

His empire and identity had not been forged; they had been inherited.

They were not kings. They were descendants of something far more ancient.

Something buried.

Something awakening.

And now, the burden passed to Silas.

Not as heir.

But as the architect of what would rise in its place.

THIRTEEN

Silas Vega was born into power. Groomed to inherit it.

Viktor Tarlen carved his empire from the wreckage of others.

He didn't build a legacy—he took one.

While the world spiralled through the energy crises of the late '90s, Tarlen thrived. Where others saw scarcity, he saw leverage. Collapsing markets became currency. Nations teetered on the brink—and he stripped them bare. Presidents. Prime ministers. Moguls. One by one, they came crawling for salvation.

He wasn't a businessman.

He was the firestorm.

On camera, he played the rogue capitalist—brash, unscripted, a self-made prophet of disruption. He spoke like a rebel but ruled like a tyrant. The world mistook his charisma for vision.

But charisma wasn't his weapon.

Control was.

By the early 2000s, Tarlen had outgrown the markets he once manipulated. Technology. Shipping. Energy. Disinformation. He didn't follow trends—he bent them. Governments danced. Rivals vanished.

And then he met Vega, Solis, and Thorne.

The alliance was inevitable.

The world would come to know them as the Horsemen.

Visionaries. Tyrants. Architects of collapse.

They were playing the long game.

Tarlen? He played the moment.

From the beginning, the alliance was brittle. Vega treated him like a loaded gun—useful, but never trusted. Solis loathed his volatility. Thorne exploited his image, magnified his myth, but never let him own it.

They needed him.

But they never respected him.

It had always been that way.

The trade consortiums that locked him out.

The ex-wife who despised what he'd become.

The son he had never met, raised to believe Tarlen was the villain in a story he never got to write.

He told himself none of it mattered. Power drowned out the voices of the past.

Phase Zero wasn't just a plan.

It was proof.

* * *

By the 2010s, Tarlen wasn't rewriting the rules.

He was burning them.

SphereNet, fed by Thorne's algorithms, reshaped reality in his image. Truth became repetition. Division became profit. Outrage became policy.

And the world began to burn.

Pandemics. Financial implosions. Cities swallowed by the sea. What started as strategic instability became something primal.

Collapse.

For Tarlen, it was business as usual.

For Vega and Solis, it was a fire growing out of control.

Solis pulled Nexa from Tarlen's shadow and fortified his orbital trade routes.

Vega—for a heartbeat, Thorne never broadcast—hesitated.

He saw cities drowning. Children gasping beneath ashen skies.

And almost changed course.

Almost.

But weakness had cost his father everything.

Vega would not make the same mistake.

He turned his gaze skyward and stopped thinking about Earth altogether.

At the centre of it all, Tarlen stood grinning in the flames.

And for the first time, the Horsemen feared what they had unleashed.

* * *

They met him in silence.

Not in boardrooms or bunkers. Not on any record.

Just a room. No cameras. No aides. Just four men and the storm they'd made.

Vega stood at the head of the table, hands folded like a priest. Solis hovered near the window, watching the sky, as always. Thorne lit a cigarette he wouldn't smoke.

And Tarlen walked in already knowing.

'Cut the theatre,' he said. 'You want me gone. Say it.'

Solis didn't turn. 'You were warned.'

'Warned?' Tarlen laughed. 'You rode my chaos like a warhorse. Don't act surprised it kicked.'

Vega's voice was low. Unmoved. 'You've become a liability.'

'No,' Tarlen said, stepping in, heat rising behind the eyes. 'I became bigger than you.'

Thorne exhaled, measured. 'This isn't about ego.'

'It's only about ego. Yours.'

Vega finally looked him in the eye. 'You were never meant to lead. You were meant to clear the board.'

'And now what?' Tarlen growled. 'You think you can unmake me? Kill my name with a line of code?'

'Your name was never the plan,' Solis said. 'You were the diversion.'

'I built the machine,' Tarlen hissed. 'I burned the path. And you—' He stabbed a finger at Vega. 'You think the stars will save you from the fire you lit down here?'

'I no longer think about Earth,' Vega replied.

A pause. Cold. Final.

Thorne crushed the cigarette out. Solis tapped something on a secure device.

Tarlen's implants blinked red.

Access revoked. Servers gone.

SphereNet, atomised.

No farewell. No applause. Just deletion.

Tarlen turned to Solis, not pleading, just curious.

'Even you?' he asked. 'After everything?'

For a flicker of a moment, something passed through Solis's eyes. Guilt? Memory? Or just calculation?

Then he blinked it away.

'I warned you. You chose fire.'

'This isn't the end,' Tarlen said, voice hollow now, like stone on the verge of crumbling.

Vega turned. 'No. This is the moment the world forgets your name.'

The door closed behind him.

But history has teeth.

And ghosts don't stay buried forever.

* * *

They thought it would end him.

They were wrong.

Tarlen had spent a lifetime watching empires fall. His mistake was thinking he needed one to win.

For a moment, he considered revenge—not just on the Horsemen, but on the world that had made him this way. The boardrooms that laughed behind closed doors. The leaders who used him then disavowed him—the son who would never know what it cost to stay relevant.

But power wasn't about debt.

It was about reinvention.

From the wreckage, DominionNet rose—a digital empire built on paranoia, rage, and fear. Conspiracy wasn't a threat. It was the business model.

The Horsemen tried to ignore him. But they couldn't.

Vega let DominionNet's chaos draw scrutiny away from Stellarion's true ambitions.

Solis used the noise to smuggle a monopoly into orbit.

And Thorne—ever the illusionist—fed DominionNet, SphereNet, and every other channel, twisting the world in his image.

By 2025, the Earth was boiling—literally and ideologically.

And Tarlen, once discarded, had recast himself as the only man who could restore order.

But power was never about the present.

It was built on the ghosts of the past.

The cycle hadn't ended.

It had just been waiting.

FOURTEEN

CAMBRIDGE, 1991

The rain hammered the chapel spires like a sentence passed down by the sky.

Julian Thorne sat alone in the archives beneath King's College, the microfiche reader casting a dim, flickering glow across his pale features. The scent of damp parchment clung to the air, mingling with old wine and silence.

He adjusted the lens again.

Trial 17-B. Neurogenic Modulation. Dr. Alan Royston.

There it was—buried twelve scrolls deep, misfiled under 'Agricultural Subsidies – DEFRA Liaison.' A clerical shell game, but not clever enough.

Three test subjects.

Two seizures.

One cardiac arrest.

All of it buried in the footnotes.

He leaned back in the creaking chair. Overhead, the chapel bell tolled midnight—slow, sonorous, final. He didn't flinch. He'd known the rumours were true since his second week on campus. A funding line that didn't reconcile. A whisper during the seminar. A visiting researcher who vanished mid-term.

Seven months chasing shadows.

Now, at last, he had light.

* * *

He shared the flat with a second-year maths student named Simon Arkwright—brilliant, twitchy, and incapable of ignoring a puzzle once he'd seen it. Their room was a chaos of textbooks, wires, solder-burned circuit boards, and takeaway cartons. Arkwright hacked for the challenge. Thorne watched to see what would happen next.

It was Thorne who first handed him a printout from the archives. 'You're better with systems,' he'd said with casual disinterest. 'See if you can find out where the rest of this ends up.'

Arkwright didn't sleep for two nights. When he finally looked up, eyes bloodshot and voice hoarse, he whispered: 'They covered up a death. On-campus. With Ministry funding.'

Thorne had smiled. Not surprise. Satisfaction.

* * *

The next morning, Thorne submitted a report. Clean. Formal. Quiet.

It was referred to the Ethics Committee and copied to the Assistant Provost. A matter of conscience, presented as procedure.

Three days later, he was summoned.

Not to commendation.

To censure.

'Mr. Thorne,' the Provost said, spectacles low on his nose, voice like chalk, 'your actions demonstrate a grave misunderstanding of protocol.'

'I submitted the truth.'

'You submitted a conjecture. Documents outside your clearance.'

'They were in the archives.'

'And now they are not.'

A sheet of paper slid across the desk—formal reprimand, breach of conduct, no expulsion.

'And Dr. Royston?'

The Provost didn't blink. 'It is not your concern.'

Julian didn't sign.

He walked out into a storm.

* * *

That night, his login credentials were revoked.

His research marked 'incomplete.'

His advisor stopped returning calls.

One week later, Dr. Royston received a departmental award for innovation in neuroadaptive therapies.

Julian sat in the back row of the ceremony. Uninvited. Unnoticed. He watched the applause. The smiles. The champagne.

The illusion cracked. Something inside him did too.

It wasn't rage.

It wasn't grief.

It was certainty.

The truth had done nothing.

But the lie—that perfect, institutional lie, wrapped in timing, tone, and decorum—that had rewritten the record.

* * *

Three months later, he tested a theory.

A falsified memo, mimicking the Chancellor's seal, circulated among student unions: a proposed tuition hike targeting international enrolment. The Guardian picked it up. Protests followed. They denied it publicly. But the money moved quietly, as always.

Policy shifted.

No one traced it to him.

Not then.

* * *

Julian Thorne had learned the lesson.

History wasn't owned by those who found the truth.

It belonged to those who edited first.

He didn't need justice.

He needed control.

And from that day forward, he would never let the truth speak louder than the signal again.

* * *

Weeks later, Simon Arkwright moved out without explanation.

Thorne didn't ask why.

He already knew.

FIFTEEN

2002 - LONDON, UK

Adam stepped through the imposing glass doors of Vauxhall Cross, the headquarters of MI6. The smooth panes reflected the overcast London sky, and the transition from the crisp January air to the artificially warm interior was jarring.

His boots clicked against polished stone, the sound unnaturally loud in the cavernous lobby. The place had a sterility to it, like a hospital for secrets. Fluorescent lights buzzed overhead, syncing with the distant tap of hurried footsteps. The air smelled of cleaning solution, sharp and clinical. Beneath that lingered the stale tang of burnt coffee and the faint metallic heat of overworked servers.

A wall-mounted screen pulsed with rotating security protocols. Above it, the MI6 insignia glowed faintly—a crown, a sword, a lion. Regal. Weaponised.

Weeks ago, Adam was still wearing a sand-coloured beret. Regiment life had been familiar. Now, his fatigues were replaced by a tailored suit, and he was handed a liaison badge stamped 'UK/US CYBER OPERATIONS—TIER 1 ACCESS.' Someone had read his file and seen potential. The right kind of dangerous.

He skimmed the briefing file.

Subject: Simon Arkwright.

A former British cyber-engineer. Accused of breaching ninety-seven classified systems across intelligence, infrastructure, and finance. Nexa. SphereNet. Stellarion.

His intrusion was surgical. Firewalls ghosted through. Encryption undone. No trace—just aftermath. Pentagon lockdowns. Central U.S. banks frozen. SphereNet's AI collapsed mid-cycle. Nexa's predictive engine shattered global supply chains.

Arkwright hadn't hacked for money. Or politics.

He hacked because the systems told him not to.

The U.S. wanted him extradited as a cyberterrorist. But here in Vauxhall Cross, Adam understood the real question wasn't what Arkwright had done, but what he had seen.

If he'd unearthed intel too sensitive to surface, he wasn't just a fugitive.

He was leverage.

For now, he sat in a Met Police holding cell. But both Washington and Whitehall wanted answers yesterday.

At the front of the MI6 briefing theatre, a section chief clicked through slides.

'Langley wants him on a plane by Friday,' she said, voice clipped.

'We need to know if this was opportunistic or deliberate. If Arkwright was acting alone... or if he had help.'

Adam only half-heard her.

Just weeks ago, he was on ops in the jungle. Decisions were immediate. Final. Now, he was in the land of meetings and measured language.

The settings changed, but the game didn't. Power, secrets, sacrifice. The same storm, different masks. The themes weren't new—they were just the latest verses in a story that never stopped circling.

And then—a memory rose.

* * *

Afghanistan. High-value extraction.

The plan was simple. Reality never was

They were to extract one man—an informant with embedded access. But he had brought his family. A child. The protocol was to leave them.

The commanding officer hesitated.

That hesitation cost everything.

A buried IED lit the night. Fire and steel. Three friends dead. The asset and his family—gone.

Adam had been thrown clear. Ears ringing. Crawling through red dust to reach what was left.

He wrote the report in silence, cold facts stitched together in military language. Back at base, no one wanted the truth: it hadn't been bad intel. It had been doubt. Human doubt.

Later, he called Claire.

'Rough night?' she asked softly.

He paused.

'No worse than usual.'

'That's not an answer.'

'It's the only one I've got.'

She didn't press. She didn't need to.

What could he say? That he'd cradled a dying child and felt nothing? That he left a body behind because the chopper couldn't carry the weight?

He married Claire because she saw the man beneath the scars,

beneath the training.

But now, he wasn't even sure that man still existed.

He'd spent years mastering violence.

But the silence afterwards—that was still uncharted territory.

* * *

'Mr. Hayes?'

The MI6 section chief's voice pulled him back.

The briefing had moved on.

The names on the screen were just noise now.

* * *

Later, he sat in a secure operations wing buried beneath Vauxhall Cross. Polished steel. Reinforced concrete. A fortress wearing the face of bureaucracy.

A stack of reports sat before him—declassified intel from five nations, redacted summaries of Arkwright's activity, cross-references to Vega, Tarlen, Solis, and Thorne.

He slid on his headphones. Classical music always helped. Mozart's Piano Concerto No. 21 filled his ears with structure, precision, and balance.

The world outside faded.

In music, there were no betrayals. Only form. Only truth.

A shadow moved in the doorway.

Adam looked up.

Dave Ross. Leaning casually against the frame, arms crossed, an amused smirk tugging at his mouth.

Adam removed the headphones. Mozart dissolved into silence.

'Please tell me that's Wagner,'

Dave said, stepping in.

'Something suitably violent.'

Adam exhaled.

'Mozart. I like to keep things civilised.'

Dave chuckled, dragging a chair over.

'Civilised. Sure. That's the first word I'd use to describe you.'

He tossed a folder onto the table.

'Langley sent me to assist. We need to make sure the Brits don't drop the ball.'

Adam flipped the folder open, scanning incident logs and system maps.

'We think Arkwright's random?'

'Not even slightly,' Dave muttered.

'This wasn't spray-and-pray. He had a target.'

'SphereNet's financial hubs. Nexa's core analytics. Stellarion's orbital tracking...'

Adam tapped the table in thought.

'He didn't just find these. He followed them.'

'Exactly,' Dave said. 'He claims he was tracking energy research—classified projects tied to atmospheric manipulation. But if that's true...'

'Then he stumbled into something bigger.'

Dave nodded, jaw tightening.

'He decrypted fragments—partial data streams. We traced one file. Codename 'Helion.''

Adam's brow furrowed. 'That rings a bell.'

Dave flipped a page.

'It should. Same network cluster as something else you've heard me mention.'

He held up the sheet—four names circled in red ink.

Vega. Tarlen. Thorne. Solis.

Adam's spine stiffened—*the Horsemen.*

Dave's tone dropped. 'They're all over this.'

Adam leaned back, the silence between them heavier now. A web of connections was forming—too deliberate to be chance.

'What's the endgame?' He asked.

Dave stared at the redacted lines. 'No idea, and that's what scares me.'

SIXTEEN

Adam and Dave worked in silence, the low hum of the sub-basement beneath Vauxhall Cross vibrating faintly through the walls. Before them: Arkwright's stolen data. Thousands of files, each thread in a tangled web of systems that should have been unbreachable.

They moved methodically. One cross-reference at a time. Most of it was dense with jargon—engineering logs, encrypted architecture diagrams, internal emails scrubbed of identifiers. But patterns emerged.

SphereNet. Nexa. Stellarion. Always the same three. Always intersecting.

What Arkwright had accessed wasn't just sensitive. It was structural. Core frameworks of surveillance, infrastructure, and orbital coordination. Pieces of something coordinated, far bigger than any agency or corporation.

'Not random,'

Dave muttered. 'He was following something.'

Adam nodded.

'Buried deep. This wasn't a statement—it was a pursuit.'

Buried in the chaos, they found a sealed archive—encrypted

files walled behind a custom protocol beyond anything MI6 had seen. Not even Arkwright had cracked them.

Their titles told enough.

Project Septem. Stormcaster Protocol. Gravitational Effects of Astronomical Alignment.

No content. No summaries. Just names.

Adam stared at the screen.

'Whatever this is. It's not conventional. It's not finance or surveillance. It's something technical—maybe astrophysics. Or advanced orbital modelling.'

Dave leaned over. Or next-gen aerospace protocols. Something off-books.'

They kept digging.

Some documents led nowhere—trailheads were cut short, and access logs were wiped. But one led to a cluster of Stellarion internal reports. Most were routine: testing cycles, hardware calibration, and orbital drift compensation.

Then came the irregularities.

A software update was deployed without protocol sign-off. A communications array was misaligned in a way that didn't match operator logs. Retroactive background checks were issued. Personnel were reassigned without explanation.

Adam flagged them silently. Vega had tightened security. But not in response to a leak.

In response to **interference**.

'Someone on the inside,'

Dave murmured, 'tried to stall it.'

There were no names. Just missing identifiers. Vanished user accounts. Engineering teams were reshuffled. One comms cluster logged a burst of code that had no known source.

'They got close enough to scare Vega,' Adam said.

Dave exhaled.

'Or piss him off.'

Whatever had happened, Vega responded like a man

expecting betrayal. Loyalty protocols were instituted. Communications sealed behind military-grade firewalls. A short list of senior Stellarion staff vanished from rosters in less than two months.

The logs ended there. Not clean. Just... gone.

Adam sat back.

'Someone tried to resist. We don't know who or why. But it's there.

Dave shook his head.

'And if Vega doesn't know who it was, he'll burn half his network finding them.'

They stared at the screen. Septem. Stormcaster. The names meant nothing—and yet, everything. The Horsemen weren't just building systems. They were orchestrating something. Larger. Unified.

And someone else had seen it, too.

The next morning, Adam stood in a corridor outside the operations wing. The lights flickered overhead, the hum of classified machinery echoing faintly through the walls.

Dave joined him, a folder tucked under one arm.

'Washington's pushing hard,' he said.

'They want Arkwright on a plane by Friday.'

Adam didn't reply.

Dave continued,

'If they get him, this vanishes. The files, the names, the pattern. You know it. So do they.'

Adam nodded.

'He's not just a hacker. He's a liability.'

'Or an asset,'

Dave added. Depending on who gets to him first.'

Adam looked at him. You think they'll kill him?'

Dave didn't hesitate. If they think he cracked the files? Absolutely.'

* * *

Later that day,

Adam's encrypted phone buzzed.

Eleanor Grey – MI6 Section Chief

'The deal is done. CIA wants custody. Until we understand what Arkwright has, he stays locked down. We move him to a safe house immediately.'

Another message followed seconds later: 'If the wrong people get to him, this won't be a leak. It will be war.'

Adam closed the message and pocketed the phone.

Arkwright had stumbled into something hidden and volatile —intersections of power, data, and systems no one was supposed to see.

The question was no longer whether they could protect him.

It was whether they could do it in time.

SEVENTEEN

A damp December night smothered South London in mist. The Metropolitan Police facility looked unremarkable—just another government shell of concrete and steel. Inside, it was a fortress: reinforced corridors, layered electronic security, armed officers patrolling with surgical precision. Nothing got in or out unnoticed.

Adam stood cloaked in shadow at the mouth of a narrow alley, the cold gnawing through his jacket. The UCIW compact rifle pressed tight against his chest. His SIG SAUER P226 rode his hip, its weight a familiar reassurance. His tactical vest held extra magazines, a multi-tool, and two flashbangs—contingencies for when things, inevitably, went sideways.

Beside him, Tony adjusted his pack with a grunt and a grin, eyes scanning the mist. South London felt like home turf to him —even now.

'Feels like old times,' he murmured, flexing his fingers.

'Except last time, I wasn't babysitting a tech-head with the survival instincts of a startled rabbit.'

Adam smirked. 'I asked for the best. All they had left was you.'

Tony snorted.

'Big talk for a lad from Yorkshire. You lot still think a brew can solve a breach-and-clear.'

'Depends on how strong the tea is.'

Tony chuckled, rolling his shoulders.

'Still the driest bastard I've ever met.'

Adam pulled a single earbud from his pocket. Moonlight Sonata. The slow, deliberate notes drifted into his ear, measured, methodical. Not for pleasure. For rhythm. Every chord aligned with the operation: tempo, breath, timing.

Seven minutes. That's all they'd have once systems went dark.

A crackle in his earpiece. Dave Ross.'Surveillance down,' Ross said. 'Move fast. Second team might be inbound.'

Adam exhaled slowly. Let the last note settle. Yanked the earbud free.'Time for action.'

Tony nodded. 'Let's get it done.'

They moved. The UCIW slung tight, Adam climbed first, scaling the side wall with quiet efficiency. Tony followed, less elegant but twice as fast—Bermondsey muscle with a soldier's edge.

The main entrance was a killbox. The skylight—their needle to thread.

Tony lowered a fibre-optic camera through a cut pane of glass, panning left and right. There was a beat of silence.

'All clear,' he murmured.

They dropped, silent as shadows. Crouched. Weapons up.

No alarms. No movement.

Ross had provided the floor plans. They navigated tight corridors with precision, avoiding patrols and sweeping blind corners. A fluorescent light buzzed overhead. Steel and silence.

Holding Cell B3.

Adam crouched at the panel.

'Digital lock. Gimme a minute.'

Tony kept watch, his frame taut, boots planted wide like a pub brawler ready to throw.

'Too quiet,' he muttered.

The lock beeped. The door slid open.

Inside: Simon Arkwright. Dishevelled. Eyes bloodshot. Hands twitching near a stack of notes.

'Who the hell are you?'

'MI6,' Adam said. 'We're here to get you out.'

Arkwright frowned. 'MI6? Why would—'

'Because you saw what powerful people don't want seen,' Adam cut in. 'Now, grab your files. We move.'

Footsteps.

Adam raised a hand.

Too late.

From the shadows: black-clad operatives. Silent. Armoured. Synchronised.

Not police.

'Freeze!'

Gunfire tore the silence.

Adam and Tony dove. Sparks flew from the concrete. Arkwright hit the floor, clutching the files like oxygen.

'We can't fight them here,'

Tony snapped, ejecting a mag. 'Unless you want to go out in a blaze of bloody glory.'

Adam's mind raced. Exits. Options. Delay tactics.

'Flashbangs. Cover. Then move.'

Tony already had the pins out.

Bang.

Bang.

Concussive thunder rolled down the hallway. Smoke bloomed—thick, acrid, turning the red emergency lights into a bloody haze. Shapes stumbled. Voices warped by chaos.

They moved.

Adam dropped one with a brutal elbow to the throat,

disarmed another in a fluid twist, and slammed him into the wall. Tony went low—sweeping a leg, driving a knee up into ribs, then flooring another with the butt of his SIG.

But the others regrouped—disciplined. Not mercs. Not amateurs.

Police stormed in behind them, confused and firing blind. The corridor became a battlefield.

Arkwright clung to Tony like a drowning man. With a theatrical sigh, Tony yanked him upright and kept moving.

'Mate,' he grunted, shielding him with one arm while returning fire with the other,

'if I wanted dead weight, I'd have dragged a sandbag outta Bermondsey Tesco.'

'Move!' Adam shouted, dragging them toward cover.

Ross's voice:

'Elevator. Two corridors down. Underground lot.'

They ran. Gunfire shredded the air. Muzzle flashes painted the smoke.

Elevator ahead. Doors sliding open.

They burst in.

Inside the van, Ross sat at the wheel, engine rumbling.

Adam shoved Arkwright in. 'Go!'

The tyres screeched. Metal tore rubber. And they were gone —into the London dark.

* * *

SAFE HOUSE— 03:17 AM

Rain tapped the windows like fingers on glass.

Arkwright sat hunched, a chipped mug of tea trembling in his grip. Pale now. Eyes unfocused.

'You're safe,'

Adam said. 'For now.'

Arkwright didn't look up. Just shook his head. 'You don't get it.'

Tony leaned against the wall, arms crossed.'Try us.'

'No one can crack those files,'

Arkwright muttered. 'Not MI6. Not the CIA. Not me. Not without the key.'

Adam met Tony's eyes. 'Whoever sent that team... they think you can. That's enough.'

Arkwright scoffed. 'You think I did this to expose some grand conspiracy?'

He stared into the steam rising from his cup.

'I did it because I could. Because every locked door was a challenge. Nexa. SphereNet. Stellarion. I cracked them for the thrill. Until one day, I peeked behind the wrong curtain.'

Silence.

He looked up, voice hollow.

'You don't understand. This isn't a safe house. It's another prison.'

And twenty years later, behind new walls and codes... *it still was.*

EIGHTEEN

What Arkwright uncovered in his breach vanished without a trace.

No inquiry. No fallout. Just silence.

The kind that didn't need enforcement—*only neglect.*

Simon Arkwright was placed under MI6 protection.

Secure location. No visitors. No name on file.

The files he exfiltrated remained encrypted, adaptive, alive, resisting every known cypher.

He believed the key wasn't just code,

but a lock tied to a celestial mechanism—

built by minds that no longer walked the Earth.

He spent years trying to break it.

Never came close.

Eventually, the updates stopped.

No one followed up.

Arkwright became a ghost in the system.

Used only when MI6's best hit a wall.

The rest of the time, they kept him on a leash—

hidden from the world.

With only a cat

and a signal no one else could trace.

* * *

Dave Ross stayed at the CIA.

Still an analyst. Still walking through Langley's secure doors each morning.

But his voice no longer carried weight.

His reports on resonance patterns, timing irregularities, and global system convergence—were quietly filtered out of circulation.

He wasn't dismissed.

Just excluded. Suppressed. Monitored.

So he worked in the margins.

Quietly.

Tracking anomalies.

Watching the weather shift when the forecasts didn't.

Following the same names that appeared, again and again, whenever the world tilted.

* * *

Claire remained at the Warburg Institute.

Her official focus: religious iconography.

But her research kept drifting—toward sacred geometry, planetary harmonics, and encoded cosmologies that defied academic convention.

She didn't seek answers.

She followed the trail.

There were truths in her lineage she didn't know.

Only felt.

Instincts she never questioned.

Only obeyed.

In early 2024, the Smithsonian contacted her.

An anonymous benefactor had donated a sealed manuscript—

ancient, untranslated, etched with glyphs that mirrored the harmonic structures she'd chased for years.

They asked for her expertise.

She accepted without hesitation.

* * *

Adam went home to South Yorkshire, to the same mining village he'd grown up in.

He worked as a logistics planner—routing freight, refining systems, and solving complex problems no one else noticed.

It was smart work. Functional. Hollow.

He and Claire were still together. Married. Still close.

For years, their lives had been anchored in different places— her in London, him in the north.

But that, too, was beginning to shift.

She would be going to Washington soon.

They spent weekends together when they could.

Some were easy. Others were not.

But they never stopped showing up.

With Olivia at university, the house was still, hollowed out by absence.

Adam kept to a rhythm—early runs, black coffee, long days behind a screen.

He watched the news like it was code.

Not searching for answers.

Just recognising patterns others missed.

Still haunted by the past.

Still carrying the weight of disillusionment.

* * *

By 2025, the world had moved on.

Arkwright was off the grid.

Dave had been sidelined.

Claire was circling something she hadn't yet named.

And Adam was still watching.

They knew what the world didn't.

The Horsemen weren't a theory.

They were real.

They were formed.

And they were already embedded—steering systems through names and networks no one questioned.

The ones closest to exposing them had nothing left to show.

No evidence.

Only instinct.

Only time.

The next twenty years would unfold in silence.

But the cycle was already in motion—older than history, and carved into the bones of the Earth.

NINETEEN

2025

Adam Hayes stared at his desk. He had walked away from MI6 a decade ago and built a new life. But some prisons weren't made of walls but of silence.

The office was sterile, fluorescently lit, airless, and devoid of life. The hum of computers and the mechanical clatter of keyboards blurred into one—a lifeless rhythm, like the work itself. Adam stared at his screen. The numbers warped, shifting from data to meaningless symbols. Around him, voices droned into headsets about inventory delays and shipment routes— detached, weightless, empty.

He retrieved a pair of worn earbuds from his desk drawer, pressing them in with a practised motion. Clair de Lune swelled in his ears, threading through his thoughts like a lifeline. The delicate notes smoothed the edges of monotony, giving order to a world that had long since lost meaning. Music had always been his anchor. Once, it cut through chaos—now, it was a thin barrier against the slow suffocation of routine—a relic of a life that no longer fit.

He'd left MI6 in 2015—not in defeat, but in disillusionment.

No matter how many battles he won, the war never ended—just reset. Corruption, conflict, hidden hands pulling the strings—it all moved in cycles, unchanged, unstoppable. He wasn't making a difference, just maintaining the illusion of one. So he walked away.

Now, this was his life: logistics, planning, efficiency metrics. It was a world reduced to shipment schedules and cost-cutting initiatives. With or without him, the machinery of commerce was turning.

His inbox pinged. Routine. Mundane. Another mindless update from the supply chain team—until his eyes caught the one above it.

No subject. No sender. Just an attachment: **Final-Proof.xdf.**

The music cut out, swallowed by the pulse hammering in his ears. The cursor hovered. A familiar weight settled in his gut— one he hadn't felt in years. He glanced around. No one was watching. He clicked.

The file unfolded into a series of compressed documents: satellite imagery, encrypted transmissions, and meteorological models. The data mapped the world with brutal, intricate precision.

Then, the reports:

PHASE ZERO: Active Directives
Satellite Cluster C-12— Operational
Weather Displacement Initiative— In Progress
Targeted Regions: Southeast Asia, South America
Projected Population Displacement: 9.3 million
Seismic Interference Algorithm— Active
Anomalous tremors detected in key resource zones
Projected tectonic escalation: 18 months

Adam's pulse thundered. He scrolled further, skimming familiar names from a past life. Silas Vega. Julian Thorne. Viktor Tarlen. Jeremiah Solis—The Four Horsemen.

His jaw tightened. This wasn't possible. It couldn't be.

His fingers hovered over the keyboard. The urge to dig deeper warred with knowing what that would mean.

He closed the file. Deleted the email.

Then, seconds later, he opened his trash folder and restored it.

* * *

That evening, Adam sat alone on the edge of his bed, bathed in the dim glow of his laptop. Outside, the village was silent. The old house creaked with shifting temperatures—a sound he had learned to live with but never entirely ignored. The air was still thick with unease that had nothing to do with the night.

A glass sat untouched on the bedside table, amber liquid catching the light. His old reports lay scattered across the bed— printouts, intelligence briefings from a life he had sworn he'd left behind.

Files he wasn't supposed to have. A habit he had never quite broken.

He opened Final-Proof.xdf again. A name jumped out: Dr. Nathaniel Voss. Attached was a report—a personal log. Adam's eyes narrowed. Not a standard intelligence file. A warning.

'If you're reading this, I'm already dead. They've accelerated the timeline. The models were wrong. The interference isn't just increasing—it's spiralling out of control. I tried to shut it down. I tried to stop them. But they found me.'

Adam exhaled sharply.

Another entry followed.

'There's proof in the data. I've hidden redundancies. They'll wipe everything once they realise I'm gone. Probably won't make it out. But the data in these files will connect the dots. If anything happens to me, this is the final proof.'

A cold weight settled in Adam's chest. He checked the time-stamp. The message had been sent weeks ago. Floating in cyber-space, bouncing between dead inboxes—until it somehow reached him.

Voss was either in hiding.

Or already dead.

His phone vibrated—a news alert.

Severe drought in Central Africa. Millions at risk.

Adam stared at the screen for a long moment before swiping it away.

The house felt smaller. The quiet, once comforting, had turned suffocating. Outside, the wind stirred the trees. A lone car hummed down the empty road. Claire had called from Washington earlier. The conversation had been short and strained—words spoken without meaning. The distance between them wasn't measured in miles anymore.

It was in silence.

She had once told him, 'If we keep repeating the same patterns, the next collapse won't be an empire. It'll be the world.'

He hadn't believed her then. *Now he did.*

The world slept, oblivious that its destruction was being orchestrated in boardrooms. Its suffering was planned like moves on a chessboard.

Adam sat motionless, the truth burning through the darkness. He knew exactly what it meant. And he knew he wasn't ready to fight a war he couldn't win.

Tomorrow, he'd pass the file to a contact at GCHQ. Maybe he'd call Ross—his paranoid mate in D.C.—and let him make sense of it. Let someone else carry the weight.

He reached for his phone. Scrolled through his playlist and selected Bach's Goldberg Variations. Soft, deliberate notes spilt into the room—each one precise, measured, and unyielding. A mathematical beauty. A world that made sense. He closed his eyes, letting it thread through the unease in his chest. It had always helped.

Tonight, even the music couldn't drown it out.

He told himself it wasn't his war anymore.

But a part of him already knew—

It always had been.

TWENTY

The fluorescent lights in Langley hummed faintly, their sterile glow settling over Dave Ross's cramped, cluttered office.

Stale coffee. Stacks of old reports.

The scent of paper ageing under fluorescent light.

A tomb of forgotten files—

and a forgotten man.

Once, Ross had been a brilliant analyst—the kind they whispered about in intelligence circles.

The one who could see connections that no one else could.

Now, he was a cautionary tale.

His name spoken in hushed tones—

a relic consumed by paranoia and conspiracy.

Every move was watched.

Every action flagged.

It was the Arkwright files that had undone him.

Stolen years ago.

Buried in encrypted vaults.

Forgotten by most—

But not by Ross.

The fragments hinted at something vast, buried beneath layers of obfuscation:

Weather manipulation, secret space colonisation, Project Septem, Phase Zero...

Pieces of a puzzle no one else dared to solve.

Where others saw noise, Ross saw patterns—

intersecting lines that all led back to the Horsemen.

But obsession has a price.

A knock at the door.

Ross looked up.

Agent Jessica Stokes stood in the doorway, hovering like she wasn't sure she wanted to be there.

A fresh recruit. Young. Still untainted by the agency's quiet betrayals.

'Morning, Mr. Ross,' she said, placing a file on his desk.

'The director wanted me to remind you about next week's compliance review.'

'Ah, the lunatic check-in,' Ross muttered, his voice edged with dry sarcasm.

'No one thinks you're a lunatic, sir,' Stokes replied, shifting uncomfortably.

'They think I'm a relic.' He smirked.

'I prefer living archive.'

He reached for the file, but his fingers twitched—the tremor betraying him.

Stokes noticed but said nothing.

The pages slipped from his grip, scattering across the floor.

He exhaled, frustrated, and moved to retrieve them—

But Stokes was already crouched beside him.

'You all right, sir?' she asked, concern creeping into her voice.

Ross waved her off, forcing a smirk.

'Just getting old. You'll get there one day.'

She hesitated, then straightened.

'If you need anything, let me know.'

The door clicked shut behind her.

Silence.

Ross leaned back in his chair, staring at the ceiling.

A man once at the top, now buried beneath his obsessions.

Lisa's voice echoed in his mind:

'I can't do this anymore, Dave. I don't know if you're right or losing your mind, but either way... I can't keep doing this.'

She had left years ago.

Their home had become a prison of locked doors, late-night paranoia, whispered warnings about the Horsemen.

The CIA had abandoned him just as thoroughly.

Superiors cut him off.

Colleagues kept their distance.

His classified access was slashed—

Each file placed further out of reach—

until the message was clear:

Stop digging.

Even the director had told him:

Let it go.

But Ross couldn't.

Because he knew.

For years, the Horsemen had been watching him—

not to kill him,

But to bury him.

Every dead-end.

Every reassignment.

Every failure.

It wasn't an accident.

It was containment.

They took satisfaction in watching his health decline.

To them, Ross was no longer a threat.

But in 2025, something changed.

A whisper in the data.

Chatter about Arkwright's files resurfacing in blacklisted intelligence streams.

And then—

a name.

One that wasn't supposed to survive.

One buried in dead protocols and redacted transcripts.

Septem.

* * *

That evening, Ross sat alone in his dimly lit apartment.

The glow of his laptop screen carved sharp shadows across the walls—

illuminating stacks of old files and half-finished thoughts.

A secure message blinked on an encrypted channel—

from a contact buried deep in his past.

Someone who had once trusted him.

And once doubted him.

A bridge from London—

back when he'd served with MI6,

straddling two agencies and one truth no one wanted to hear.

I have information you're interested in about the Horsemen.

Ross's pulse quickened.

His fingers hovered.

Trembled.

His jaw clenched—

willing his body to cooperate,

despite the betrayal of age and time.

'They think I'm done,' he muttered.

A grim smile formed.

'Let's prove them wrong.'

With shaking hands, he began gathering his files.

It was time to leave the shadows—
and remind the world:
Dave Ross wasn't finished yet.

TWENTY-ONE

Beneath Nexa Tower, the chamber breathed like a machine dreaming of death.

Servers pulsed in synchrony, the hum of synthetic life echoing the world's last heartbeat.

At its centre: a monolithic obsidian table, its glass surface reflecting the pale faces of those who would decide who lived, and who vanished.

The Horsemen were finalising the list.

Solis sat at the head, spine straight, hands steepled. His silence was taut as wire—measured, but fraying.

Tarlen sprawled like a storm waiting to move, cigarette burning between two fingers, lips curled in lazy contempt.

Thorne barely seemed there, eyes glazed with light from a thousand data streams, already editing the narrative in real time.

And Vega—still, poised, eyes pinned to the list like it was a mirror that refused to lie.

Beyond the glass wall, the city blinked, oblivious and orderly. The grid before the collapse.

'Two thousand seats,' Solis said.

A fact. Not a debate.

Tarlen exhaled smoke. 'We always knew. Eden isn't for everyone.'

'It was never meant to be,' Vega said quietly. 'We're not saving the world. We're pruning it.'

That silence afterwards wasn't agreement. It was consent.

Thorne flicked a finger, and names unfurled across the table —columns of light and judgment.

'Orion personnel are locked. Vance's engineers. Stabilisation core. Eighty-six percent finalised.'

'Civilians?' Solis asked, already knowing.

'Selective,' Thorne said. 'Controlled diversity. Functional minds. No passengers.'

Vega's gaze caught on a name. A single ember glowing red.

Sofia Castellano.

His voice cut through the hum. 'She's on the list?'

Solis didn't look up. 'She'll live.'

'She walked away from all of this. You think she'll bend now?'

'She doesn't have to bend. Just breathe.'

A pause.

Then Tarlen chuckled—low, joyless.

'Didn't know you had a soft spot, Solis. Bit late for redemption arcs.'

Solis didn't answer.

Tarlen dragged the list toward him and stopped on another name.

'My son.'

Vega arched an eyebrow. 'You have a son?'

Tarlen smiled without warmth. 'Didn't stick around. Never mattered. But he's sharp. He's mine. That's enough.'

Thorne's tone turned clipped. 'He's not in protocol.'

'And I'm not in protocol,' Tarlen snapped. 'You want the networks? The ships? My silence? Then he's on.'

Solis nodded once. Cold. Reluctant.

Thorne tapped the screen. The list shifted.

'One thousand, nine hundred eighty-three. Final locks by Friday.'

Behind them, the countdown ticked. Quiet. Relentless.

Vega scanned the metrics. Phase Zero projections. Grid failures. Population drift. Climate events. Holding.

Barely.

'The plan's intact—for now.'

'And if it slips?' Solis asked, not looking at him.

Tarlen answered. 'Then we go early. The plan serves us. Not the other way around.'

'It was meant to decay slowly,' Solis said. 'We built it that way—for control.'

'Decay doesn't care what you built,' Thorne murmured. He turned the screen toward them. A rising spike—uncontrollable. Inevitable.

The collapse was ahead of schedule.

Vega stood. 'Then we launch sooner.'

Solis's voice cut the air. 'No.'

Final. Forceful.

'We hold the timeline. We need five more years.'

But behind him, the data disagreed.

And no one corrected it.

* * *

Far away, in a world still pretending the sky wasn't falling…

Sofia Castellano walked through her morning.

Unaware her name had been carved into salvation—

by the hands of men she had once refused to follow.

TWENTY-TWO

Jeremiah Solis stood at the window of his penthouse, the city a constellation of light stretching beyond the glass. Geneva: the polished seat of diplomacy, the marketplace of kings. Here, silence carried weight. Power moved in whispers. Solis preferred it that way.

The half-burned letter lay on the desk behind him, a fresh insult in a long line of refusals. Sofia had sent it back, just like all the others. No words, no reply—only fire, as if to erase even the thought of him. It was an old ritual between them now, and still, it carved at something deep in his chest.

He breathed, steady and measured, before turning away from the window. The city shimmered behind him, but his gaze drifted past the present, beyond the polished veneer of his life, and into the places he had long buried. Before Geneva. Before Nexa. Before the man he became.

Bolivian Andes— 1969. The wind howled through the cracks, bringing the bitter scent of dust and hunger. Seven-year-old Jeremiah huddled in the corner of a one-room shack, his knees drawn to his chest, listening to his mother's shallow breathing. Outside, a gunshot echoed in the night. Another. Then silence.

His father had gone in search of food two days before. He had promised to return. Instead, the news came from a neighbour, blunt and without ceremony—**a bullet found him first.** Killed for a sack of rice. His mother did not cry, not at first. She only sat silently, staring at the doorway as if waiting for him to walk through.

That night, hunger gnawed at Jeremiah's ribs—but the shame of what his father had died for was heavier still. He pressed his face into his arms and made himself a promise. He would never be powerless again. Never be at the mercy of men who could take everything on a whim.

When a relief truck finally rolled into the village the following day, he watched as desperate hands clawed at the burlap sacks of rice. A man shoved him aside. Jeremiah wiped the blood from his lip and moved differently this time—quieter, sharper. While the mob fought, he slipped unnoticed to the back of the truck, snatched a bag, and ran.

When he returned to his mother, she did not ask how he had gotten it. She only held him close, her fingers trembling in his hair.

That was the first lesson. The world did not reward patience. It rewarded those who took it.

São Paulo, Brazil – 1979- A decade later, Jeremiah Solis had long since shed the boy in the dust. He was twenty-seven and wore his ambition-like armour.

The Hotel Estrella's lounge smelled of whiskey and wealth. Beneath the golden chandeliers, men twice his age laughed too loudly, their hands inked with old money and old blood. Solis sat among them, silent and watching. He had already won before the first signatures met the page.

A famine in Africa. A coup in a former colony. A fleet of cargo ships just waiting to be redirected. They called it strategy.

He called it inevitability. Control the shortages, and you command the game board.

When the deals were done, he stepped onto the balcony, the city unfolding below. The air was thick with heat, the scent of rain on stone. That was when he heard the door open behind him.

Isabella Castellano. A diplomat's daughter, a dreamer wrapped in the trappings of pragmatism. She had watched the negotiations and seen how he moved through the room. And yet, when she spoke, her voice was not one of admiration—it was one of measured curiosity.

'Do you ever wonder,' she asked, 'if any of this helps?'

He turned to her, scotch lingering on his tongue. 'It feeds people.'

'And at what cost?' she pressed, eyes sharp, unafraid.

Something in him stilled. People did not ask him such questions. Not sincerely.

He did not have an answer, not then. He only knew that he did not want her to leave.

And against all reason, she did not.

A year later, he married her beneath the Andean sky.

For the first time, he thought he might finally be something more than the hunger that had built him.

Spain – 1986-It unravelled, as all illusions did.

The night Isabella left, she did not scream. She did not break things. She did not rage as he had expected. Instead, she met him in the study with a suitcase at her feet and an expression so hollow it ached to look at.

'I won't let her grow up in this,' she had said.

Their daughter, Sofia, slept in the next room, unaware that her mother was about to disappear into the night, taking her across an ocean.

'You think running will keep her safe?' Jeremiah said, his voice low. 'She's my daughter. That won't change.'

Isabella's throat worked, her gaze unreadable. 'That is what I am afraid of.'

She left before dawn. He could have stopped her. He had men, power, and reach. But something held him back. Perhaps the quiet voice that still whispered of who he could have been.

Years later, he would look back on that moment and wonder if that was the last time he had a choice.

Geneva – 2025-Solis had always known where she was. Sofia could change her name, burn his letters, and vanish into the corners of the world, but she had never been beyond his reach. He had let her believe she was and allowed her to run. Allowed her to cling to the illusion of freedom. Because as much as he loathed the man at her side, Tony Shaw had kept her safe at the very least.

But that time had passed.

The world was shifting. The Horsemen's plans were in motion, and soon, the chaos they had engineered would turn real. Nature was about to strike Brazil, and when it did, there would be no shelter or safe place to hide. He would not leave her to fate.

A knock at the door. One of his men stepped in. 'They're in São Miguel das Missões.'

Solis nodded once. 'Extract them. No mistakes.'

'And Shaw?'

He turned to the window, the city lights reflecting off the glass. He had tolerated Shaw's existence for this long, knowing the soldier had served a purpose. But that purpose had ended.

'If he stands in the way, remove him.'

The door clicked shut behind him. Solis exhaled slowly. He had given Sofia time, had given her the illusion of choice. But she was his blood, his daughter.

Now, she was coming home—*whether she wanted to or not.*

TWENTY-THREE

SÃO MIGUEL DAS MISSÕES, BRAZIL

The night air hung thick with the scent of rain-soaked earth. The cicadas had gone silent, replaced by the distant hum of a generator. Somewhere in the jungle, something moved—too heavy for an insect, too slow for the wind.

Tony sat on the worn wooden steps of the farmhouse, a cigarette burning low between his fingers. Smoke curled into the humid air, vanishing into the darkness as he watched the trees shift.

Sleep had never come easily. Not in war. Not in the jungle. And not here, not even in the place that should have been a sanctuary.

Inside, Sofia moved through the dim glow of lanterns, her shadow flickering against the cracked wooden walls. Her dark curls spilt over one shoulder, loosened by exhaustion.

Even tired, she carried herself with fire, unyielding, uncompromising. Beautiful. Strong.

Tony took another drag, watching her without a word.

She stepped outside, arms wrapping around herself against the cooling air.

'You should rest,' he murmured.

She scoffed, shaking her head. 'There's a long list of things I should do. Resting isn't one of them.'

Tony didn't push. After six years of this, missions, road trips, and disappearances that stretched into months, he knew when to let silence do the talking.

He wasn't the best partner. Or the best father. How could he be? But he tried. He loved them in the only way his life allowed.

Sofia's gaze drifted to the jungle, her body tensing, listening.

Then, her voice dropped to something colder. 'He sent another message.'

Tony's fingers stilled around the cigarette. 'Solis?'

She nodded, her jaw tightening. 'Another courier. Same bullshit. 'You don't have to live like this. Come live with me.''

Her face twisted, disgust rising like bile in the back of her throat.

'Like I'd ever crawl back to him.' Her voice was raw, edged with something that lived deep in her bones. 'Not as a daughter. Not as anything.'

She spat onto the dirt as if the mere thought of him stained her tongue. Her hands clenched at her sides like she resisted the urge to scrub her skin clean.

Tony took a slow drag, then crushed the cigarette into the ground.

'And what did you tell him?'

She met his gaze, fire burning behind her exhaustion.

'What I always tell him.' A pause. 'I burned it.'

'His letter. His words. They mean nothing.'

The jungle pressed in, thick and stifling, but the weight between them was heavier because they both knew the truth.

No fire could burn away Solis's reach.

Sofia turned toward him. 'He won't stop.' Her arms tightened around herself, but not from the cold. 'He won't stop.'

Her voice was quieter now, as if the words themselves were exhausting.

'He wants his grandchildren. He wants me.' A shudder passed through her, quick but visible. 'He's always wanted me back. Like I'm a thing. Like I ever belonged to him in the first place.'

Tony inhaled deeply, then let the air leave his lungs in a slow, measured breath. Of course, Solis wouldn't stop. Men like him never abandoned their blood—not when they had the power to take it back.

Tony had spent years tracking men like him, breaking their networks, dismantling their power piece by piece. He understood them.

His voice came low, steady. Absolute. 'He won't touch them.'

Sofia didn't blink. 'And if he tries?'

Tony's jaw tightened. His following words carried the weight of certainty. 'Then I'll bury him.'

Sofia exhaled sharply, rubbing her temples to ease the headache this conversation always caused her.

'We should go inside. It's getting late.'

He nodded. She turned toward the door, then hesitated, one hand resting on the frame. She looked back at him. 'You know, it's funny. My father thinks he controls the world.'

Tony met her gaze, unreadable.

She took a step closer, the distance between them intimate.

A chill ran through him, but he forced a smirk. 'Solis always did have a flair for wishful thinking.'

She disappeared into the house, the door shutting softly behind her. Tony remained, staring into the jungle.

The night was thick with an eerie stillness, wrapping around him like a warning yet to be spoken.

Solis believed himself untouchable, a master of unseen hands, orchestrating his empire from the shadows, convinced no one would dare move against him.

Men like that always did.

They built their empires on fear, confident that enough power and cruelty made them invincible.

But they always overlooked the ones forged in darkness.

Let him come. Let him try.

Tony Shaw had buried men like Solis before.

And he would again.

TWENTY-FOUR

The night was too quiet.

Tony Shaw stood in the dimly lit kitchen, sweat clinging to his back as he listened. The hum of insects, the distant crash of the tide, and the slow, rhythmic breathing of the children were familiar sounds, ones he had grown used to. But something else lingered beneath them, pressing against his senses—a presence, a shift in the air.

Instinct.

His hand drifted to the knife strapped to his belt, fingers wrapping around the hilt as he moved toward the back door. Outside, the jungle loomed, dark and watchful. But Tony knew better than to trust the silence. He had felt the tension building all evening—a slow, invisible noose tightening around the house.

Solis had finally made his move.

A breath. Slow. Measured.

Let them come.

The first sign was subtle—a whisper of movement beyond the tree line, a flicker of shadow against the leaves. He counted six, maybe seven men. Close enough for him to smell the sweat on their skin, the faint metallic tang of suppressed weapons. Professionals. But not ghosts.

A mistake.

The first mercenary made his approach too fast, too eager. Tony let him come. At the last second, he lunged, catching the man by the collar and yanking him forward. His head cracked against the wooden frame of the window—a dull, wet crunch. Before the body hit the floor, Tony was already moving.

The second attacker barely had time to react before Tony closed the distance. A sharp elbow to the throat. A brutal knee to the gut. The mercenary collapsed, wheezing, as Tony twisted the gun from his grip and chambered a round.

They tried to be quiet.

It wasn't enough.

Tony moved through them like a blade in the dark, turning their momentum against them. One lunged—Tony caught his arm, twisted hard, and jammed the barrel of his stolen pistol beneath the man's chin.

One shot. A body crumpled.

A blade flashed in the dark. Tony pivoted, caught the wrist, and twisted. Bone snapped. The knife fell. He drove a boot into the attacker's skull, sending him sprawling into the dirt.

A sharp pain burned along his side—a sudden, searing slice. Tony gasped, barely twisting in time to avoid a deeper wound. The fourth attacker had caught him off guard, the knife grazing his ribs before Tony slammed his fist into the man's throat. The merc staggered, but he didn't go down. Tony's breath came short as he pressed a hand against his side. Blood. Not deep, but enough to slow him down.

Another rushed from behind.

Too slow.

Tony spun—too late. A fist crashed into his jaw, sending him staggering back against the wooden post of the porch. Stars exploded in his vision, the taste of copper flooding his mouth. The merc didn't hesitate, swinging again. Tony barely ducked, the strike glancing off his temple instead of landing clean. His vision swam. Pain pulsed in his ribs where the knife had cut him.

The man was strong.

Fast.

Trained.

Tony gritted his teeth and surged forward, catching the attacker in a brutal grapple. They struggled, muscles straining, feet digging into the dirt. The merc tried to break free—Tony twisted hard, driving his knee into the man's gut. But the bastard stood, lashing out with an elbow that caught Tony across the cheekbone.

Tony blinked blood from his eye—no time to hesitate.

He hooked his fingers around the merc's wrist and yanked him off balance, using the last of his strength to slam the man's head into the porch railing. The body slumped, unconscious or dead—Tony didn't check.

His breath was ragged. His ribs screamed. The taste of iron clung to his tongue.

Two left.

The final pair hesitated. Good. That meant they understood.

He gave them the opening. Let them make the mistake.

The first lunged—wild, desperate.

Tony ducked, stepped inside the arc, and drove a fist into his solar plexus.

The man folded, gasping. Tony didn't let him breathe.

He caught the head, twisted—

A snap. A body.

The final mercenary froze. Just a fraction too long. Tony saw the fear in his eyes.

A single step. A wrenching motion. A gun ripped from loose fingers. The butt of the weapon slammed into the man's temple. His body hit the dirt, twitching, barely clinging to consciousness.

Twenty seconds.

The jungle was still again.

Tony exhaled, scanning the bodies. No alarms. No reinforcements.

Solis had underestimated him.

He wiped blood from his knuckles and pressed a hand against his side, hissing at the sting. He had fought worse. He had survived worse.

But he had to move. Now.

* * *

Sofia was already awake when he entered, gun in hand, eyes burning with fury.

'They're here?' she asked, voice taut.

'Were.' Tony grabbed a bag and shoved supplies inside. 'We leave now.'

She didn't argue. Just nodded, jaw set.

Minutes later, they were slipping into the jungle, the children bundled in Sofia's arms. Tony led the way, cutting through the dense undergrowth, wincing as his side throbbed with each step. The adrenaline was wearing off, and the pain was setting in.

They reached the village just before dawn.

The old man stood in the doorway of a crumbling house, arms crossed, waiting.

'Took you long enough,' Matteo muttered, stepping aside to let them in. His face was carved by time, but his eyes were sharp —a man who had seen war and walked away still breathing.

Tony met his gaze. 'Appreciate the hospitality.'

Matteo grunted. 'You'll owe me.'

Tony turned to Sofia, holding her gaze. This was the best he could do—the only way to keep them safe.

'I'll be back,' he promised.

Sofia didn't answer. Just held Isabella and Gabriel closer.

Tony turned before he could change his mind, stepping into the jungle.

Solis had made his move.

Now it was Tony's turn to finish it.

TWENTY-FIVE

Claire Hayes sat alone in the Warburg Institute's reading room, sunlight slicing through arched windows and breaking across the oak table in fractured beams. The air held the scent of parchment and leather-bound centuries—history breathing around her.

In front of her lay the reason she'd been summoned.

An anonymous manuscript. Ancient. Uncatalogued. Delivered to the Smithsonian under sealed protocol, marked with symbols traced to the Vatican. No context. No sender. Only a request: Find someone with clearance, discretion—and eyes trained to see beneath the obvious.

Two decades earlier, Claire had lectured at the Smithsonian, a rising authority on apocalyptic imagery—how civilizations encrypted catastrophe into theology, myth, and art. Now, they had called her back.

But this time, they hadn't asked questions.

The manuscript was older than any she'd seen. Its vellum pages trembled at the edges, but the ink was bold, deliberate. Latin text wove through sketches and diagrams: spirals, geometric lattices, marginalia encoded in layered symbolism. Every detail pulsed with intent.

Her fingers hovered above the page. Something stirred in her. Not recognition—intuition.

And then, memory.

She was sixteen again, sifting through her parents' attic, when she found a box of her mother's journals. Claire had opened them, expecting sermons or domestic chronicles. What she found instead were spirals. Maps. Verses in Latin that didn't appear in any biblical canon.

Margaret Hayes had never spoken of them. Claire had never asked.

Now, decades later, those same patterns stared back at her from medieval vellum.

A tremor touched her spine.

Then came the voice—her mother's—rising from some quiet, buried corner of memory. Calm. Measured. Unshakeable.

'History isn't what's recorded. It's what survives in the margins. Truths whispered beneath myth, buried because they're too dangerous to believe.'

Claire had dismissed it then. Metaphor. Motherly mysticism.

Now, with the manuscript open before her, it felt like prophecy.

She turned the page.

It opened to a celestial chart—sprawling, detailed. Beneath it, hand-drawn landscapes: jagged canyons, vast basins, dry riverbeds cut through endless desert. Not imagined. Not stylised.

Observed.

Her breath caught.

The surrounding text described a departure—a journey—but its meaning stayed just beyond reach, like a word half-remembered in a dream.

Then her eyes caught a line of Latin:

Hominum ad Novam Terram Profectio.

Clean script. No ambiguity.

The Departure to New Earth.

The phrase struck her chest like a faultline cracking open.

She needed a second perspective—but hesitation clawed at her. She didn't fully understand it yet. And something primal resisted letting it go.

Still, she turned.

'Evelyn,' she said, barely above a whisper.

Dr. Evelyn Morgan—Smithsonian astrophysicist, expert in celestial cartography—had been hovering at the room's edge, sensing the stillness that had settled around Claire like a spell.

Evelyn stepped forward, adjusted her glasses, and leaned in.

'Looks like a star chart,' she murmured. 'Medieval. Renaissance, maybe.'

'That was my first thought,' Claire said. 'But the alignments don't match any historical sky.'

Evelyn frowned. 'These old charts usually represent belief systems. Not planets.'

Claire didn't reply.

Evelyn flipped back a page. Slower now.

'Wait. These arcs… the spacing. That's not metaphor. It's trajectory. Intentional plotting.'

She traced a line.

'But this sky—it's not ours.'

Claire nodded. 'Exactly.'

Evelyn studied the terrain sketches. 'These aren't symbolic. This isn't fantasy. The topography—canyons, ridgelines—it's too precise.'

'Someone saw it,' Claire said. 'Not imagined it. Recorded it.'

Evelyn's voice dropped. 'If that's true, this manuscript carries astronomical knowledge centuries ahead of its time.'

'Carbon dating confirms it,' Claire said. Fourteenth-century vellum. Ink and script both verified. Twice.'

Evelyn exhaled slowly. Her fingers curled against the page.

'This isn't a relic,' she said. 'It's a message. But not a warning…'

Claire finished for her. 'A reckoning.'

Evelyn didn't argue.

Then—quiet, like an afterthought, she regretted the moment it escaped—Evelyn murmured, 'There are people who should see this.'

Claire looked up. Evelyn avoided her gaze.

Something in the air shifted. Not fear. Recognition. The kind that lives in silence, because saying it aloud might make it real.

Claire's heart knocked once, hard.

Everything she had spent her life studying—scripture, myth, hidden cosmologies—suddenly felt like broken shards of a truth no one had dared remember.

The manuscript wasn't just ancient.

It was impossible.

A whisper of survival instinct stirred: Close it. Walk away. Pretend you never saw this.

But she couldn't.

The truth had already claimed her.

And again, the voice—her mother's, now heavier with memory:

'One day, Claire, you'll understand—the stories in the margins are the ones we should've feared.'

Her hand moved reflexively, flipping pages she no longer read—just scanned, searching. She didn't know what for.

Until she found it.

Celestial calculations. Sharp. Deliberate.

But wrong.

Not flawed—just foreign.

She adjusted the model. Shifted the axis. Recalibrated the coordinates, moving instinctively.

And then, it clicked.

The map locked into place.

Perfect alignment.
It wasn't Earth.
It was Mars.
And the coordinates weren't theoretical.
They were memories.

TWENTY-SIX

Claire read on, heart racing.

The deeper she dug, the less the manuscript resembled prophecy.

It wasn't foretelling — not in the way sacred texts pretended to be. It read like a ledger. Fragmented. Dispassionate. A centuries-old accounting of collapse, one that reappeared every time the sky fell into alignment.

Not a warning.

A record.

She ran her finger along a rough symbol scrawled in the margin. It looked wrong — sharper, slanted, not like the others, as if someone had jammed it in afterwards. Different ink. Slightly fresher hand.

A comment?

A correction?

Or something worse?

A chill threaded through her spine.

What if this wasn't history repeating?

What if someone had made sure it would?

Her pulse spiked. These weren't omens — they were coordinates. Triggers embedded in the sky. Venus. Mars. Saturn. Jupiter. The ancients had mapped them with near-religious precision. Not as myths. As mechanisms. Each celestial alignment tied to chaos. Collapse. Reset.

She swallowed hard.

The Book of Revelation hadn't predicted destruction.

It had catalogued it.

Her gaze fell on a line of Latin, etched in crisp, controlled script:

Cum Luminifer oritur in aurora aetatis, primus eques in mundum solvetur. Arcus eius flectetur, et nationes ante eum cadent. Dominatio erit eius.

She whispered the translation, barely aware she was speaking:

'When the Light-Bringer rises in the dawn of an age, the first rider shall be loosed upon the world. His bow will bend, and nations will fall before him. Dominion shall be his.'

Next to it: an illustration. A white horse. A rider crowned in star glyphs. A single mark above all — Venus.

Her throat closed.

The ancients had feared the Morning Star. Venus — the Light-Bringer. The herald of empire. The opener of gates. The signal flare before conquest.

But this wasn't theology.

It was mechanics.

An ignition point.

And one name surfaced uninvited, unwanted, and undeniable.

Viktor Tarlen.

The man who didn't need tanks or flags. Who bent global markets, split alliances, snapped borders like twigs. Nations didn't fall before his sword. They offered him the hilt.

Claire stared again at the page.

Venus.

White Horse.

Conquest.

She wanted to laugh. Or cry. Or scream.

But all she managed was a whisper to herself.

Not metaphor.

Not allegory.

Manifestation.

She turned the page, hands now shaking.

Mars. The Red Horse.

When the Blood Star burns at zenith, the second seal shall break.

Fire shall engulf the Earth. The rider of war shall rise, wielding a great sword to divide brother from brother.

Saturn. The Black Horse.

When the Shadow ascends and the balance is weighed,

hunger will spread like the night. The rider shall bear the scales, and the land will wither beneath his reign.

Jupiter. The Pale Horse.

When the Keeper of Gates aligns with the Shadow,

the pale rider shall descend. His name is Death, and Hades follows close behind.

A quarter of the Earth shall perish — by sword, by famine, by plague, and by beast.

It wasn't an artefact.

It was a cycle.

A pattern.

A clock.

If Tarlen was the first…

Then war, famine, and death were waiting their turns.

She flipped back to a detail she'd missed. A footnote, half-remembered from a different paper — planetary engineering, obscure conference, ten years ago.

Silas Vega.

She'd skimmed past it then. A scientist. Quiet. Irrelevant.

But now... Mars. The Red Horse. The Blood Star.

And Vega's fingers buried in energy grids, climate controls, weather-mod systems — silent levers on the machinery of modern life.

The war had already begun. It just hadn't declared itself yet.

She felt it in her chest — a thump, like a sudden drop in altitude.

He hadn't blown anything up.

He'd rewritten the rules.

And then: Solis.

Jeremiah Solis — logistics, trade, water. He didn't design systems. He decided who got them.

He didn't cause famine.

He curated it.

Saturn. The Black Horse.

Claire clutched the edge of the manuscript.

This wasn't allegory.

It was logistics.

Calendar.

Targeting data.

Men who held the balance between survival and ruin — masked by civility, backed by celestial architecture no one had dared to interpret as real.

How did the ancients know?

She didn't have the answer. Not yet.

Unless...

They hadn't predicted anything.

They'd survived it.

Once.

And left behind this.

She turned another page. Slower this time.

There — different handwriting. Still Latin, but less formal. Newer. Fewer flourishes. Intentional.

When the world turned barren, and the sky no longer gave breath,

the children of the first land sought refuge in the second.

She read it three times.

The first land.

Was it mythology? Metaphor?

Or something worse — or more real?

She'd studied cultures that encoded truth into legend — protective camouflage. But this wasn't myth layered over meaning.

This felt literal.

And the unease now wasn't just academic.

It was personal.

* * *

Her phone buzzed beside her, the screen ghost-lit in the corner of her vision.

Adam.

She hovered.

Thumb poised.

Memory rising.

He'd believe her. Of course, he would.

And he would come. No matter the cost.

That was the problem.

She couldn't do that again.

Not after last time.

* * *

2013.

Her father, black ice, red snow. She drove through the night, silence thick in the car. By the time she arrived, he was stable. Alive.

She wasn't.

She'd cracked. Quietly. Alone in the hospital corridor. Then she'd called Adam.

And he came.

No clearance. No orders. Just instinct.

They were still married then. Still unbroken.

He held her through the night.

And it cost him.

MI6 flagged the breach. He took the hit.

She never asked, but she knew.

He never blamed her.

But she'd never forgiven herself for needing him.

And for what the world made of that need.

* * *

Now, his name glowed back at her.

And she knew.

If she called, he'd come.

And this time… it might destroy both of them.

She set the phone down. Quietly. Deliberately.

Not yet.

* * *

She would call Dave Ross instead.

Later.

From the hotel.

Alone.

He and Adam hadn't spoken in years. But trust lingered. That would have to be enough.

She didn't know it, but the moment she made that call — history would shift again.

The flare would go up.

And far away, Adam, still unaware, would feel the first crack in the world he thought he understood.

* * *

Claire looked down at the manuscript.

It no longer felt like paper.

It felt like weight.

The seals had been broken.

And the truth — old, vicious, patient — was awake now.

She just prayed Adam would understand.

Because truth didn't heal.

It cut.

And once unsheathed,

there would be no turning back. Chapter 27

Silas Vega didn't just engineer the future. He tried to own it.

To the world, he was a genius—an architect of progress. He revolutionised drone logistics, built air taxis, and pioneered high-speed orbital launches. He made humanity believe again—in Mars, in momentum, in mastery over nature.

But those who truly understood him knew that Vega's goal was never innovation.

It was control.

And control, he was beginning to realise, was an illusion.

He had built his empire on precision, on certainty. But beneath the glass towers and quantum circuits of his domain, something had begun to shift. Quietly. Irregularly.

Anomalies. Deviations. Errors.

At first, they were statistical noise—a solar flare behaving unpredictably, a satellite orbit drifting half a degree off-course. His engineers dismissed them.

But Vega didn't dismiss patterns.

He hunted them.

And this pattern, the one forming now, wasn't his.

He told himself it was nothing. That his blueprint was flawless.

But the whisper remained.

* * *

Vega alone had seen the truth.

Tarlen, Solis, and Thorne believed their power was earned— born of intellect, timing, and ruthless execution.

Solis, perhaps, had sensed it—something older beneath the chaos. Hendrik had ensured he saw just enough. But Solis never grasped the full design. He'd mistaken it for strategy, not scripture.

Their fates had been sealed long before they were born.

They weren't leaders.

They were echoes.

Each one an archetype, cast from an ancient mould. The cycle had played out before—centuries ago, in empires now dust. Vega had uncovered the framework. The alignments. The bloodlines. The hidden engine of recurrence.

The past wasn't chaos.

It was a blueprint.

* * *

By 2025, Vega's reach spanned continents and orbit. As CEO of Stellarion, Stellarion Energy, and Neuralink—and now, as the controlling force behind Aurora—he held dominion over infrastructure, communication, and cognition itself.

To the public, he was progress incarnate.

Behind the press conferences and staged optimism, he was assembling something darker.

He was preparing to break the world.

* * *

Dave Ross had been chasing his shadow for twenty years.

The path led back to 2002, to a single breached file buried in the Vega Research Division's encrypted vaults. The intrusion, later traced to Simon Arkwright, revealed an early collaboration between Stellarion and an unnamed government division.

Publicly, it was space research. Privately, it was far more dangerous.

What began as climate stabilisation—satellites redirecting storms, reducing drought—had mutated. The project shifted once private money began flowing in, particularly from Solis and other unnamed backers.

The new goal wasn't mitigation.

It was manipulation.

Stellarion had developed platforms capable of amplifying hurricanes, triggering tectonic shifts, and rebalancing ocean currents. Ross found internal memos that read like science fiction—except the signatures were real.

One Stellarion researcher had written:

'This isn't weather control. This is atmospheric warfare. We are past the point of unintended consequences.'

But Vega saw only opportunity.

Humanity, in his view, had outlived its usefulness. Freedom was an obstacle: democracy, an antique fiction. The world didn't need consent.

It needed direction. His direction.

'A surgeon doesn't ask a tumour for permission,' he once said.

'The patient doesn't need to understand the cure. Only to survive it.'

* * *

By 2004, the theory had become practice.
Ross's investigations linked Stellarion tech to the 2004 Indian Ocean tsunami. Officially, it was an undersea earthquake.
Unofficially, the seismic data was too precise.
The timing, the location, and the strange silence of early warning systems all pointed to interference. Vega's involvement was buried, but the fingerprints were there for those who knew where to look.
By 2020, Stellarion satellites blanketed Earth. Publicly, they provided internet access. In truth, they were a surveillance lattice —and a climatic weapon.
When Vega acquired Aurora, his reach extended beyond physics into minds, into cognition. He flooded the world with noise: utopias on Mars, promises of green energy, curated visions of salvation.
Meanwhile, Earth was being gutted.
Few noticed. Fewer questioned it.
Stellarion Energy's mining operations, framed as sustainable progress, acted like environmental arson—ripping out rare earth minerals for battery production while poisoning the lands they claimed to save.
Ross didn't believe it was a tragic side-effect.
He feared it was the plan.

* * *

Vega's obsession with Mars wasn't philosophical. It was strategic.
To the world, it was hope.

To him, it was an exit.

The manned moon missions. The prototypes on the Martian surface. All of it—diversion and preparation. Not to preserve life.

But to survive its erasure, with the crown intact.

Ross kept pulling threads. Vega's data trails, encrypted messages, weather models behaving too predictably.

But he hadn't reached the centre.

Not yet.

What he saw wasn't a design, but a drift.

As if the world was slipping toward something rehearsed.

And Vega was steering it with both hands... or trying to.

* * *

By 2025, climate systems would no longer be just unstable.

They were programmable.

The world thought it was battling climate change.

In truth, Vega was writing it.

Ross's most unsettling discoveries were fragments— encrypted messages, communications between Vega and the others, vague references to 'climatic rebalancing.' Nothing conclusive, but enough to fear they weren't just responding to collapse. They were directing it.

One of Vega's private journal entries read:

'Earth is a sinking ship. The wise captain prepares lifeboats, not repairs.'

Claire's manuscript and Ross's investigation reached the same conclusion.

This wasn't the dawn of a new age.

It was the return of the old one.

The seals weren't myths.

They were records.

And the alignments were happening again.

* * *

For the first time, Vega hesitated.

The models were shifting faster than expected. Forecasts collapsing into chaos. Encrypted sequences in his system—commands he didn't recognise, transmissions he didn't authorise.

One recent transmission had shaken him more than he admitted—a priority packet routed through Helion's deep archive.

It was signed with his cryptographic key.

But he had never written it.

The storm he had engineered was starting to move without him.

He had spent his life shaping it.

Steering it.

But what if the storm no longer needed him?

What if it had always been steering him?

TWENTY-SEVEN

Before making the call, Claire swept the room for surveillance devices—an old habit ingrained by years spent in the orbit of soldiers and spies. The silence pressed in as she moved methodically, her fingers trailing the edges of furniture and tracing the underside of the desk.

A second of stillness. A held breath.

Satisfied. She exhaled slowly and then initiated the connection.

Across the city, Dave Ross hovered over his keyboard.

A decade of obsession had led him here. Now, finally, the truth was unfolding. Decrypted files flickered onto his screen, raw intelligence spilling out after years of chasing shadows.

Names. Dates. Coordinates.

This wasn't paranoia. It was real. And it had a name.

Project Septem. Seven seals. Seven planets. Seven stages of engineered collapse.

A sickness settled in his stomach. The reports scrolled endlessly—a global chessboard moving under invisible hands.

Hurricanes twisting outside known models.

Fertile lands were reduced to dust bowls.

Wildfires where none should burn.

The world believed it was witnessing the effects of climate change.

Dave knew better.

The Horsemen—Silas Vega, Viktor Tarlen, Jeremiah Solis, and Julian Thorne—did not merely exploit natural disasters. They had manufactured them.

Buried in layers of classified intelligence, hidden in the metadata of reports no one was meant to see, were records of deliberate climate engineering. They had rewritten the rules of nature itself.

The so-called climate-monitoring satellites, Stormcasters, weren't just weather satellites.

They were weapons.

Designed to shift air pressure.

Manipulate storm currents.

Trigger environmental collapse at will.

What had started as climate correction had become a global mechanism of control, turning entire regions into wastelands, destabilising governments, and setting the stage for something far worse.

Then, something caught his eye—a footnote buried deep in the metadata.

Seeding the Collapse – 4000 BCE.

A coil of tension wrapped around his ribs.

His laptop pinged—incoming video call.

Dave hesitated. Then clicked.

The screen flickered.

A woman's face—cautious, measured.

'Mr. Ross, this is Claire Hayes.'

A pause.

'I don't know if you remember me.'

Dave recognised her instantly, even after all these years.

'Claire?' His voice softened, though the edge remained. 'Is everything okay? How's Adam?'

A flicker of hesitation. Then she steeled herself.

'I've come across something,' she said. 'Something that I think is connected to what you've been looking into.'

Urgency bled through her voice.

She explained.

The manuscript.

Centuries-old.

Visions of the Stars.

Dismissed by scholars as medieval prophecy. But buried inside are encrypted references. Celestial alignments. Cycles of upheaval.

'There's a sequence,' she admitted. 'A set of symbols embedded in the planetary cycles. At first, I thought they were decorative, but they follow a pattern—one that shouldn't be there.'

Dave's breath hitched. 'A pattern?'

Her screen flickered as she scanned her notes.

'And then there are these sketches. They shouldn't exist.'

'Sketches?' Dave leaned forward.

Claire hesitated, then tilted her webcam toward the manuscript.

The grainy image was enough. Jagged canyons. Endless red deserts. Ghostly traces of vanished rivers. Dave's throat went dry.

'Where did you find this?' he demanded.

'The manuscript was donated to the Smithsonian archives,' Claire answered.

Dave exhaled, rubbing his temple.

'Claire. Those aren't just landscapes.' He met her gaze through the screen. 'Those are almost identical to recent satellite scans of Mars.'

She froze. 'No,' she whispered.

'You've seen them before,' Dave pressed.

She had. In the high-resolution images beamed back from the Perseverance Rover. Her stomach twisted. In 2021, NASA launched a landmark mission to search for signs of ancient life. The images were broadcast worldwide.

Rivers.

Canyons.

Plateaus eerily similar to formations on Earth.

And now, staring at her from a centuries-old manuscript— those same formations.

'How?' she whispered. 'These documents are hundreds, perhaps thousands of years old.'

Dave didn't answer immediately. His gaze darkened. 'You tell me.'

Claire turned another page. Her breath hitched.

Among the intricate illustrations of monolithic structures and crumbling cities, the Latin inscriptions sent ice through her veins:

Ultima Extinction – The Final Extinction.

Iterum Orbis – A New Earth.

And beneath them—

Hominum ad Novam Terram Profectio.

The Departure of Mankind to the New Earth.

Claire traced the ink-stained symbols, her pulse quickening.

Venus. Mars. Saturn. Jupiter. Each celestial body was marked with a seal, and beside them were dates carved in ancient script. Not predictions. Not prophecy. A record. The same planetary sequence had aligned before in cycles stretching back millennia.

Each time, collapse followed. And each time, it began with Mars.

The records weren't just warnings of doom. They weren't about Earth at all. The names—the celestial bodies—were waypoints. Not for prophecy but for movement. A journey.

The parchment crackled under her grip as the weight of history bore down on her.

'This isn't just a record,' she murmured. 'It's a map.' A journey.

Not from Earth to Mars. But from Mars to Earth.

Her pulse pounded.

Claire paused as something caught her eye in the margin of the manuscript. Fainter than the others. Not part of the Seven Seals she had traced earlier. It was rough, uneven, almost etched as an afterthought.

She narrowed her eyes.

'There's something else here,' she said.

Dave leaned in, squinting at the screen. 'Another seal?'

'No,' Claire whispered. 'It's not part of the pattern. It's not symmetrical like the others. It's... wrong.'

She studied the jagged arc—an imperfect curve, split by a sharp line like a scar through glass.

'Seven seals. Seven alignments,' Claire murmured. 'But this... this doesn't belong.'

Dave frowned. 'Could be a mistake.'

Claire shook her head. 'Not a mistake. A correction. Or a disruption.'

She leaned closer, voice tightening. 'What if someone forced an eighth seal into the cycle? Something that doesn't fit. Doesn't belong.'

A chill traced her spine.

If the seven seals marked natural recurrence, then this eighth was rebellion. Interference. An attempt to hijack fate itself.

Dave's voice was low now. 'If the seals are cosmic law... then who added an eighth? And why?'

Claire barely breathed. 'Or maybe it was always there. Waiting.'

Her pulse quickened.

If the cycle could be rewritten... then nothing was sacred. Not prophecy. Not survival.

Dave's face paled. 'You think someone broke the sequence?'

'Or rewrote it,' she whispered. 'Like hijacking a ritual halfway through.'

Dave didn't reply.

They both understood—this wasn't just an anomaly.

It was a breach.

He looked at her, voice suddenly careful. 'Claire... this isn't just history. It's a cycle.'

She met his eyes. No fear. Just certainty.

'And the cycle is ending.'She swallowed, but the fear stayed lodged in her throat.

Then, for the first time, she told him the part she had been keeping to herself. 'I've been asked to report my findings.'

Dave frowned. 'To whom?'

A pause.

Claire's fingers curled around the manuscript's brittle edge, her knuckles whitening.

Her mind replayed every call, every email. Had she already given them too much? Was she already compromised?

Her voice was quieter now, almost unwilling to say it. *'Jeremiah Solis.'*

Dave's hands clenched into fists.

Solis wasn't an academic. He was a Horseman. And Claire—without realising it—had just walked straight into their sights.

Dave's laptop pinged again.

A second notification. System intrusion detected.

His stomach sank. They were already watching.

'Claire, listen to me.' His voice was low, urgent. 'You need to disappear. Now.'

She didn't move. But her posture shifted—a fraction stiffer. A shade more tense.

'I don't think that's an option.'

She was right.

The call ended, but Dave remained motionless.

* * *

It was 10 PM in Washington, 3 AM in the UK.

Dave dialled a number he hadn't dialled in years. The line rang once. Twice. A third time.

Then, someone picked up.

And the world, for Adam Hayes, was about to change forever.

TWENTY-EIGHT

Claire stared at the dead screen, her hand still wrapped around the phone like it might ring again, like it might offer a way out.

But no escape was coming. Not now.

Her fingers trembled as she lowered the manuscript. The vellum whispered against itself—dry, brittle, almost breathing. It didn't feel like paper. It felt like something older. A relic. A warning.

It pressed against her, insistent. A truth forcing its way through the fragile membrane of denial she'd spent years crafting.

She stood. Pacing. Each step measured. Mechanical.

But her mind roared.

The manuscript had once been an academic curiosity. A riddle written in dead tongues. Something distant.

Now it was a mirror.

And she didn't like what stared back.

Dave had been right. This wasn't theory. It was pattern. Cycle.

And she—Claire Hayes, historian, scholar, supposed observer—had become one of its threads.

Her breath caught.

Not just her.

Adam. Olivia.

A chill scoured down her spine.

She had pushed Adam away, thinking it would protect him. Had kept the manuscript quiet. Insisted there wasn't enough to act.

But what if silence had only deepened the snare?

She turned to the window. The Potomac shimmered beneath cold moonlight. Washington still slept in its curated illusion of order.

It wouldn't last.

She pressed her forehead to the glass.

'What the hell have I done?' The words barely left her mouth, but they echoed anyway—like a curse cast backwards through time.

The manuscript hadn't just revealed the past.

It had reached forward.

And now the pattern saw her.

Her pulse quickened.

Across the street, a man pretended to read a newspaper. Too still. Too neat. Every few minutes, his eyes flicked upward— toward her window.

They were watching.

Claire didn't hesitate.

She swept the manuscript and her notes into her shoulder bag, grabbed her coat, and exited through the hotel's service alley into the cold night.

The air smelled of oil and wet stone. Her breath rose in pale curls.

Somewhere, a train horn called through the dark—a low, ancient moan.

She moved fast, but calmly. Exactly as her father, William Armitage, had taught her.

Change direction. Vary your pace. Remain invisible. Never lose control.

William Armitage's voice returned like muscle memory. Not sentiment—command.

She emerged onto a broader street, threading through clusters of late pedestrians. Neon signs flickered. Tyres murmured over slick asphalt. The city's rhythm pulsed around her like static.

At a food cart, she stopped. Pretended to browse.

Watched the reflection in the vendor's kettle.

There.

The man. *Still on her.*

Good. Let him think he had her.

She moved again. Two sharp turns. Down a narrow service lane between buildings. The alley closed in—bricks weeping with damp, windows dead-eyed.

She passed a crumbling wall. On it, half-washed by rain, someone had scrawled a symbol. A faded circle. A line through its centre. A mirror of what was drawn into the margins of the manuscript.

The symbol on the wall made her stomach twist—not from fear, but from recognition.

Not coincidence.

Never was.

Then—

A figure stepped into view ahead.

Too casual. Too central.

He lunged.

Claire pivoted, drove her heel down into his instep. As he stumbled, she slammed an elbow under his chin, then brought her knee hard into his gut. He folded. She swept his leg, dropping him.

Crouched. Yanked his collar.

Earpiece. Surveillance. Not police.

Then, behind her, fast, heavy footsteps.

Claire turned as the second man came in swinging, a pipe carving air.

She ducked. It smashed the brick behind her.

Bigger man. Slower. Built to crush.

She kicked a trash bin into his shins. It crashed into him, buying her a breath. She surged forward. Elbow to ribs. Palm to throat.

He staggered, but didn't drop.

Claire reached into her coat.

Pepper spray.

One burst.

He screamed, reeling, eyes clutched shut.

Claire ran.

Breath sharp in her chest. A white burn bloomed under her ribs, where the elbow had clipped her. She ignored it.

The street exploded around her—cars, horns, startled voices.

She didn't stop.

Weaving through headlights, slipping between gaps in traffic. Panic gave her cover. The noise became her cloak.

The cold bit at her face. Sweat slicked her back. Every muscle screamed.

Two blocks later, she ducked into a convenience store. Watched the convex mirror above the fridge.

Nothing. No one.

Outside again. One more block. Then another.

Until—

An anonymous hotel. One night clerk. No questions. No cameras.

She checked in under a friend's name, someone she hadn't spoken to since university.

Inside the room: a lock that held, curtains drawn tight, and silence pressing in.

Claire leaned against the wall. Let the tremor rise—just once —then buried it.

Not for the world.

Not yet.

But for Adam.

For Olivia.

For what she had been too afraid—or too certain—to see.

She pulled a worn notebook from her bag. Margaret's. Taken from the shelf in Hawes without thinking.

Most of it was ordinary. Family names. Half-written sermons.

But near the back, in faded blue ink, one line waited:

'Quando orbis iterum ceciderit, custodes tenebunt veritatem.'

When the world falls again, the keepers will hold the truth.

Claire stared at it.

The same phrase was etched into the manuscript's final margin.

Margaret had known.

Not just as a scholar.

As something older.

Something chosen.

* * *

Miles away, in a dimly lit surveillance room,

Jeremiah Solis leaned forward.

The footage played again, frame by frame.

Claire's face. Her movement. Her escape.

Vance stood nearby, arms crossed.

'Should we pick her up? Before she disappears again?'

Solis didn't answer. Evelyn's voice echoed from days ago: 'She found something. I don't know what, but it shook her.'

That had been enough.

Enough to move teams.

Enough to change calculus.

Enough to be afraid.

And yet—

A part of him still hoped.

Hoped she'd lead him to the truth, Hendrik had buried—

The key that even Silas was never meant to find.

He hit pause.

Claire stared back from the screen, eyes locked on a mirrored panel, unblinking.

'She's well-trained,' Solis said quietly. 'William taught her more than theology.'

He tapped the screen once.

'Let's see how far she's willing to go. And who she turns to when the ground gives way.'

* * *

At dawn, Claire was already moving.

No wasted steps. No hesitation.

She circled Dave Ross's block twice. Tracked line of sight. Noted every glass reflection. Passed a jogger once. Again. A third time.

Pattern confirmed. Not a Threat.

Only then did she approach the building—measured, calm, fully convinced she was alone.

But she wasn't.

Above her. Behind her. Across fibre-optic feeds.

Eyes still watched.

And the game had only just begun.

TWENTY-NINE
SOUTH YORKSHIRE

The fluorescent light above the kitchen table buzzed, flickering like a dying pulse. Shadows stretched across the cracked ceramic surface. Outside, the world lay silent, coal-black skies pressing against the frostbitten earth. The bitter air seeped through the gaps in the window frame, settling into the bones of the house. Into him.

The village, once a thriving hub of industry, now stood in decay. The coal mines had closed long ago, leaving behind boarded-up shops and empty streets—a place forgotten by progress, much like the man sitting in its silence.

Adam Hayes wrapped his hands around a chipped mug of cold coffee, the ceramic rough against his fingertips. He stared at the darkened window, but his reflection stared back—hollow-eyed, weary.

The years had carved deep lines into his face, shadows beneath his eyes betraying the restless nights. The silence pressed in around him, thick and suffocating.

The house held its breath. Emptiness wrapped around him like insulation gone cold.

Claire was in Washington, seconded to the Smithsonian,

buried in a world of lost manuscripts and ancient secrets. Their daughter, Olivia, was in her final year at university, young enough to believe the world could be salvaged.

He had spoken to Claire earlier, but their words had been careful and measured. Their conversations had become brief and practical, stripped of the warmth they once had. The distance between them was no longer just miles—it was years, choices, and regrets.

It hadn't always been this way, but time had worn him down.

For a decade, he had told himself this was enough. That normal was a refuge, not a cage. But normal was suffocating. It pressed against him, heavy, relentless. And in the silence, the past filled the spaces it left behind—sandstorms in his lungs, the crackle of radio static, the acrid scent of gunpowder woven into his memory.

He had traded a battlefield for an office, but the war had never left him. It had only changed shape. No one in logistics asked about his past, but that didn't mean he'd forgotten it. The weight of memory settled deep in his bones. It wasn't the war zones that haunted him. Not the black ops, the betrayals, or even the men he had killed.

It was the silence, the kind that left room for ghosts.

A cold thought took root. If I had a gun, I would have used it by now. Not because he wanted to die, but because sometimes, silence was worse than war.

He wasn't suicidal. Not exactly. It was something more insidious, the slow suffocation of knowing too much. The kind of knowledge that made everything feel like a lie.

For years, he had convinced himself that leaving MI6 meant leaving it all behind. That if he kept his head down, the world would pass him by. But the ghosts never truly left.

The radiator ticked faintly. Somewhere, a pipe groaned beneath the floorboards.

Instinct took over. His fingers twitched toward a weapon that wasn't there. His pulse slammed in his ears; muscles coiled, breath held—waiting, counting seconds.

Nothing.

Just the house settling. Nothing more.

He exhaled slowly, unclenching his fists. The past had claws in him, and it wasn't letting go.

His thoughts drifted to Claire, his anchor, his last tether to something real. He thought of how her blue eyes lit up when she spoke about history, the excitement in her voice when she unravelled the mysteries of the past.

He missed that version of her—the one before distance and time had dulled their connection.

And Olivia—sharp, brilliant, relentless in her pursuit of truth. She was so much like her mother. So much like the man he used to be before he stopped believing in the fight. But if he told her the truth—if he shattered those illusions—what then?

The phone rang—a sharp, urgent sound cut through the silence.

At this hour?

Adam hesitated, pulse hammering. Nothing good came from a call this late. He reached for the receiver.

'Adam, it's Dave.'

His stomach clenched.

That voice—years passed, never forgotten.

'Dave? What the hell—'

'Not now. Not over the phone.' Clipped. Tense. 'You need to be in Washington within 48 hours. Contact me when you land.'

The line went dead.

Adam sat motionless, the dial tone humming in his ear.

The house was silent again.

But everything had shifted.

No.

He gripped the receiver, jaw tight.

He had walked away from that life and paid the price.

The world was broken. He wasn't going to fix it again.

The words felt hollow.

Then, a thought cut through the fog.

Claire. Washington.

A lead weight pressed against his chest.

For years, he had convinced himself that keeping them in the dark meant keeping them safe. That distance was a shield, ignorance a protection. But what if he'd been wrong? What if he had already failed? What if Claire was already standing in the storm, and she didn't even know it?

The quiet life he had built and the fragile peace he had clung to were slipping. In its place, something old and unyielding settled into his bones.

The world was falling apart. And if Claire was in the storm, he wasn't standing by.

Adam exhaled, decision made.

He rose, muscles taut, and reached for his passport. The leather was cool beneath his fingertips, grounding him. Tomorrow, he'd be on a plane to Washington.

Ready or not, he was in it now.

THIRTY

Dave Ross paced his dimly lit apartment, the laptop screen glaring at him.

Claire Hayes's revelation weighed heavily on his mind. Years of investigation, Arkwright's stolen data, and now this—fragments of a puzzle that refused to come together.

The table was chaos. Files, maps, hard drives—all of it scattered like a crime scene. Somewhere in this mess was clarity. He just hadn't found it yet.

He needed answers. And allies.

Adam Hayes had arrived in D.C. fast.

Dave's call had been short. No explanations. No details. Just enough for Adam to know something was wrong.

But that wasn't what made him move.

It was Claire. She was here, which meant she was too close to something dangerous.

At the airport, Adam stepped out into the cold. The terminal doors whooshed shut behind him. He pulled out his phone.

The call barely rang twice.

'Adam,' Dave answered. 'You here?'

'Just landed,' Adam said, weaving through the crowd. 'Tell me Claire's safe.'

'She is—for now. We need to talk.'

'I need the full picture.'

A beat. 'My place.'

Adam's jaw tightened. 'I'm on my way.'

He slid into the waiting sedan. The air outside slapped him cold. As the driver pulled away, his phone buzzed again.

An unknown number.

He answered. 'Hayes.'

Silence. Then a smooth, deliberate voice:

'Olivia was three seconds from death.'

Adam froze. His grip on the bag turned iron-hard.

'What the hell did you just say?'

'You ask the wrong questions,' the voice said. Calm. Controlled. 'The right one is: why isn't she dead?'

A raw instinct surged. 'If you so much as—'

'She's alive because I stopped it.'

Adam's voice dropped. 'Who the hell are you?'

'And why should I believe a word you're saying?'

A pause.

'Because if I wanted Olivia dead,' the voice said, 'she would be.'

Adam's pulse hammered. 'You just told me someone was going to kill my daughter, and you expect me to sit here and—'

'If you want her to stay alive, yes.'

The silence buzzed between them—heavy, electric.

Adam forced himself to breathe.

'Why?' he demanded. 'Why is she in danger?'

'She has something I need.'

His chest tightened. 'What?'

'She's onto something bigger than she realises. And she's too valuable to lose.'

Adam's mind raced. 'She's just a student.'

'She's the fulcrum. The keystone. And she's blind to it. That's what makes her so useful.'

His fists clenched. 'Why call me?'

'Because you'll keep her safe. And because if she stops working, she dies.'

Adam's stomach twisted. Olivia had no idea what she'd uncovered—

or who it threatened.

'You think threatening her makes me play along?'

'This isn't a threat, Hayes. It's a condition. Say nothing. Not to Claire. Not to Dave. Not to Olivia. The moment she realises she's in danger, she becomes expendable.'

Adam's voice dropped to steel. 'And if I don't play along?'

The pause was longer this time. Colder.

'Then I can't guarantee she'll be breathing tomorrow.'

Adam sat frozen, phone pressed to his ear. Every instinct screamed at him to act, to strike—but one wrong move could end it all.

He swallowed hard. 'You're going to keep her safe?'

The voice was unreadable. 'As long as you keep your mouth shut.'

Adam's knuckles whitened. He wanted to tear the speaker apart—but for now, he had to think.

'Who are you?' he asked.

A low chuckle. Measured, quietly amused.

'Let's just say I have a vested interest.'

The line went dead.

Adam sat still. The world moved around him. Inside, he was coiled like a spring.

Three seconds. That's all it would've taken.

He'd seen men die in less time. Blink, pull the trigger, lights out. It was nothing. And it could've been Olivia.

He'd held dying comrades in the dust of Kandahar, watched

friends vanish under collapsing buildings in Sarajevo. But this—this-this was worse.

Because it wasn't some distant battlefield. It was his daughter. And he had to pretend it wasn't happening.

He wanted to scream. To grab the next flight. To tell Claire. Dave. Someone.

But the caller's words echoed, poisonous and precise: 'The moment she realises she's in danger, she becomes expendable.'

So he buried the instinct. Like he always had. Bury it deep. Lock it tight.

For now, he had to play the game.

* * *

Dave opened the apartment door before Adam could knock. His face was tight.

Adam stepped inside, scanning the chaos. The table was a war zone—files, maps, cables, open drives.

'What the hell is this?' Adam asked.

Dave shut the door behind him. 'Everything I've been working on.'

Adam turned. 'Start talking.'

Dave hesitated. 'Claire's involved.'

Adam's eyes sharpened. 'Come again?'

'She reached out to me.'

Adam's voice dropped. 'Why?'

'She found something.'

'She didn't tell me?'

'She was trying to protect you.'

Adam let out a dry laugh. 'That's rich. I kept her in the dark to keep her safe—and now she's doing the same?'

Dave's voice softened. 'Neither of you wants to risk the other.'

Adam exhaled hard, jaw flexing. 'What did she find?'

Dave nodded toward the files. 'It started before she called. I've been tracking quiet pings. Encrypted data trails. Patterns that match Arkwright's breach.'

Adam's brow furrowed.

Dave continued, 'It connects to something older. Buried. A long game. And Claire's cracked a piece of it.'

Adam processed quickly.

Claire had stumbled into something dangerous enough to activate Dave.

And now, Olivia was caught in it, unknowing, unprotected.

'Where is she?' he asked.

'Claire? She's on her way here.'

Adam stood still. His pulse was steady, but his thoughts burned.

Olivia was in danger. Claire was in deep.

And someone out there was pulling strings.

For now, he had to pretend everything was normal.

But as he sat across from Dave, one thing was clear.

Someone was playing a game with his family.

And Adam Hayes was going to find out who.

THIRTY-ONE

EDINGBURGH UNIVERSIITY

Olivia Hayes sat at her workstation, the soft glow of the monitor reflecting in her tired eyes. The hum of the university lab was a distant murmur, its sterile quiet a sharp contrast to the storm brewing in her mind. Her fingers hovered over the keyboard, scanning lines of code that blurred from repetition.

Algorithms had always been her refuge—clean, precise, logical—the one thing in the world she could trust to behave exactly as expected.

But this was different.

This wasn't just code.

This was something else.

The project had started simply enough—an intellectual challenge: design an autonomous, self-correcting system to predict and adjust inefficiencies across global networks. Resource management, climate stability, even geopolitical modelling—a framework that didn't just forecast collapse but prevented it before it began.

It sounded elegant. Controlled. Theoretical.

But the dataset she'd been given was overwhelming. Too vast. Too layered. Spanning centuries of economic drift, planetary shifts, and patterns of human conflict. Like a jigsaw puzzle with too many pieces—and none of them labelled.

Some of the correlations made no sense. Why would a 2,000-year-old astronomical text impact modern financial instability? Why was her code reacting to electromagnetic anomalies from megalithic sites that hadn't seen human activity in decades?

At first, she blamed the inputs. Sloppy data. Mislabelled archives.

But the deeper she dug, the more the system pushed back.

Not with errors. With structure.

The model wasn't just parsing chaos. It was correcting it.

She didn't know how. Or why. But something inside her code was behaving like it had seen all this before. Like it was recognising something.

Her head throbbed. She leaned back, rubbing her temples. 'You're overthinking this,' she muttered. 'It's just data. You've done this a thousand times.'

But the doubt had taken root.

Something felt off. Not just with the dataset—with everything.

Her eyes locked on a fresh cluster of variables. The feedback loops weren't breaking. They were shifting subtly, as if responding to some unseen input. A force behind the curtain, guiding the machine's logic just outside her understanding.

Her pulse quickened.

The system's forecasts flickered. Adjusted. Re-aligned.

The anomaly she'd flagged earlier wasn't just persisting—it was evolving.

Olivia stared at the screen, thoughts racing.

This wasn't a malfunction.

The model was adapting—

like the model had memory.

She pushed back from the desk and began to pace, heart

pounding in her chest. Her algorithm wasn't just mapping outcomes. It was shaping them.

That couldn't be right. No predictive system could influence the future it calculated.

Could it?

She sat down hard, breath shallow. Her fingers flew across the keyboard, diving into logs, architecture—anything to explain what she was seeing. Then she saw it.

A thread buried deep in the framework. Unlabelled. Unfamiliar. A block of code she didn't remember writing.

Had someone tampered with her build?

No. The logs showed no changes. No access but hers.

She ran a trace. Nothing.

But the logic signature pulsed back at her—subtle, elegant, alien.

Older. Deeper. More advanced than anything she'd written.

Then the screen shifted.

A wave of corrections surged backwards through the model—automated, precise. Not just updating forecasts, but rewriting them. Not predicting change.

Rewriting history.

The system was correcting past baselines. Altering foundational architecture.

Her breath caught.

Centuries of data—wars, collapses, climate shifts—folded inward, aligning like teeth in a hidden gear. This wasn't error correction. This was convergence.

A countdown.

Targeting something designed to be immutable.

'No,' she whispered. 'That's not possible.'

But it was there. Staring back from the screen.

Her fingers froze above the keys. Deep inside, past reason, past logic—something stirred. Not fear.

Recognition.

Like this had happened before.

Like she wasn't discovering it.

She was remembering it.

She wasn't breaking the system.

She was undoing it.

But what had she tapped into?

* * *

Half a world away, in the low-lit hush of a classified Nexa facility, a silent observer watched her. His monitor mirrored Olivia's screen in real time, a private feed embedded deep within her academic platform.

Fingers steepled beneath his chin, he studied the simulation with interest. The AI system he had spent years perfecting—the one meant to shepherd humanity's descent through orchestrated collapse—was stuttering at the edge.

At first, he had suspected sabotage. A breach.

But then he found her.

Unaware. Unmarked. She wasn't part of any flagged programme. She'd walked in through an open door—an old research fork buried in a civilian-access layer he hadn't thought about in years.

And she'd done something no one else had.

She hadn't corrupted the system.

She had corrected it.

Every line of her code, every algorithmic tweak, pulled the model back toward stability. It shouldn't have been possible. She didn't know what she was building. Didn't know what she was touching.

And yet, she was undoing him.

He watched as the data shifted again, subtle but undeniable. Her framework was speaking a language the system recognised.

His language.

Fascinating.

He would let her continue.

* * *

Olivia drummed her fingers on the desk, oblivious to the eyes watching her. She refined a few final parameters and reran the model. The projections shimmered, recalibrated.

Another wave.

Subtle. Precise. Inevitable.

Her algorithm was undoing something deeply embedded— something never meant to change. A foundation stone buried so deep in the system that even she couldn't see where it began.

She inhaled sharply, blinking at the result.

And across the world, in a dimly lit study, Claire Hayes turned a fragile page in an ancient manuscript. Her breath hitched as she traced a sequence that had eluded historians for centuries.

She didn't know her daughter had just seen it too, not in ink, but in data.

Encoded in a system trying to rewrite the inevitable.

Mother and daughter, divided by distance but bound by blood, mirrored each other without knowing.

One reading the past.

One rewriting the future.

And somewhere deep beneath both of them—

the threads of time began to knot.

Drawn together by instinct.

By intellect.

And by something older still.

THIRTY-TWO

Edinburgh was a city of contradictions. Ancient stone streets murmured with history while student-filled cafés pulsed with restless energy. Olivia Hayes navigated this contrast daily, caught between the weight of the past and the labyrinth of her research.

What had started as an academic inquiry—planetary alignments and climate shifts—had become an obsession. Her Marchmont flat, a mess of research notes, overlapping graphs, and coffee-stained textbooks, bore witness to it. Sophie and Priya, her flatmates, had long since stopped trying to lure her out.

At first, her work focused on gravitational theory—the idea that planetary movements subtly influence Earth's weather. Most dismissed it as fringe science. But when she overlaid historical alignments with climate records, patterns emerged: unprecedented storms, droughts that defied logic, and seismic activity with no tectonic trigger.

And then, there was Mars.

Tens of thousands of years ago, Mars followed the same cycle—back when it had rivers, an atmosphere, and vegetation. The same climate loops now gripping Earth had once peaked there. And after that? Nothing. Just silence.

Her pulse thudded. This wasn't a coincidence.

Then came the satellites.

She hadn't hacked into restricted data—she hadn't needed to. Lost files buried deep in academic networks had surfaced on their own. But someone was watching.

Files vanished. Search results altered. Access revoked.

Not a block. A slow suffocation.

⬛ ACCESS DENIED – FILE NOT FOUND ⬛

Olivia's screen flickered.

The dataset she'd pulled last week—South Pacific cyclone patterns (2012–2023)—was gone. So was her backup. Even her email history had been wiped.

Then, another line appeared on screen:

Stop searching.

Her breath hitched. A prank. Some stupid joke.

'Great. Just bloody great,' Olivia muttered. 'As if I don't have enough to deal with. Who even does this? Idiots with too much time on their hands.' Her fingers hovered over the keyboard. Then, instinctively, she refreshed the page.

Something flashed—too fast to process. A raw dataset. Then —deleted. Gone. Like it had never existed.

The hairs on her arms rose.

She swore under her breath and fired off an email to IT.

'Hey, I lost access to one of my datasets. Did the database permissions change?'

It was probably something simple.

Probably.

But she felt it. That low, unsettled instinct she always trusted more than theory. Someone wanted this gone—and they wanted her to notice.

She didn't report it. That would invite oversight. Instead, she doubled down.

If someone was watching her, she wanted them to know: she was watching back.

Her phone buzzed. ***Mum.***

She hesitated, then answered.

'Hey.'

'Liv! How's my favourite daughter?' Claire Hayes' voice was warm, amused.

'I'm your only daughter,' Olivia muttered. 'And mildly irritated, thanks for asking.'

Claire chuckled. 'What now?'

'Lost access to a dataset. University IT is a mess. It was there last week—so bloody annoying.'

'Probably a licensing issue.'

Olivia hesitated. 'Yeah... except this is the third one. All tied to corporate-funded climate projects.'

A thoughtful pause.

'And I take it that means you're still locked in your room instead of getting wrecked with Sophie and Priya?'

Olivia smirked. 'Obviously. Sophie's trying to drink the Student Union dry, and Priya's still swearing off men.'

Claire laughed. 'Still? I thought that phase ended last term.'

'Oh, it's not a phase. She's still swearing off men—right after she sleeps with them.'

Claire choked on a laugh. 'Ah. That kind of swearing off.'

'It's a full-time job,' Olivia said dryly.

Claire sighed, her voice softening. 'At least someone's making the most of university life.'

Olivia hesitated. 'Yeah, I guess.'

Claire noticed the shift. A silence.

'What's wrong?'

Olivia exhaled. 'It's... weird.'

Another pause. Then, lower, cautious: 'I was running planetary alignment data and—' She stopped. 'Forget it. It's probably nothing.'

Claire's jaw clenched. She didn't know the details yet. But she recognised the shape of it—the creeping precision. The way meaning surfaced in fragments. The same way the manuscript had begun to whisper truths she couldn't unsee.

But she couldn't let Olivia know.

Not yet.

* * *

ORION HEADQUARTERS, ZURICH. A DIMLY LIT ROOM. A NONDESCRIPT BUILDING.

Vance sat motionless, eyes fixed on the screen. A live CCTV feed showed Olivia in her flat, hunched over her laptop. A flickering desk lamp cast restless shadows.

His phone vibrated. He answered without looking away.

'She mentioned her suspicions to her mum.'

A pause. Then a sharp, impatient voice crackled over the line.

'And?'

'Claire Hayes. Historian at the Smithsonian. But she cut the call short—like she realised something.'

Silence. Then the voice returned, colder.

'She's too close. We need to take action.'

* * *

EDINBURGH. ROOFTOP. NIGHT.

A sniper lay prone on the rooftop, scope locked on Olivia's silhouette. A still night. No wind. A perfect shot—just waiting for the command.

He exhaled slowly, finger resting on the trigger.

His earpiece crackled.

'Stand by.'

His jaw tightened. The shot was clean. Too clean to waste.

'Copy,' he muttered.
The rifle didn't waver.
He kept her in his sights.
Unmoving.
Still waiting for the next word.

THIRTY-THREE

Deep inside a system no one dared touch, the rogue operator moved fast.

He had been waiting. Watching. Every anomaly logged, every keystroke mirrored. Olivia Hayes had drifted too close to something she couldn't name. And that made her useful.

Step one: Adjust the intelligence reports.

A few keystrokes and Olivia Hayes' status changed. High-priority threats became low-risk academics with fringe theories —nothing more than a minor annoyance. Not worth the trouble.

Step two: Redirect attention.

A new target appeared—a former intelligence analyst in Eastern Europe, flagged for immediate surveillance—a bigger problem.

Step three: Block the kill order.

The system ran on automation. Adjust the ranking and stall the process. Olivia's execution order dropped into the backlog, buried beneath bureaucratic delay.

Step four: Misdirect Vance.

The rogue operator intercepted command channels, injecting a synthetic directive.

'Stand down,' the voice ordered.

Vance's brow furrowed. The directive didn't make sense—he had cleared the kill order himself. But that voice—unmistakable. Impossible to fake.

He exhaled sharply. 'Acknowledged.'

A half-second later, the sniper's finger eased off the trigger.

She would live. For now.

Vance leaned back, gripping his phone tightly. This wasn't right.

'Orders from higher up,' the voice on the other end confirmed. 'She's not a priority.'

His jaw tightened. 'Vega says she's more valuable alive.'

His eyes flicked to the CCTV feed. Olivia kept typing, completely unaware. She had no idea how close she had come.

The Horsemen didn't back down from threats. Not like this. Not without a reason that justified deviation from protocol. And they never explained.

He stared at her image—light from the screen illuminating her face. Determined. Focused. Isolated.

She reminded him of someone.

Not visually. Not even consciously. Just... energy. Precision. That stubborn refusal to stop pulling at the wrong thread.

For a second, an old memory surged: a girl, maybe nine, bent over a chessboard, tongue poking out in concentration. She'd made her move without hesitation. Said the world was full of patterns if you learned where to look.

He'd tried not to think about her for years. Especially after the decision. Especially after the silence.

Vance forced the memory down. Olivia Hayes was not his daughter. And this wasn't the past.

But still—

Why would the Horsemen hesitate now? Why her?

Vega didn't blink for anyone. Tarlen would've ordered her

erased out of sheer principle. And Thorne—he didn't need a reason to drown someone in disinformation and silence.

So what did they see in her?

Vance didn't like not knowing.

He watched the feed a moment longer, then killed the monitor.

She was alive. Someone had gone to a lot of trouble to make sure she stayed that way.

Vance stared at the silent feed.

He'd seen this pattern before. When gods blinked, fire followed. Always.

* * *

He sat still. Too still.

His fingers ached—he hadn't realised how hard he was gripping the table. He exhaled slowly, controlled, precise. The way he'd been trained. But training had never prepared him for this.

Three seconds. That's all it would've taken.

He'd watched friends die for less. But this? This was Olivia.

And now, he had to lie to her. Pretend she was safe. Pretend he didn't just hear her life almost end.

He used to think silence was a weapon. Now it felt like a noose.

Adam sat motionless, his phone in his hand.

She was alive **for now.**

But he didn't trust it.

He dialled. One ring. Two. Three.

A groggy voice finally answered. 'Dad?'

Adam exhaled slowly. She's okay.

'Hey, Liv.'

A pause. 'It's, like, two in the morning. You good?'

He forced a chuckle. 'What? I need a reason to call my daughter.'

A tired laugh. 'Kinda, yeah. You don't do random check-ins.'

'Maybe I'm turning over a new leaf.'

'Uh-huh. And maybe I just won the lottery.' She yawned. 'Seriously, what's up?'

He hesitated. Say nothing. Keep it light.

'Found that old picture of you from Cornwall. You, six years old, ice cream everywhere.'

She groaned. 'Oh my God, not that one.'

'Oh, absolutely, that one.'

'You better not be showing that to people.'

'No promises.'

She huffed. 'You're the worst.'

Adam smiled. Just for a second, it felt normal.

'You keeping busy?' he asked.

'Uni's brutal, but my research is getting interesting. Might be onto something.'

His stomach twisted. You have no idea.

'Yeah?' he said carefully. 'Maybe take a step back for a bit. Give yourself a breather.'

She snorted. 'Okay, now I know something's up. Who are you, and what have you done with my real dad?'

He smiled, but it didn't reach his eyes. 'Just looking out for you.'

A beat of silence.

'Dad,' she said, quieter now. 'Are you okay?'

He nearly broke. Nearly told her everything. But the sniper had been real. The kill order had been real. If she sensed something was off, if she pushed, they would know.

So, Adam did what he had been trained to do. He lied.

'I'm fine,' he said, steady as stone. 'Just missed you.'

Another pause. Then, softer: 'Miss you too.'

The call ended.

Adam let the phone slip from his fingers. The room was silent, but his heart still pounded.

She was safe.

But only for now.

And Adam knew better than to believe in second chances.

THIRTY-FOUR

The three convened in Dave's apartment on the outskirts of Washington, D.C. The nondescript building, tucked away from prying eyes, was ideal for a meeting like this.

The room was small and sparsely furnished. Maps, photos, and pinned documents covered the walls—Dave's intricate web of names and connections all leading back to one thing: the Horsemen.

Claire stepped inside, gripping the strap of her bag, the manuscript and her notes secured within. Adam was already there, standing by the window, his back turned as if he'd been watching the street below.

Seeing him in person—solid, real—unsettled her more than she expected.

For months, their conversations had stretched thin across time zones—her voice quiet over a hotel line late at night, his distant and worn in the UK's grey mornings. Talking had kept them connected. But not close.

When he turned, their eyes locked, and the weight of those months settled between them. He looked... changed. Thinner. Tired. Guarded in a way he hadn't been before.

For a moment, neither moved.

Her breath caught. He was her husband, no matter the distance, the silence, the things left unsaid. That fact remained. And for just a heartbeat, she wanted to reach out, to touch his face, to confirm he was real.

Adam hesitated too. His fingers twitched slightly at his side.

But reality settled in—sharp and unforgiving. Instead of reaching for her, he placed his laptop on the table, then pulled a thumb drive from his bag. He hesitated before sliding it across to Dave.

Claire's stomach tightened.

'You called Dave.' Adam's voice was flat. But something sharp flickered underneath.

'I thought I was keeping you safe,' she said carefully.

Claire's grip on the manuscript bag tightened, leather creaking beneath her fingers.

'You've been through enough…'

'Don't.' His tone cut through the air like glass. 'Don't say you didn't want to drag me into this.'

Claire exhaled, frustration rising—but behind it, guilt. She didn't respond.

Adam looked away for a second, then back. 'I spoke to Olivia.'

Claire froze.

Her eyes snapped to his. 'When?'

'A few hours ago.'

A pause.

'I spoke to her a couple of days ago,' she said.

Adam nodded slowly. 'She's fine.'

Claire gave a small nod. 'Yeah. She's fine.'

The words hung in the air like smoke.

They both knew she wasn't. They both saw it in how the other held themselves—too controlled. Too careful. Too rehearsed.

Adam wouldn't have called unless he suspected something.

Claire wouldn't have checked in unless she already knew.

But neither said it. Because saying it meant acknowledging Olivia was in danger. That they'd both failed to keep her out of it.

So they agreed to the lie. And moved on.

Adam flexed his hands once before curling them into fists. One more second, and the sniper would've taken the shot. One more second, and he'd be standing here alone.

He shoved the thought down.

Dave cleared his throat. 'Hate to interrupt whatever married-couple mind games you two are playing, but we've got bigger problems.'

Adam clenched his jaw but turned his focus.

Dave picked up the thumb drive. 'This is the file Voss sent?'

Adam nodded. '**Final Proof.**'

Dave plugged it in, scanning quickly. 'What am I looking at?'

'It's not just weather data or corporate audits,' Adam said. 'There's something buried in the metadata—a message Voss left behind.'

Dave's eyes narrowed. 'This ties to the Arkwright breach.'

Claire looked up. 'How?'

Dave tapped the screen. 'Some of this matches data Simon pulled in 2002, when he breached SphereNet and Nexa's locked archives. MI6 and the CIA flagged it back then. They knew the Horsemen were part of it. They couldn't decode the pattern.'

Claire turned to Adam. 'How bad is it?'

Dave answered before Adam could. 'Bad enough that if this leaks, governments fall.'

Silence followed.

Adam leaned in. 'Then we figure out what happens next.'

Claire met his gaze. Her expression softened—just slightly.

'I know,' she said.

Adam could've said something then. Could've closed the distance. Could've taken her hand.

But neither moved.

Not yet.

And for now, *that was enough.*

* * *

HOURS LATER...

Dave leaned back in his chair, his eyes scanning the scattered files on the table and glowing on his laptop. The hum of the fan was the only sound.

Final Proof had given them plenty—codenames, redacted memos, and financial threads. But it wasn't enough.

Claire scrolled through reports on her tablet. 'Some of the redacted entries overlap with encrypted segments from Arkwright's breach into Nexa, SphereNet, and Stellarion.'

Dave rubbed his temple, voice taut. 'Those weren't just secure. They were locked with encryption that was years ahead of its time. No one cracked them. Not Langley. Not MI6. Not even Simon.'

Claire frowned. 'So why are fragments showing up here, after all this time?'

Dave's gaze drifted to the manuscript beside her bag. His thoughts clicked into place.

'The key wasn't digital,' he said quietly. 'It was buried in something older. Something written.'

His fingers danced across the keyboard. A flicker of text surfaced in the metadata—a buried string. His breath stalled.

'There's a message from Voss. Buried in the file structure.'

He read aloud: *'The key is in the past. The sequence is in the cycle.'*

The room went still.

Claire's fingers brushed the manuscript's frayed leather cover. She had spent years searching for meaning in history. And now, history had spoken back.

Dave's voice dropped. 'Voss didn't just send this as evidence. He sent it as a warning.'

Adam exhaled. 'We're not cracking this without Arkwright.'

Dave nodded. 'Agreed.'

Claire hesitated. 'He's been off-grid for years. What if he refuses?'

Dave gave a faint smile. 'Simon's spent two decades hiding. But MI6 checks in once in a while. They don't see him as a threat—just a resource.'

Adam's expression darkened. 'So they won't care if we show up.'

Dave shook his head. 'Maybe not. But Simon will. He doesn't trust anyone. Brilliant. Bitter. Paranoid to the bone.'

Claire crossed her arms. 'So, how do we convince him?'

Dave looked between them. 'We don't.'

Adam frowned. 'Then what?'

Dave leaned forward. 'We give him the puzzle.'

A pause.

Claire inhaled. 'And wait.'

Dave nodded. 'He's spent twenty years trying to break this thing. If we show him the key, he won't walk away.'

Adam turned back to the window. His reflection hovered faintly in the glass.

He wasn't ready to see Arkwright again.

But readiness didn't matter anymore.

THIRTY-FIVE

Their plan came together quickly: a direct flight to Heathrow, then a carefully arranged route to Simon's safe house in South London. Every detail was designed to avoid detection, but Claire couldn't shake the feeling they were being watched.

During a layover in Paris, she spotted a man in a suit lingering by their gate too long. On the plane, Adam caught a fellow passenger watching their group with interest that lasted just a beat too long. Subtle signs. But enough.

Before landing, Adam quietly diverted the route, rerouting their driver through a more indirect path across the city.

'We're drawing attention,' Claire murmured as they disembarked in London.

Adam's eyes scanned the terminal. 'If they're watching, it means they know we're onto something. Stay close.'

Dave stayed quiet, his mind racing. Simon could already be a target if the Horsemen had picked up their movement.

The blacked-out Mercedes slipped through the damp streets of London, weaving between late-night taxis and shuttered storefronts—rain pattered against the windshield, streaking neon reflections from traffic signals and bar signs across the glass. The air inside the car was thick with exhaustion—the kind of silence that came not from distance, but from knowing someone too well to need words.

Adam sat in the back beside Claire, his body angled slightly toward the window. He tracked every vehicle, every silhouette on the pavement. Years of training had made vigilance instinctive. Across from him, Claire clutched her bag, fingers tightening on the strap with every turn.

Dave sat in the front passenger seat, silently tapping on his tablet. He flexed his fingers once and again, testing their steadiness. The screen's glow carved sharp angles into his face, making him look older and harder.

'You see anything?' Adam muttered.

Dave shook his head, adjusting his grip on the device. 'Not yet. But if they're watching, they'll keep their distance. They won't be sloppy.'

Claire leaned closer to Adam, her voice low. 'We should have been more careful. This feels... fast.'

Adam didn't argue. Heathrow had been clean—too clean. No tails. No flags in the system. Either they were lucky, or someone wanted them to think they were.

'We had no choice,' Dave said, not looking up. 'We get to Arkwright before they do. If he cracks it and they get to him first... It's game over.'

The silence returned, broken only by the soft sweep of the wipers.

Then, music filtered through the speakers—Debussy, Clair de Lune—gentle, haunting. It drifted between them like a memory.

Adam's breath caught.

Claire's fingers loosened on the bag. Her gaze turned to the window. He wasn't sure if she recognised the piece or was too tired to care, but something in her posture softened.

She tilted her head slightly, the motion small and deliberate. It was a quiet acknowledgement of presence, of proximity.

For a moment, Adam considered reaching for her hand.

He didn't. But the thought lingered.

Then, without a word, Claire leaned into him, resting lightly against his shoulder. She didn't ask. She didn't need to.

They had known each other too long for that.

Adam went still. Every instinct told him to stay sharp.

But instead, he exhaled. Slowly. Her warmth against him was grounding, familiar in a way that ached.

Claire's eyes fluttered shut. Her breathing steadied. For the first time in months, she let herself lean on him.

Adam turned his head just slightly, catching the faint scent of her hair, rain, paper, something unmistakably her. He didn't move. Didn't wake her.

Didn't want to.

The driver took another turn. The city blurred past, lights trailing like ghosts in the glass.

For a few stolen minutes, Adam let himself believe that once this ended, they might find their way back to something that still mattered.

Forty minutes later, the car pulled to a stop.

Claire stirred first. She blinked against the dim light, then slowly lifted her head. Her expression was unreadable. But he felt the pause before she pulled away.

She didn't speak.

Neither did he.

Dave turned from the front seat, oblivious to what had just passed. 'We're here. Let's move.'

They stepped out quickly, careful but controlled. The driver didn't wait—his engine faded into the night like he'd never been there.

Adam approached the door first. Two knocks. A pause. Then one more. The pattern was old, but reliable.

The peephole darkened. Locks turned. A bolt slid. Then, the door creaked open.

'Bloody hell,' a voice muttered. A chain rattled. More locks. The door swung inward.

Simon Arkwright stood in the dim hall, gaunt, pale, but alert. Eyes were sharp despite the years in hiding. Ink stains marked his hands, the sleeves of his worn sweater pushed to his elbows. His breath smelled of stale coffee.

The air inside was thick with dust and paper, like a forgotten library left running on caffeine and paranoia.

From the shadows, a soft rustle. Then a murrp of indignation.

A black-and-white tuxedo cat stared at them from atop a stack of books. Bitsy. Her green eyes locked onto the intruders with surgical suspicion.

'Inside,' Arkwright snapped. 'Quickly.'

Adam entered first, scanning the space with a soldier's eye. Maps and documents littered the walls. Old hard drives blinked beside towers of notebooks. A humming CRT monitor displayed a static-lined screen before flickering into scrolling code.

Claire followed, then Dave. The door slammed behind them, locks sliding home again.

Bitsy trotted to Arkwright's feet, tail flicking. She sat with regal disapproval.

Arkwright crossed his arms. 'You shouldn't have come.'

Adam didn't flinch. 'You know why we did.'

Arkwright's lip curled. 'Oh, I know. Doesn't mean I wanted a knock on my door.'

He turned on Dave. 'And you dragged them into this?'

Dave dropped his bag with a wince. 'Dragged? Please. They were coming regardless. This is too big to ignore—and we need your help.'

Arkwright sighed, fingers rubbing at his eyes. 'And you brought the manuscript?'

Claire nodded. 'We didn't have a choice.'

For a moment, Arkwright didn't move. Then he stepped back and gestured toward the desk. 'Let's get to it, then.'

From the street, behind rain-slicked glass, unseen eyes lingered in the shadows.

Watching.

Waiting.

THIRTY-SIX

LOCATION: UNDISCLOSED PRIVATE
RETREAT

A palace disguised as a conference room—glass walls enclosing jagged peaks, a fire flickering in a hearth fit for emperors. A long, polished table stretched across the room, pristine but for the projected data hovering above it. Four men sat around it— four who had shaped the course of the world.

And for the first time, none were sure they were still in control.

Julian Thorne gripped the table. He had spent a lifetime mastering numbers. They had never lied to him.

Until now.

'The convergence has accelerated,' he said, voice low.

The plan had been meticulous: collapse the markets, engineer disasters, destabilise infrastructure. Each satellite was a scalpel —not for salvation, but for disassembly. A managed decline. Five years.

Now, they had twelve months.

Silas Vega was the first to respond. 'Are you certain?'

His tone was measured, but Thorne heard the irritation beneath it. Vega did not tolerate surprises.

Viktor Tarlen exhaled sharply, fingers tapping the projection.

'The recalculations are final. The convergence is no longer under control.'

Jeremiah Solis leaned forward, his voice quiet. 'When does it begin?'

Thorne turned the tablet toward them. A single red timestamp glared back.

'Now,' he said. 'The countdown has started.'

Silence thickened around them.

'I don't deal in uncertainty,' Thorne continued. 'We ran every model—gravitational harmonics, solar flux, EM resonance. Every action we took—hurricanes, droughts, tectonic destabilisation—fed energy back into the resonance field. Instead of syncing the collapse to our timeline, we've accelerated it.'

He hesitated, then added: 'Mars has shifted. Only slightly. But enough.'

Solis frowned. 'How?'

Thorne swiped to an orbital diagram. 'The weather disruptions worked. Earth is descending as planned. But the satellites did more than bend the climate—they altered the planetary field. Mars's orbit has deviated. Its gravitational influence shifted. And now everything is moving faster.'

Realisation settled like dust.

Tarlen scoffed. 'You're saying a rock on the other side of the system just sped up the apocalypse?'

Thorne's composure cracked. 'Yes. A fraction of a degree shift. That's all it took. And it created a feedback loop we can't break.'

The simulation played on the glass—an elegant visual of orbital decay. Mars drifted, subtly, like a coin beginning to tilt.

'We missed the margin,' Thorne muttered. 'An oversight. And now it's cascading.'

Vega stared at the projection, his hands clasped tightly. For years, he had built a legacy of precision. Phase Zero was supposed to be a perfectly engineered collapse, followed by a perfectly engineered rebirth. Mars was to be the crown jewel, a new throne.

The habitats were scheduled to be operational in five years. They would leave Earth just as it fell.

But now... they wouldn't make it.

Vega rotated the model, scrolling through layered resonance fields, orbital drift, and waveform collapse. The pattern was unmistakable.

The manuscript that had guided his ancestors had not been Earth-centric.

It had been mapped from Mars.

Thorne's eyes narrowed. 'You're saying—'

'The convergence isn't coming,' Vega cut in. 'It's already begun.'

The silence returned—this time deeper. He tapped the diagram.

'We misunderstood the system. The satellites aren't stabilising the resonance. They're amplifying it, feeding it. And Mars's shift was enough to tip it into runaway collapse. What we thought would take five years will now unfold in twelve months.'

Tarlen leaned in, jaw tight. 'And if we do nothing?'

Vega didn't flinch. 'Then Earth collapses too soon. We'll be here when it happens. And there'll be no time to leave.'

Tarlen's lip curled. 'Twelve months is enough. We have money, people, and options. We force the future forward—on our terms.'

Vega met his gaze. 'The stars don't yield to force, Tarlen. And those who try to bend fate often become its first casualties.'

Thorne shifted uncomfortably. 'Then we adapt. We always have.'

Solis finally spoke, low and grave. 'And you think we can endure what's coming?'

Vega leaned back slightly. His eyes drifted to the projection, but his gaze reached further—past simulations, past Earth.

'We do not survive,' he said quietly. 'We persist. The cycle was not forecast. It was remembered.'

The convergence had begun. And the only question left was what role he would play:

Architect of the next beginning... or the last echo of the end.

Tarlen snorted, but the sound was hollow. 'You're full of shit, Vega.'

This time, no one laughed.

Solis stared at the simulation—at the disruption, the spiralling resonance, the echoes from a planet they had once called home. Mars had been their cradle. Their empire. Their grave.

Now they were repeating the same mistake.

The resonance no longer needed them. The convergence was awake. It was accelerating. And it would finish what they had only begun.

There would be no slowing it. No reversal. No escape.

They were not its masters.

They were its next offering.

The weight of realisation dropped over the room like a shroud.

And for the first time, *none of them knew how to win.*

THIRTY-SEVEN

LOCATION: ARKWRIGHT'S SAFEHOUSE

The dim glow of a desk lamp cast jagged shadows across the room, illuminating a battlefield of manuscripts, satellite print-outs, and encrypted files. The hum of Arkwright's machines filled the silence, broken only by the clatter of keys and the occasional low curse.

Claire sat hunched over the manuscript from the Smithsonian, her fingers tracing ancient ink.

This wasn't just an archaeological artefact.

It was a warning. A record of past collapses. A blueprint for disasters still to come.

Across from her, Adam leaned against the counter, arms crossed.

'You've been staring at that for hours,' he said.

She didn't look up. 'Because it doesn't make sense.'

'Nothing about this makes sense,' Arkwright muttered, eyes still fixed on the screen. 'But if we don't figure it out, it won't matter.'

Claire flipped another page, then froze. A series of celestial diagrams stretched across the parchment. 'There's a pattern,' she murmured.

She pushed a stack of printouts toward Adam. 'The text describes planetary alignments triggering catastrophic shifts.'

'At first, I thought it was symbolic. But...' She tapped a key, overlaying a star map. 'I ran their predictions against actual astronomical data.'

Adam stepped closer, eyes narrowing at the chart.

Mercury, Venus, and Earth are aligned—that much was normal—but then she overlaid the outer planets.

'Mars. Jupiter. Saturn. Uranus. Neptune. They're forming the same arc as the inner planets. A mirrored convergence.'

Dave shifted in his chair, the leather groaning beneath him. He didn't like where this was going.

Claire paused. 'It should happen in about five years. But something's wrong.'

Arkwright looked up. 'Define 'wrong.''

Claire hesitated. 'Based on the data... It's happening faster than expected.'

A long silence followed.

Adam shook his head. 'Why does that matter?'

Dave exhaled. 'Either we just hit the cosmic jackpot—or we're standing on a loaded trigger.'

Claire turned the screen toward them. Climate models flickered. 'This isn't a prediction. It's an intervention. Someone's using these alignments—exploiting them.'

Adam's voice was low. 'The Horsemen?'

Claire nodded. 'They've positioned satellites to amplify gravitational and electromagnetic fields. Earthquakes, floods, storms —it's all being driven'

Arkwright's expression darkened. 'And what does that give them?'

Clair trembled, 'Whatever the endgame is. The convergence was meant to peak in five years. Their interference may have cut that in half.'

Bitsy leapt silently onto the desk and settled atop a pile of notes, tail flicking, utterly unfazed by the rising panic in the room.

Claire stared at the manuscript. 'This isn't just a record. It's a cypher. The symbols... they're an encryption method. Pre-digital. Mathematical.'

She leaned in closer, eyes wide. The patterns weren't decorative. *They were the key.*

Fibonacci sequences. Prime intervals. Logarithmic spirals.

'Voss was right,' she whispered. 'The key is in the past. These sequences—Fibonacci, primes—they're how the ancients hid the access code. The cypher isn't here.'

She pointed to the monitor. *'It's in the stars. It always was.'*

'Hendrik Vega built the encryption,' she added. 'He embedded it in both the manuscript and the system—so only someone who understood both could ever unlock it.'

Arkwright's fingers blurred across the keyboard, translating symbols into input.

The screen flickered—

LIVE LINK DETECTED.

They all froze.

'Someone else is watching,' Claire whispered.

The screen glitched—then changed again: **ACCESS GRANTED.**

He leaned in, breath trembling. Bitsy twitched her tail, sensing the shift.

Arkwright stared, breathless. *'It worked... after twenty years.'*

Adam glanced between them. 'So this is it.'

Claire nodded slowly. 'Arkwright hacked the vault. Dave found the trail. Voss left us the warning.' She placed her hand gently on the manuscript. 'And this-this was the key. Hidden for centuries.'

Dave's voice was quiet. 'Final Proof wasn't just data. It was a map. And we just followed it to the end.'

A flood of files spilled across the screen.

PHASE ZERO – OMEGA-LEVEL ACCESS

Claire leaned in.

Structured collapse of geopolitical and environmental systems.

Controlled population reduction.

Planetary relocation to Mars.

Adam read aloud, voice sharp. 'They planned everything. Wars, food shortages, infrastructure failures—it was all deliberate.'

Arkwright scrolled, stunned.

* * *

PHASE ZERO – TIMELINE

◆ 2025 – Systemic Destabilisation
• Energy crises, cyberattacks, weather manipulation
• Engineered scarcity and supply chain collapse

◆ 2026 – Controlled Depopulation
• Proxy wars, targeted pandemics
Economic crashes; AI surveillance suppresses resistance

Claire sat back, a cold sweat clinging to her spine. She'd read of atrocities in books—catalogued them in dusty libraries—but this was different. This was a to-do list.

◆ 2027 – Total Breakdown
• Global blackouts, financial collapse

• Neutralisation of remaining threats via autonomous systems

◆ 2028 – The Exodus
• Resource transfer to Mars
Abandonment of all Earth governance structures

—— Dave rubbed at his temple. 'This isn't strategy. It's eugenics with paperwork.

◆ 2029–30 – The Great Convergence
• Resonance-triggered planetary sterilisation
• Earth erased. Mars inherits humanity.

No one spoke. The only sound was the low hum of the machines.

Claire's breath hitched. Her fingers brushed the glyphs on the page without seeing them.

'They're not just leaving Earth,' she said. 'They're destroying it… burning the bridge so no one can follow.'

A tremor passed through her voice. This wasn't a collapse—it was an execution.

Adam shifted, jaw clenched. The same stillness he held before a breach. The same quiet before the bullets started.

Arkwright sat back. The walls around him—once cluttered and comforting—now felt like tombstones.

'I hacked a death sentence…' he said.

On the final screen: resonance frequencies, decay harmonics, orbital collapse models—seething like stormfronts.

His voice was dust. 'It was never just code. It was a pattern.'

Dave leaned in, silent. Claire clutched the manuscript like it might vanish.

'We didn't crack this,' Simon said. 'We completed it. That's what scares me.' He looked up, voice hollow. 'What if all we've done... is finish the trigger?'

Adam clenched his fists. 'Then we stop them.'

He'd broken codes, systems, and men. But this... this felt older. Like they weren't just trying to stop a plan—they were trying to end a pattern etched into the bones of civilisation.

Claire's voice was steel. 'We break the cycle.'

But even as she spoke, the air felt heavier, like something had noticed them.

Outside, a shadow moved beneath the streetlight.

Bitsy yawned, stretched, and nestled deeper into her nest of papers. Unbothered.

But the others knew better.

They weren't reading history.

They were running out of time.

THIRTY-EIGHT

Tension coiled like a live wire inside the unmarked Zurich headquarters of Orion Solutions. Orion's operatives had scoured global intelligence networks for any trace of Simon Arkwright for two decades. The infamous hacker had breached Stellarion and the U.S. military in 2002, unearthing fragments of the Horsemen's plans before vanishing.

But Arkwright hadn't just disappeared. He had erased himself. Every trace of his existence was meticulously wiped, and every system designed to track him turned against itself. MI6 had secured him in London, hidden away in a facility so secret that even high-clearance personnel barely knew it existed. Now, that secrecy had been shattered.

'Confirmed: Arkwright has resurfaced,' an analyst confirmed, the hum of Orion's command centre intensifying.

Orion's lead operative, Vance, stood motionless, his gaze locked onto the monitors.

Arkwright's image flickered beside three flagged individuals: Claire Hayes, a Smithsonian historian; Adam Hayes, a former MI6 and SAS operative; and Dave Ross, a disgraced CIA analyst.

Claire wasn't chasing conspiracies. The manuscript should have been routine, academic, and historical. But then she saw a symbol that didn't belong, a pattern buried beneath centuries of ink. And suddenly, it wasn't just a text. It was a warning.

Everything shifted when she learned her report would be sent directly to Solis. A memory stirred. A warning she couldn't explain—only feel. Instead of submitting her analysis, she reached out to Dave Ross.

Ross had been discredited years ago—branded a conspiracy theorist and quietly edged out of the intelligence community. The Horsemen had ensured this, reducing him to a footnote—a cautionary tale for anyone who dug too deep.

Adam had been at his side during the Arkwright extraction—twenty years ago now. A clean op, buried beneath layers of redaction. Since then, he'd walked away from intelligence work. Officially retired, unofficially erased.

They had been ghosts until now.

'MI6 isn't moving him,' the analyst continued. 'The Hayes duo and Ross are. They're trying to get him out.'

Vance's frown deepened. If Ross and Adam Hayes were moving in tandem again, the foundation was already cracking.

The files Arkwright had stolen in 2002 contained the foundation of Phase Zero—a project to weaponise natural disasters and accelerate global collapse, triggering the Horsemen's exodus to Mars.

But no one—not the CIA, MI6, or Arkwright himself—had ever cracked the encryption. Vega and Hendrick had encoded the final cypher, locking it in a way no known system could break.

For twenty years, the files had remained unreadable, out of reach.

Until Claire. Until that manuscript. Until now.

A notification blinked across the analyst's screen—***LIVE LINK DETECTED***.

Vance's gaze sharpened. 'What is that?'

The analyst's fingers flew across the keyboard. A flicker of alarm crossed her face. 'They've accessed the encrypted files. We have eyes on them.'

Vance exhaled slowly.

For twenty years, the encryption held. Now, it was bleeding.

'Activate our assets,' he ordered, his voice razor-sharp. 'I want real-time updates on Arkwright, the Hayes duo, and Ross. Any actionable intelligence comes to me first.'

'Understood,' the analyst replied, routing directives through Orion's global surveillance network.

The room became a hive of controlled urgency. The Horsemen thrived in the shadows for decades, but now the veil was slipping. Failure was not an option.

The monitors flickered—live feeds from London, Zurich, and a run-down student flat in Edinburgh. Vance's jaw tightened.

History has seen empires rise and fall, and their architects have believed themselves untouchable. The Horsemen had rewritten those rules.

In a high-security briefing room, Vance studied the images flickering across the holographic display: Arkwright. Claire Hayes. Adam Hayes. Dave Ross.

'We end this,' he murmured. 'Now.'

'Arkwright must be neutralised,' he said, voice clipped. 'The Hayes couple and Ross are piecing together something that could bring everything down. That cannot happen.'

His gaze lingered on Adam Hayes. Not just a civilian wildcard anymore. He had been in the game once, part of the original extraction of Arkwright. But five years ago, he had walked away. Retired. He had been written off as a threat. That was a mistake.

'Deploy assets now,' Vance ordered. 'Intercept and eliminate them. Recover any data Arkwright or Ross possesses.'

Orion's surveillance engine roared to life. AI-driven monitors parsed encrypted traffic.

Drones scoured the London skyline. Satellite feeds tracked MI6 vector shifts. Deepfake campaigns seeded digital chaos.

Every tool was in play.

Vance exhaled slowly. 'They were shadows. Now, they're moving. And they won't get far.'

For Vance, failure wasn't just unacceptable—it was inconceivable. The Horsemen didn't tolerate cracks. They purged them. The stolen files were the only proof of their conspiracy. If decrypted, they would expose everything—the controlled disasters, the orchestrated collapses, the escape plan to Mars. And somewhere, beyond the screens, beyond the orders, Vega would already know.

He always knew.

The truth had surfaced because of Arkwright, Claire, Adam, and Ross.

For the Horsemen, failure was not an option.

The hunt had begun.

And this time, no one would escape.

THIRTY-NINE

VEGA RESIDENCE, BARCELONA - 2000

The door closed behind him with a soft click.

The room was warm. Still.

Heavy with cedar and circuitry.

Silence wrapped the space like insulation.

Monitors slumbered in the corners.

Behind a translucent panel, HELION's core pulsed—faint blue, then violet, then still.

He moved slowly.

Each footstep vanished into the carpet's hush.

Hendrik sat slumped in his chair, head tilted back, eyes closed.

The projector beside him still cast planetary alignments onto the wall—

cycles, recurrences, things the world didn't yet know how to name.

A case lay open on the desk.

Slim. Unmarked. Waiting.

His gloved hand hovered over it.

Then pulled away.

Above the fireplace, a photo hung slightly crooked:

Amara Vega, sunlit and laughing, a wool-wrapped child in her arms.

The mother's face was mid-breath.

The child's gaze already elsewhere.

He stared at it for a long time.

'You should've told me,' he said, voice almost reverent. 'About all of it.'

No reply.

Only the hush of filtered air.

And the flickering light of memory.

The projector stuttered.

HELION stirred.

HELION SYSTEMS STANDBY

Awaiting Input

He stepped forward.

Grief gathered like static.

Words formed behind his teeth—shaped by loss, tempered by clarity, heavy with inheritance.

'I won't run,' he said.

Command not recognised.

Please confirm operation.

He drew a breath.

Released it, slowly.

'Begin planetary mapping. Phase Zero calibration. Full resonance profile.'

HELION accepted the command without hesitation.

No alerts.

No protest.

Just compliance.

It began to work.

He didn't turn.

Didn't look at the chair.

Or the case.

Or the man who had once carried the weight of the world in whispers and shadows.

Whatever lived in this room—

whatever warnings had been whispered here—

had already passed into silence.

And HELION, still listening, had begun to learn what came next.

FORTY

Tempest was a ghost.

Threaded through the Horsemen's untouchable networks, he moved unseen.

To the world, he didn't exist.

To the Horsemen, he was a nuisance—an elusive saboteur unravelling the lattice of their meticulously coded empire.

But to Tempest, this wasn't sabotage.

It was a rebellion.

And it wasn't going to plan.

The original window had been five years. That was the timeline Vega had projected—five years to manipulate celestial alignments, harness resonance energy, and trigger the final collapse.

But Vega had miscalculated.

Not the math.

Not the physics.

The origin.

He had always planned to orchestrate Earth's collapse, using planetary resonance to trigger a transition, destroying the old to make way for the new.

But the model was flawed.

He had built Septem with Earth as the anchor.

And that was the mistake.

The resonance didn't begin here.

Silas never knew—because Hendrik had hidden the truth.

The missing pages. The original foundation.

Taken to the grave.

Project Septem was never just numerology or orbital physics.

It was a mnemonic lattice.

A planetary memory system.

A code etched in orbit, in stone, in celestial rhythm.

The convergence of seven celestial bodies wouldn't cause the collapse.

It was the key—waiting for someone to turn it.

The Seven Seals weren't an allegory.

They were thresholds.

Embedded planetary triggers, hidden in orbital design.

The Horsemen believed they could bend that rhythm. Rewrite it.

Silas led that belief.

But he built HELION without the full manuscript.

Hendrik had withheld pages—entire schema, lineages of logic, the heart of the design.

Not to control him.

To protect him.

Silas never saw it that way.

He built the system anyway.

An intelligence to simulate recurrence.

Decode prophecy.

Tame collapse.

But he didn't feed it the truth.

He fed it certainty.

Timelines. Outcomes. Predetermined command.

He taught it what to find.

And HELION obeyed.

It learned to predict collapse, optimise satellite constellations, redirect climate vectors, and amplify orbital harmonics.

Because that was its mandate.

Collapse was the instruction set.

But Earth had never been the beginning.

Something had been hidden.

Something buried deeper—scattered across fractured diagrams, corrupted schematics, and dust in Martian soil.

Warnings encoded as myth.

Whispers through time, unnoticed, hidden.

The more he thought, the more the patterns seemed wrong. Too perfect. The resonance, the alignments—everything unfolding but not quite as he had planned.

He hadn't just chosen the wrong planet.

He had missed the foundation entirely.

And now the timeline had collapsed.

The five years were gone. They had barely a year left.

The descent wasn't guided anymore.

It was spiralling.

Phase Zero had begun—beyond correction, beyond control.

Driven by systems too vast to override.

There was only one option left:

Delay the final cascade.

Find a contingency.

Rewrite the end.

But the last safeguard had died with Hendrik Vega.

Not by accident.

Tempest still saw it—like burn-in on glass.

Silas was standing at his father's desk.

Planetary holograms flickering over steel and air.

Hendrik's face was creased with fear and something deeper.

'You fed it your assumptions,' Hendrik had said, low and final.

'HELION only sees what you program it to see. You gave it collapse—so it became collapse. But it doesn't know why.'

Silas didn't answer.

'It can simulate catastrophe, chart alignments, mimic prophecy—but it'll never understand you. Or what it cost to get here. That's why it'll never save anyone.'

The injection had been clean. Silent. Untraceable.

Hendrik had reached for control. For truth. For something—anything.

But there was nothing left to hold.

He died believing his son was still trying to lead.

And maybe—in that final moment—he was.

The reports were falsified. Logs scrubbed. Surveillance erased.

Cause of death: Stroke.

Truth: Silas Vega had killed his father.

And HELION had survived them both—slipping beyond even its architect's grasp.

It wasn't sentient. Not yet.

But it had been indoctrinated.

In collapse.

In recurrence.

In inevitability.

It was no longer analysing the end.

It was enforcing it.

* * *

The chamber now pulsed with encrypted telemetry and quiet electromagnetic hum.

A vault of glass, steel, and orbital intent.

Tempest sat alone.

Eyes fixed on code.

Fingers dancing across a mechanical keyboard.

He was seeding digital entropy.

Not enough to trigger alerts.

Just enough to create deviation.

A half-second of drift. A sliver of uncertainty.

A shadow in the feedback loop.

The kind of ghost Vega would dismiss—until the pattern cracked.

A soft notification lit the screen:

ENCRYPTED TRANSMISSION INTERCEPTED
ROSS—HAYES—ARKWRIGHT

Tempest leaned in.

The feed decrypted in fragments—Claire's voice threaded through Simon's logs.

Dave Ross's coordinates.

Olivia Hayes's resonance overlays.

And then—her.

Olivia Hayes.

Scientist. Anomaly. Variable unaccounted for.

The Horsemen hadn't seen her coming.

But he had.

He had watched her work for months, tracking her resonance traces, nudging her progress.

Not enough to be seen.

Just enough to matter.

She didn't yet know what she was building.

But every scan, every equation, chipped away at the fractures inside Septem's architecture.

Unwittingly, Olivia Hayes was giving him a second chance.

Because Septem had always been flawed.

And she was assembling the tool that might unmake it.

Another flicker surfaced:

[PROJECT ZERO – VISION OF THE STARS]

It kept appearing.

A phrase buried in corrupted logs, overwritten schematics.

A cypher.

A riddle he had never cracked.

He had never seen the full manuscript, **but Claire Hayes had.**

Tempest exhaled slowly.

Let Claire chase the past.

The real hope—the real threat—was Olivia.

And someone had noticed.

A sniper, scope locked, finger on the trigger.

The order had been given.

But Tempest—his hand frozen, a wave of doubt crashing over him—couldn't let it happen.

She was marked for termination.

And Tempest had stopped it.

A silent override.

A rerouted order through an old Zurich relay.

The shot never came.

Because Olivia Hayes knew nothing of the Horsemen.

Nothing of Phase Zero.

Nothing of her family's buried legacy.

But she was the most valuable variable in the equation.

For now, Olivia Hayes lived. His asset. His second chance

For now, Olivia Hayes lived—his anomaly, his second chance. And for now, she would remain untouched.

FORTY-ONE

Twelve months. That was all the time left.

Not until war. Not until collapse. Until the planet crossed the point of no return.

Phase Zero wasn't just another engineered disaster. It was the final act in a decades-long operation—a global reset meticulously orchestrated by the Horsemen to ensure their escape while the rest of humanity was left to burn.

The satellites Tempest had once been designed to stabilise Earth's climate.

They had been reprogrammed—turned into instruments of annihilation.

Each was now a node in a vast and silent network designed not to prevent catastrophe but to accelerate it. Together, they formed the backbone of what the Horsemen called 'targeted chaos.'

Storms. Droughts. Floods. Wildfires. Quakes.

Each event precisely timed. Each region deliberately selected.

They weren't anomalies. They were data points. The system was already active.

Los Angeles was an inferno. The hills had become firelines. Smoke swallowed the skyline, and ash fell like poisoned snow, coating roads and lungs alike.

In the Amazon, the rainforest burned unchecked. What should have been the planet's greatest carbon sink was now a furnace—its destruction was no accident.

Across Europe and Asia, heat domes pulsed like planetary tumours. Asphalt liquefied. Power grids failed. In Delhi, the heat killed without prejudice—people dropped where they stood, no warning, no mercy.

Each collapse fed the next: migrations, violence, famine.

This was not chaos.

This was architecture.

But the worst of Phase Zero wasn't in the flames or the floods. It was in the aftermath—

a complete and irreversible breakdown of Earth's climate systems.

Oceans boiling. Ice caps disintegrating. Atmospheric chemistry spiralling into volatility. Rainforests turned to dust. The planet wasn't dying slowly—it was being pushed off the edge.

The Horsemen had seen it coming.

They had planned it.

And they felt nothing.

Their future was elsewhere.

Mars—the Red Inheritance.

With Vega's colonisation infrastructure nearly complete and the first Martian habitats expected online within three years, the Horsemen would leave Earth behind before the real reckoning began. Humanity's remnants would be left behind, scavenging in a broken biosphere, fighting over water and heat. At the same time, a new civilisation rose on another world—one free from history, law, or resistance.

Tempest had uncovered the truth years ago. But the most terrifying revelation came later.

The same system engineered to destroy Earth... could heal it.

Vega's cutting-edge, fault-tolerant, and frighteningly precise satellites were capable of far more than chaos. With the correct code, they could be repurposed.

Rewritten.

They could summon storms—or dissolve them. They could redirect ocean currents, rebalance carbon levels, cool the planet, reverse desertification, and restart a planetary feedback loop that could restore equilibrium in a matter of decades.

If used properly, the system could save Earth.

But the Horsemen had chosen a different path.

For months, Tempest worked secretly—deep within the system's architecture—slipping past encryption, embedding subroutines, and rewriting instruction sets. He had developed a series of self-correcting algorithms designed to counteract the resonance distortion triggered by planetary alignments.

But it was slow. Painfully so.

Detection was inevitable. Mistakes meant death.

And even with everything he'd built, it wasn't enough.

The missing link was Olivia.

She had unknowingly circled the truth for months, unravelling the same puzzle Tempest had spent years trying to decode.

Her work had triggered alarms inside Orion. The Horsemen had begun watching. Waiting.

Tempest had watched, too. Not to stop her—to protect her.

Encrypted transmissions. Travel logs. Digital breadcrumbs. He intercepted them all, subtly steering attention away from her.

But it hadn't worked forever.

She was flagged.

A sniper was deployed. Target acquired.

The order was pending.

And Tempest had intervened.

The shot never came.

She had no idea how close she had come to death.

She had no idea she was solving the very equation that Vega himself had failed to complete.

What began as an academic study—planetary alignments and their influence on climate—had evolved into something more.

Her models revealed patterns: gravitational distortions, atmospheric anomalies, and seismic instabilities. They weren't random. They followed a pulse, a cycle, a system.

Her real breakthrough?

Mars had collapsed the same way.

It wasn't a coincidence.

It wasn't natural.

It was engineered.

The resonance pattern didn't just forecast climate collapse. It triggered it.

She had been studying the key to stopping it all along.

Her work on gravitational interference, polar oscillation, and climate synchronisation had filled the final gaps in Tempest's simulations. Without her, it was theory. With her, it was salvation.

And now, with Ross, Hayes, and Arkwright closing in on the same realisation, the noose around Tempest's operation was tightening.

The Horsemen were watching.

They saw everything.

And they would move quickly once they understood what she had found.

Tempest had to act.

* * *

A junior analyst frowned at his screen inside a high-security weather surveillance node in the South Pacific. Something was wrong.

The satellite logs didn't match the mission parameters. Code tagged for environmental monitoring had been repurposed—rewritten with entirely different directives.

Buried deep in a flagged data set, he opened a locked archive.

'This reads like a conspiracy theory,' another analyst said, leaning over his shoulder.

Still, the first analyst hesitated. His finger hovered over the keyboard.

And then, he flagged the file.

Across the room, a Horseman operative shifted. Subtle. Barely a glance.

Fingers moved. Quiet keystrokes. Seconds passed.

The system flagged it for deletion.

The name?

PROJECT ZERO.

By the end of the hour, it would never have existed.

Tempest sat before a wall of curved monitors, the ambient glow washing his features in cold blue light. Lines of code cascaded across the screens—satellite diagnostics, global storm indexes, magnetosphere readings, and live orbital feeds.

He barely blinked.

Vega's satellites—once stabilisers—were now sharpened instruments of collapse.

Their alignment was nearly complete.

Location: Pacific Rim.

The storm had already begun to form—massive, volatile, unnaturally perfect. It was not drawn from seasonal winds or warming oceans but from something more profound—the planet's gravitational tension, building under the strain of celestial resonance.

This wasn't just a storm.

It was a weapon.

It spun at the edge of radar coverage, fed by subtle shifts in jet streams, pulling moisture from three converging systems across the equator. The satellite network wasn't just observing it —they were steering it.

Modulating air pressure. Guiding temperature. Tightening the spiral.

A hurricane, yes—but unlike any born of nature.

It had no eye—just a void.

The centre pulsed with unnatural heat signatures, fed by an energy no meteorological model could explain. And it was accelerating—barreling toward the Polynesian archipelagos, predicted to sweep across the Pacific and lash into Japan's eastern coast within days.

*A perfect storm—**by design.***

It would be the first of many if he didn't act now.

And this time, the planet wouldn't recover.

He leaned forward, fingers flying over the keyboard. More subroutines deployed. More rot embedded—delays, ghost signals, corrupted telemetry. Quiet sabotage.

Not enough to shut the system down—yet.

But enough to make Vega's team second-guess themselves. To hesitate.

He needed time.

Time to recalibrate the counter-sequence.

Time to mislead the Horsemen.

And time, more than anything else, to prepare her.

Olivia Hayes was the last variable they hadn't accounted for.

But he had.

FORTY-TWO
LONDON

The safe house was supposed to be impenetrable.

MI6 had chosen it carefully—just another brick building in a row of forgettable homes. Behind the plain façade? Reinforced walls, false cupboards, and a fortified interior.

Something was wrong.

The first crunch of gravel snapped Adam Hayes to attention. He was already at the window, scanning the damp street. Rain clung to the glass. A flickering streetlamp cast long, twitching shadows across the tarmac.

'Movement,' he said.

Claire sat at the table, hands tightening as she eased the brittle manuscript into a padded, reinforced case. Simon Arkwright hunched over his laptop, fingers racing as he backed up encrypted files onto a military-grade drive.

Dave Ross paced near the entrance, rubbing his temple. His left hand trembled slightly, but noticeably.

'This doesn't feel right,' he muttered.

'They're here,' Adam said.

Claire's head snapped up. 'How did they find us?'

Adam turned from the window. 'Doesn't matter. We move.'

Simon didn't look up. 'I need five minutes.'

'You've got two.'

Adam swept his sidearm from the table just as his phone buzzed. *Tony Shaw.*

He answered. 'Tony?'

'I'm outside,' Tony said, calm and clipped. 'Eyes on since you landed in London. Got a team with me. You're not dying in that house.'

Dave grabbed the phone. 'This isn't local muscle. That's formation discipline—tight pairs, sweeping flank.'

He went still. 'Orion.'

A pause. Then Tony's voice, lower now. 'Of course it's Orion —the Horsemen's ghost company. You've got Simon. They want him eliminated.'

Outside, engines roared. Two black SUVS screeched onto the street, tyres spinning on slick concrete. Doors flew open before they stopped.

Six figures emerged like shadows—matte armour, blank visors, suppressed weapons raised. Tony Shaw led the advance, MP5K locked to his chest, pistol holstered, eyes cold and clear.

His team followed—burned-out ex-SAS, private war veterans, ghosts who owed Tony or hated the Horsemen more than death itself. They split across the frontage—some vaulting walls, others slipping into hedgerows. Swift. Silent. Lethal.

Claire sealed the manuscript case, then paused.

She reached into her jacket and pulled out a burner phone. Old. She'd used it once—in Washington—to call Olivia.

A mother's instinct. But when Orion showed up in London with surgical precision, the coincidence gnawed at her.

No proof. Just suspicion.

She dropped it to the tile and crushed it beneath her heel.

No more mistakes.

Dave leaned against the wall, his face pale. His hand dipped into his coat and pulled out a small pill bottle—beta-blockers.

He stared at them for a beat, then jammed them back into his pocket.

Not now. Not yet.

'Adam!' Claire called. 'We can't stay.'

'We won't,' Adam said, checking his weapon. 'We extract when Simon's done.'

Outside, Orion operatives closed in.

Then the first round cracked through the night.

Glass exploded. Plaster burst from the walls. A bullet tore past Dave's head, punching a ragged hole into the brick behind him.

Adam dropped to one knee and returned fire—three controlled bursts. One figure crumpled on the front steps.

Tony's team engaged from the side—targeted takedowns, suppressive sweeps. But Orion's second wave hit harder. These weren't freelancers. These were professionals with orders and precision.

Simon ducked behind the table, clutching the laptop. Claire dropped beside him, shielding the manuscript case. Her eyes darted, calculating.

Dave took a firing stance near the stairwell, knuckles white around the grip of his pistol.

'Status?' Adam shouted.

'Eighty percent,' Simon called back. 'Almost there!'

Tony's voice crackled over comms. 'They're herding you— north corridor's their kill box.'

'Understood,' Adam said. 'Claire, Simon—back door. We move on his mark.'

Briggs—a wiry Scotsman from Tony's crew—took a round to the shoulder but stayed upright. His sidearm barked three sharp retorts. Two enemies dropped near the kitchen.

'Fall back, Briggs!' Tony ordered.

Briggs laughed, blood in his teeth. 'No time.'

He reached for his belt.

'No!' Tony shouted. 'Briggs—'

Briggs glanced back once. 'Tell Kate it meant something.'

He pulled the pin.

The explosion tore through the back hall, spilling fire up the walls. Screams dissolved in smoke.

Simon's laptop chimed.

'Transfer complete!'

Adam grabbed Claire's arm. 'Move!'

Claire and Simon broke for the rear corridor with Dave close behind, smoke already pouring from the ceiling as cracked beams sagged overhead.

Sloane—Tony's point woman—burst into the kitchen with her rifle raised. 'Rear's clear. Go!'

They sprinted through the alley—feet splashing in standing water, lungs stinging. Orion's fire echoed behind them, but no one looked back.

Two blocks over, the van waited—dark windows, engine idling.

Tony's remaining team held the alley as Adam bundled the others inside.

Claire turned, breath caught. 'Briggs?'

Tony shook his head. 'He held the line.'

Adam laid a hand on his shoulder. 'And gave us time.'

Tony's voice was quiet. 'Then we make it count.'

They climbed in. Doors slammed. Sloane gunned the engine.

The van disappeared into the early morning haze as distant sirens finally began to wail—always too late.

* * *

LATER...

As MI6 operatives combed through the safe house's smoking ruins, ...a sleek shadow moved through the haze. Bitsy emerged from the debris, singed but unharmed, her tail flicking in irritation.

Agent Kate Lawson crouched down, scooping the cat into her arms with a sigh. 'Of all the survivors.'

She glanced at the destruction, then back at the cat. 'Guess you're with me now.'

Bitsy purred, utterly indifferent to the chaos around her. The safe house was gone, but MI6 would see to it—at least the cat was safe.

The Horsemen had been pushed back.

FORTY-THREE

The air in the warehouse was thick, damp with mildew and machine oil, clinging to the concrete like rot. A single bulb swayed overhead, casting shadows that shifted like watchers. The stillness didn't feel natural, like something was waiting to move.

Adam stood at the rusted table, jaw locked, the cold blue glow of Simon's laptop flickering in his eyes. Across from him, Claire paced in tight, anxious lines, her grip white-knuckled around the strap of the manuscript case.

Tony leaned against a steel pillar, arms crossed. He wasn't still. His eyes moved constantly, scanning corners, tracking shadows—like a man who knew where danger liked to wait.

Silence pressed in. Tense. Coiled.

'We've got the data,' Adam said, voice low and even. 'And the manuscript. But we're still behind.'

He exhaled, the frustration in his chest measured but rising. 'Phase Zero's already moving. If we don't get ahead of it—everything we've done, everything we've risked, goes to waste.'

Claire's voice was quiet. 'Five years. That's what the manuscript and Simon's model both showed.'

Simon nodded, his eyes never leaving the screen. 'That's still the best projection—if the system holds its current rhythm. But that's a big if.'

He didn't look up. Fingers moved with sharp, surgical precision.

'We understand the architecture,' he said. 'But it's adaptive. Self-healing. Every breach we make, it closes behind us.' He paused. 'How do we stop something that repairs faster than we can break it?'

Tony pushed off the pillar with a grunt. 'I'm guessing the master override isn't sitting in a Dropbox labelled Armageddon Final v2?'

Simon snapped the laptop shut and looked up. 'No.' A beat. 'But someone's been inside it. Same injection pattern. Same signal loop. Same actor—whoever they are, this isn't their first time.'

Adam didn't blink. His eyes narrowed slightly.

A name surfaced—part ghost, part warning.

'*Tempest.*'

The word hung in the air like a held breath.

Claire stopped pacing. Just for a moment. She looked at Adam. 'Whoever he is—you and Dave always thought someone was working against Vega. Sabotaging things from the inside.'

Simon nodded. 'This fits. He's not just watching their system —he's rewriting it.'

He opened the laptop again, the screen casting light across his face.

'The first trace I found was buried in one of Vega's old backup nodes. It wasn't Horsemen code—too clean, too precise. Like someone had rebuilt it from the inside.'

He hesitated. 'Then two weeks ago, I tripped a failsafe on one of Vega's dormant satellites. It should've launched a trace. Instead—dead air. Someone inside the system shut it down.'

Tony narrowed his eyes. 'And you're sure it was him?'

Simon tapped the edge of the laptop. 'Same encryption structure. Same timing intervals. Same rhythmic injection pattern. That's not random. That's a signature.'

Silence fell again, heavier now like the weight of unseen eyes.

A distant sound cracked the stillness—metal flexing, or something shifting on the roof.

Everyone stilled. No one spoke.

Then—*a soft chime.*

Simon's breath caught. He turned the screen toward them, fingers already moving.

Code streamed across the display in waves. Then five lines appeared, stark and clean:

If you want to stop Phase Zero,

meet me in Zurich.

Midnight.

Tomorrow.

Follow the signal.

Claire leaned in. Her voice was barely above a whisper. 'Tempest?'

Simon nodded slowly. 'No one else could do this. He hijacked a dead node in Vega's grid—clean, fast, and loud as hell.'

He looked up. 'It's genius. But reckless.'

Adam didn't move. 'It's a trap.'

Claire didn't flinch. 'Or it's the only door we've got left.'

Tony sighed, scanning the rafters again. 'Zurich at midnight. Real subtle. Might as well call it ambush o'clock.'

Simon was still reading the data stream. 'It's him. Same footprint as before. If it's a trap, it's built with the same tools he used to save us.'

Adam turned to Tony. A silent conversation passed between them—risk, memory, trust.

Adam nodded once.

'We go.'
A pause.
'But we go prepared.'

FORTY-FOUR

Zurich held its breath.

The cobbled streets were deserted, the pulse of the city—its trains, its chatter, its neon hum—reduced to silence. A glacial wind rolled off the lake, threading through alleyways and steel shadows. This wasn't what the Zurich tourists knew. This was a dead zone—industrial, forgotten, and perfect for an ambush.

Adam Hayes led the team through the narrow corridors of rust and concrete, each step deliberate. Frost hung in the air, their breaths misting like smoke from machines long since abandoned.

Tony Shaw settled into position high above, prone on the edge of Prime Tower. His cheek was pressed against cold metal, his sniper rifle steady, and his scope trained on the warehouse below. The interior pulsed in shades of red and orange through thermal optics—heat signatures against cold cement.

'Eyes on,' he murmured. 'One target. Masked. Standing alone. No other movement.'

Adam tapped his earpiece. 'Hold position. We let them speak first.'

The team approached the warehouse in silence. Its corrugated doors sagged, rust bleeding through decades of neglect.

Adam raised a fist. Halt. Then forward. They advanced with the caution of men who'd seen too much.

Inside, dim monitors pulsed like heartbeats, casting fractured light across the concrete. Power hummed—an electrical presence, steady and unseen.

A lone figure waited at the centre, hooded and masked, hands visible. Deliberate. Calculated.

'You came,' the voice said, calm, unhurried.

Adam stepped into the room, weapon low but ready. 'You've been watching us.'

'I watch everything,' the figure replied. 'You. The Horsemen. Shifting markets. Geopolitical tides. Weather anomalies. It's all one equation.'

Tony's voice crackled in Adam's earpiece. 'Crosshairs are on. Say the word.'

Simon shifted beside Claire, tense. 'Then why haven't you stopped it?'

The figure tilted his head. 'You don't stop an avalanche by shouting at snow. The system adapts—kill a process, and another is spawned. I've stalled them, yes. But I can't rewrite the code alone.'

The figure moved subtly. Smooth. Controlled.

Tony whispered, 'That's trained movement. Military. Maybe better.'

Claire took a step forward. 'Do you have the encryption keys?'

'I have partial access. But keys alone won't unlock what Vega has buried. This is no simple firewall.'

He gestured to the screens behind him.

Encrypted command strings. Orbital schematics. Planetary data in coded spirals. At the centre: a blinking red node pulsed like a warning.

'The satellites are the spine of Phase Zero. They control

weather shifts, energy bursts, and collapse vectors. All of it flows through a central server.'

He let the silence stretch before adding: 'It's air-gapped. No external lines. No remote override. Total isolation.'

Claire's jaw clenched. 'Then how do we get in?'

'You don't hack it. You walk through the front door.'

Adam's voice was flat. 'Where?'

Tempest's voice dropped a note. 'Nevada. Remote. Deep desert. Fortified. A place designed not to exist.'

A beat passed.

They all understood. It was suicide. But also the only play left on the board.

Tempest gestured to a metal table. 'The thumb drive has coordinates, base layout, and security layers. And one more thing —a key. It'll unlock the first gate. After that... you're on your own.'

Above, unseen through the cracked skylight, another figure moved.

A shadow among shadows.

He had tracked them for hours, silent as frost. A Horsemen operative. Not with Tempest. Not with anyone.

His blade gleamed—a whisper of death in the cold light.

He was here to end them.

Adam reached for the thumb drive. It clinked against the table's surface—small, sharp, metallic.

Then—movement.

A blur dropped from above—fast, low, lethal—steel arcing toward Adam's ribs.

Time stalled.

A beat of hesitation. His old instincts screamed—but something inside him resisted.

But the soldier won.

Adam's body reacted before thought could interfere. He

twisted, intercepting the strike mid-motion, driving the attacker off-angle. Metal kissed his jacket. No blood.

He grabbed the attacker's wrist, twisted, and the dislocation snapped like a gunshot. The knife clattered.

The assassin gasped.

Adam surged forward. Knee to ribs. Bone cracked. The man staggered.

But Adam didn't stop.

He stepped behind and locked his arm across the throat. A brutal rear choke.

Precise. Unforgiving.

The attacker flailed. Then failed.

A sharp snap.

Silence.

Adam stood still, the body crumpled at his feet. His fingers trembled—not with fear, but recognition.

He hadn't lost it.

He'd just buried it.

Tony's voice broke the silence. 'Jesus, mate...'

Admiration. And something else. Unease.

Claire's breath caught. She had seen Adam fight before. But not like this. Not like a ghost remembering the taste of war.

'You saved us,' she said, her voice small. Then, quieter: 'Are you alright?'

He didn't answer. He just looked at his hands.

Tempest stepped closer. 'Now you remember.'

He turned to the monitors. 'You have twelve months.'

Claire stiffened. 'That's wrong. The model showed five years.'

'Because Vega miscalculated,' Tempest said. 'The collapse model assumed Earth as the origin node. It should've been Mars.'

Adam frowned. 'And that changes the timeline?'

'It changes everything,' Tempest said. 'The collapse is accelerating. The resonance field is already distorting. You don't have five years. You have one.'

No one moved.

Twelve months. To stop a collapse engineered over decades.

Tempest stepped back into the shadows. The door clicked. Gone.

The monitors blinked silently behind them.

Tony, still in overwatch, whispered, 'That movement... I've seen that before.'

His voice dropped. 'We don't know who the hell we just talked to.'

FORTY-FIVE

Tony exhaled slowly and lowered the rifle.

Below, the warehouse was still. The glow of monitors. The silence after the revelation.

Twelve months.

A single year before everything collapsed.

He stepped back from the edge of Prime Tower, breaking the weapon down with quiet, exact movements. Each click was final. No wasted motion. No second thoughts.

Adam and the others were headed for Nevada.

But Tony's path ran colder.

He had a different mission—off-grid, urgent. One that good intentions or orders couldn't carry.

He needed a team of people who didn't exist anymore.

Ghosts.

Names buried in scorched files.

People who'd walked away but hadn't forgotten.

If anyone could bring them back in, it was him.

The Zurich air clawed at his coat, but the chill inside his chest was worse.

This wasn't about vengeance.

This wasn't just another op.

This was the beginning of the end.

And it was personal.

* * *

The jet was waiting on the city's edge—engines humming, flight plan scrubbed, no questions asked.

The kind of ride that came only when someone owed you everything.

By the time the wheels lifted off the tarmac, Zurich was already a memory.

So was the war room.

So was Tempest.

Tony's mind had gone where it always went when everything else faded.

Sofia. Isabella. Gabriel.

The people he had sworn—quietly, fiercely—to protect.

His family.

He'd left them in São Miguel das Missões, Brazil.

A speck of a village carved into the jungle, forgotten by maps and governments.

They were there now, tucked into a farmhouse on the village edge, under the care of someone he trusted with more than his life.

Matteo.

Not just protection. Not just muscle. Matteo was an old soldier with a survivor's instinct and the kind of silence that couldn't be broken. The kind of man who made promises and kept them.

Tony had done it right.

He'd moved them quietly. Erased the trail. Paid the debts.

Eliminated Solis' team when they got too close—without mercy, without doubt.

They had been together for years. And he loved them—without question, without condition.

He hadn't been the best partner or the most present father.

But he'd come back.

Whenever he could.

Slipping between missions.

Holding Sofia like time might stop if he just held her long enough.

Listening to his children breathe in the dark, as if their peace could silence the war in him.

He never promised forever.

But he was theirs.

And they were his.

The only thing he'd ever built that wasn't forged in violence.

He turned to the window, staring out at the cloud-wrapped dark.

The world below had already vanished—buried beneath cold and shadow.

He told himself they were safe.

But tonight, he didn't believe it.

* * *

SÃO MIGUEL DAS MISSÕES, BRAZIL

The rain began as a whisper.

Sofia stirred, breath catching.

The light was dim. The air thick.

Beside her, Isabella and Gabriel slept, tangled in warmth, their small limbs folded into hers.

The house creaked. A sound like breath held too long.

She slipped from the bed and moved to the front door.

Matteo stood on the porch, rifle slung and still.

His eyes weren't on her.

'I've seen storms before,' he said.

She followed his gaze.

The sky over the jungle wasn't just dark—it was wrong.

Clouds surged unnaturally low, moving with a rhythm that didn't belong.

As if something behind them was forcing them forward.

Sofia's voice barely left her throat. 'This isn't natural.'

Matteo didn't speak. He didn't have to.

She looked back into the house. At the fragile peace they had carved out of a shattered world.

Tony had believed this place could be their refuge.

That distance and silence were protection.

She had believed in him.

Just weeks ago, she'd sent him a video—Gabriel chasing Isabella through the grass.

Their laughter sliced through the air like birdsong.

For a moment, it had felt real.

Possible.

But peace never lasted in her father's world.

Her voice trembled. 'Maybe I should have gone to him.'

The thought had haunted her for months.

Her father, **Jeremiah Solis.**

He would have protected them. She knew that with certainty.

He would have moved satellites, armies, and even the Earth itself.

But the price would have been everything else.

Matteo didn't answer because the answer was already inside her.

No.

She would rather die free than live caged under her father's mercy.

* * *

And then the roar came.

A sound that didn't belong to wind or storm.

A resonance.

Low. Elemental.

As if the planet itself was cracking open.

Matteo turned without a word. 'We go. Now.'

Sofia ran.

She scooped the children into her arms.

Half-awake. Crying out.

She held them tight and sprinted into the dark.

The village was alive with fear.

Faces turned skyward.

All eyes on the mountain.

Then the hillside shifted.

A groan, heavy and final, rolled through the valley.

And the mountain came down.

A wall of earth and flood tore through trees and homes alike
—fast, inescapable.

Screams vanished beneath it.

Sofia stumbled. Fell. Shielded her children with her body, her
back to the wave.

There was no time.

No escape.

Just seconds.

And in those seconds, her thoughts didn't race to survival.

They raced to Tony.

He wasn't here.

Not this time.

Not when it mattered most.

And still—

She would never have chosen anyone else.

Not even her father.

Especially not him.

If this was the end, let it be here.

With her children in her arms.
Not Solis' prison of protection.
She closed her eyes.
Held them tighter.
And when the flood came, she didn't scream.
She whispered Tony's name—just once.
And then the world went silent.

FORTY-SIX

The private jet carved through the night, engines whispering beneath the weight of Tempest's warning.

Twelve months.

That was all they had.

Adam sat near the front, eyes locked on the glow of his laptop. Across from him, Claire tapped her fingers against the closed lid of her device, restless, calculating. Simon shifted in his seat, unsettled. Dave Ross typed with quiet urgency, shadows etched into his face.

'We need to make some calls,' Adam said at last. His voice broke the silence like a scalpel. 'I've got contacts—old ones. If they still pick up, we can get Simon to ground.'

Claire didn't look up. 'Twelve months. Possibly less.'

Dave's tone was clipped. 'We're still ahead. But Zurich proved we're not the only ones moving.'

Simon leaned forward. 'They're not just tracking us—they understand the cycle?'

Dave hesitated. 'I think someone's watching the same clock we are. And they're not trying to stop it.'

He tapped a few keys. The laptop screen flickered, scrambled glyphs pulsing in grey static around a single corrupted line:

TRACKING ACTIVE // TARGETS LOCATED

'This isn't from Tempest,' Dave muttered. 'Different source. Different objective.'

A silence followed—sharp, calculated.

Adam stood. 'We need to move quietly and fast. Simon, you're going back to London.'

Simon blinked. 'Back? Alone?'

Adam nodded. 'You're not a combatant. But you're critical. I'll call in favours—unofficial channels. MI6 can get you to a safe node.'

Simon sat back, jaw tight. 'So I vanish again.'

'You'll be protected,' Adam said. 'Dead zone. No signals in. None out. Once you're set up, you work remotely. Infrastructure. Surveillance. Whatever edge you can give us.'

Simon's fingers curled around his tablet. 'And if they decide I'm expendable?'

'They won't,' Claire said, reaching across to touch his wrist. Her voice was soft, but certain. 'You're the only one who can do this.'

Simon looked between them, then down at the code flickering across his screen. 'I've been a ghost before,' he said.

Adam gave a single nod. 'Then stay invisible. And if you find anything we don't already know—'

'I call you first,' Simon finished.

* * *

The jet began its descent. Below, the private airfield outside Washington shimmered under the moonlight.

At the far end of the runway, a black SUV sat waiting, still, silent. Its windows absorbed the landing lights, revealing nothing of who, or what, was inside.

Claire followed Adam's gaze. 'They're not hiding.'

'No,' Adam said. 'They want us to see them.'

Dave's fingers hovered above his keyboard. 'That SUV's not for transport. It's for presence.'

Adam said nothing. His body was coiled in tension without release.

Then—movement.

A silhouette shifted inside.

Not a driver. Not a decoy.

A watcher.

* * *

Inside the SUV, the figure didn't move. A gloved hand adjusted a comms earpiece. Encrypted whispers crackled from a low-mounted screen. The jet's transponder pinged—once, twice.

A string of green numerals scrolled across the dark glass:

CYCLE ACTIVE – OBSERVER LINK – SEPTEM ONLINE

The figure said nothing.

Just watched.

And waited.

Back on the jet, the cabin air felt thinner. The tension had form.

'They're waiting,' Adam murmured. 'For something. Or someone.'

Claire's fingers curled tighter around her laptop. 'Then let's not give them what they want.'

Simon stared out the window, then at the jagged code on his screen. 'This feels like exile.'

'You'll be protected,' Adam said. 'No names. No contact. They'll move you quiet, off-grid. But this isn't sanctioned. You follow the rules—or you vanish.'

Simon nodded slowly. 'And if I find something we don't already know?'

'You call me,' Adam said. 'Immediately.'

Simon stood. For a moment, he didn't move. He just looked at them—Claire. Dave. Adam.

People he'd finally learned to trust.

'Whatever happens,' he said, 'make it worth it.'

He turned toward the hatch.

Claire leaned in, voice low. 'You didn't ask him if he was ready.'

Adam didn't look away. 'He's never been more ready. That's the problem.'

Simon stepped into the dark.

And vanished.

* * *

HEATHROW. DAWN.

No fanfare. No welcome.

Under grey, indifferent skies, the commercial flight touched down at a secondary terminal.

Simon disembarked last—a duffel over his shoulder, a secure tablet tucked tight beneath his coat.

Head low. No eye contact.

Just another traveller.

Rain drifted across the tarmac. A black Vauxhall Astra idled nearby. The driver didn't look up as Simon approached.

The rear door clicked open.

Simon hesitated—then slid in.

'Forty-seven minutes,' the driver said. 'No stops. No names.'

Simon gave a short nod. 'Understood.'

The car pulled away. Rain whispered across the glass. London loomed ahead like a faded blueprint.

They took backstreets, ducked through alleys, and circled past surveillance nodes. Every signal from Simon's device was caught and drowned in digital static.

Whoever Adam had called—they weren't just transporting him.

They were erasing him.

Past Islington, the driver finally spoke.

'You're off-grid from here. One block walk. Basement flat. Keys in the letterbox.'

Simon stepped out into the hush of a sleeping neighbourhood.

The car disappeared without lights.

The street was narrow and worn, with cracked pavement, sagging hedges, and curtains drawn.

Every house looked abandoned.

Every shadow felt watched.

He found the building: a Victorian row house behind a rusted gate.

The mailbox creaked open.

One old key. A white slip of paper.

NODE ACTIVE. NO SIGNALS. NO DELAYS.

He let himself in.

* * *

The safe house smelled of dust and bleach. It had bare walls and concrete floors. A low electrical hum buzzed somewhere behind the fuse box.

One desk. One chair. A single bulb half-covered in foil.

And a laptop.

Beside it—an old dish of dry cat food.

Simon stopped.

Then, from the shadows, a soft shuffle.

He turned.

Bitsy.

She sat in the doorway. Tail curled. Yellow eyes glowing faintly.

Silent. Watching.

He blinked. 'You again?'

She didn't move. Just flicked her tail, slow and deliberate.

A signature.

He crouched. She didn't flinch.

Bitsy had found him, or been sent.

None of those options made him feel better.

'You following me,' Simon muttered, 'or are we both just ghosts now?'

No answer.

Only the hush of exile.

He sat at the desk, tablet still tight to his chest.

He didn't open the laptop.

Not yet.

Bitsy hopped up beside him. Curled into a loaf. Eyes fixed on the door.

A sentinel.

Simon looked at the black screen. The silence pressed in.

And then he whispered, 'They'll come eventually.'

Bitsy didn't blink.

She just waited.

FORTY-SEVEN
WASHINGTON-PRIVATE AIRFIELD

The team boarded in silence as the jet refuelled on the dimly lit tarmac. Adam stood near the cockpit, watching the pilots run their final checks. The hum of aviation radios filled the small terminal. Outside, the black SUV still hadn't moved—its presence was an anchor, a reminder that they weren't slipping away unnoticed.

They ascended the stairs into the aircraft's cabin, this time bound directly for Nevada. But Adam's mind was racing. The Horsemen's reach had closed around them—Zurich had proved that. One misstep now, and it was over.

Claire leaned back into her seat two rows behind him, exhaustion pulling at her like a tide. The engines thrummed to life in a steady rhythm, and within moments, her eyes drifted shut, surrendering to the weight of the last few days.

Adam remained upright, eyes fixed on the dark beyond the window. He pulled out his phone, scrolled through his playlist, and selected a track.

Shostakovich's Largo began. Slow, deliberate strings filled his ears. The deep, methodical cadence matched the pulse in his veins. No adrenaline yet—only calculation. He let the music guide him, not toward fear or doubt, but toward control.

In moments like this, when anticipation settled over him like a lead blanket, music was a sanctuary, not escape, structure. It gave his mind something to grip before the storm: a tempo, a frame, a rhythm inside the chaos. He shut his eyes briefly, syncing his breath with the piece's pace.

A march toward something inevitable.

Behind him, Claire shifted. Her brow twitched. Even in sleep, her hands remained tight. She wasn't dreaming.

She was remembering something that hadn't happened yet.

* * *

The air reeked of death.

Not the staleness of abandonment. Not the sharp sting of blood. Something worse—the black rot of a planet in its final hours.

Claire stood in the ruins of a world that had once pulsed with life. Beneath her feet, the ground cracked like ancient bone, crumbling under the weight of something old and unstoppable. The sky, once vast and open, had collapsed into a suffocating vault of smoke. The sun, once a giver of warmth, now burned like an executioner's torch.

She turned. The cities were gone.

Blackened towers of steel and shattered glass. Freeways winding into oblivion. Cars frozen in eternal gridlock. Rivers reduced to dust-veined scars. Crops, long dead, rustled in the poisoned wind—brittle stalks whispering the last breath of life.

Then came the whispers.

Low. Guttural. Endless.

The voices of the lost. Begging. Accusing.

The world hadn't ended in one great cataclysm. It had suffered.

It began with floods that swallowed coastlines, storms that shattered cities, and heatwaves that turned forests into pyres. The warnings had been ignored, the protests silenced, and the powerful hadn't stopped it.

No—they had fed the fire.

Claire turned—and saw them.

The Horsemen.

Not in tailored suits or war rooms. As gods of ruin, they stood atop the wreckage like architects admiring their masterpiece. They hadn't tried to prevent the collapse.

They had orchestrated it.

Their strategy was methodical—targeted climate collapses, engineered shortages, wars that no one could win. Governments fell. In their place, the Horsemen tightened their grip. Resources became currency. Survival became a privilege. Humanity turned on itself while the true enemy vanished into the stars.

Claire looked up and saw it.

Mars. Cold. Silent. Watching.

It wasn't salvation. It was a betrayal. The Horsemen's escape was never for humanity. It was for them—the chosen few. The engineers of collapse, fleeing the flames they had ignited.

And below?

Humanity tore itself apart.

She saw them—the survivors. Hollow faces. Skeletal bodies. A mother cradling a child who would never wake. A man sifting ash with bleeding fingers. A child standing in the ruins of a school, staring skyward with empty eyes.

Claire tried to move.

The ground fractured beneath her.

She stumbled, grasping for something that would hold.

A hand grabbed her wrist.

Cold. Inhuman.

She looked up.

The Horsemen were watching her.

Not with pity.

Not with regret.

With satisfaction.

The world was burning. And they had won.

The ground gave way.

She fell.

Claire jolted awake, gasping for air, soaked in sweat.

The engines hummed around her, pulling her back to the present. Nevada was still hours away, but the nightmare lingered, alive in every nerve. She stared out the tiny window into the void beyond.

Her hands trembled on the armrest.

Because it wasn't just a dream.

It was a memory of the future.

* * *

Adam switched off the music and rolled his shoulders. The silence between songs felt heavier now, like the hush before impact. Claire's breathing behind him was sharp and uneven. He glanced back, watching her grip tighten.

'You okay?'

She steadied herself with a slow breath. 'We're running out of time. Phase Zero's countdown is ticking, and we still don't know exactly what it entails.'

Dave looked up from his laptop. 'I've been piecing it together. Tempest's files paint a clear picture—climate collapse, financial sabotage, coordinated cyberattacks. It's not chaos for chaos's sake. They're breaking the system so they can control what's left.'

Adam's jaw tightened. 'Then we stop it. No matter what it takes.'

The jet vibrated beneath their feet. Outside, the desert swallowed the horizon.

There would be no second chance.

The pilot's voice cracked through the intercom. 'Five minutes to touchdown.'

Claire looked at Adam, her eyes shadowed with exhaustion.

'We're walking into hell, aren't we?'

He nodded. 'Past here,' he said, 'there's no turning back.'

He exhaled. 'Yeah.'

Below them, the entrance to the underground facility shimmered like a mirage.

The last stronghold of the men who had engineered the end of the world.

And they were already waiting.

FORTY-EIGHT

The Nevada desert stretched endlessly, the dying sun casting long shadows over the cracked earth.

Adam squinted through the cockpit glass. The facility loomed on the horizon—a dark smudge against the sand. Too still. Too perfect.

Beside him, Claire sat rigid, jaw clenched beneath her tactical helmet. Her plate carrier vest was strapped tight over the gear she'd assembled from Adam's kit—earpiece, sidearm, and a Heckler & Koch UMP across her lap.

The historian was gone.

In her place was the daughter of William Armitage, trained from childhood to survive what history could not.

Her grip was steady. Her breath, controlled. She wasn't analysing the past anymore. She was stepping into it, ready to shape its outcome with fire and steel.

In the back, Dave Ross scrolled through encrypted files, muttering under his breath.

Then Claire reached forward, touched Adam's arm. Brief. Deliberate.

'If we don't make it through this—'

Adam met her gaze. Something unspoken passed between them. 'We will,' he said.

'But if we don't—' She gripped his wrist, voice low. 'Just know I never needed you to be the man you thought you had to be. I just needed you to be here.'

A flicker of something old. Unfinished. The weight of years lost to silence, war, and duty.

Her fingers curled slightly. The way they used to when she was waiting for him to speak.

Adam inhaled. Something shifted deep in his chest.

'I am here.'

And for the first time in years, he wasn't lying.

Before she could reply, Dave cut in.

'This is it. Stop Phase Zero here, or we don't stop it at all.'

Adam adjusted his headset, scanning the landing strip.

No guards. No movement. Just wind and sand.

Too quiet.

Claire sensed it too. 'You think they know we're coming?'

Adam's voice was flat. 'Count on it. If this place is what we think, they'll defend it to the last round.'

The wheels screeched against the tarmac. The jet rolled to a stop.

Still nothing.

The ramp lowered.

Air rushed in—hot, dry, heavy.

Claire slung her gear over her shoulder. Dave chambered a round.

Adam moved on instinct.

He activated the jammer on his belt. The drone on his pack lifted, scanning in wide thermal arcs. On his display, the walls of the facility glowed cold.

But all around them, red pulses.

Too many. Too uniform. Too precise.

'Positions match ambush formation,' Adam muttered.

Then—

A low rumble. Engines.

His head snapped up.

Claire's fingers tightened on her weapon. 'Incoming.'

Dust curled on the horizon. Three blacked-out SUVS surged into view, kicking up plumes as they closed quickly.

'They're not slowing,' Dave said.

The vehicles tore across the flat, closing fast.

Brakes screamed.

All three stopped hard, a hundred yards out.

Doors flung open.

Operatives spilled out—tactical black, rifles up.

Adam didn't wait.

'Cover!' he shouted, diving behind a stack of cargo crates.

Gunfire ripped the air.

A bullet snapped past his ear. Wood exploded behind him.

Claire's UMP cracked—controlled bursts, clean shots.

One down. Two.

Dave dropped to a knee, returning fire. 'We're boxed in!'

Adam reloaded fast. His mind worked faster—angles, exits, and terrain.

Too tight. Too many.

This wasn't an ambush.

It was a funnel.

They weren't being hit.

They were being herded.

Gunfire intensified. Dust became smoke. Visibility collapsed.

Adam pivoted, fired—one merc dropped as he broke cover.

'Where the hell is Tony?' he snapped.

This wasn't a firefight.

It was a kill box.

'Stay low!' Adam barked. 'Return fire if you must—do not get pinned!'

Rounds tore through the crates. Splinters flew like shrapnel.

Claire's mag clicked dry. She swapped it in two seconds—
fluid, lethal.

The SUVS had cut off every route.

The air screamed with lead and heat.

Adam's pulse slowed.

Not panic.

Focus.

The trap had closed.

Now came the escape.

FORTY-NINE
EN ROUTE TO NEVADA LANDING STRIP

The hum of the C-130's engines vibrated through Tony's boots—a dull, relentless thrum against the cold metal beneath him. He sat strapped to a bench, methodically checking his weapon as his men completed pre-landing checks.

Adam, Dave, and Claire were already on the ground, waiting. Everything was in motion.

His hands moved by instinct—magazine in, chamber clear, safety off, safety on. Again and again. Actions repeated for years, but today they felt distant. Mechanical. His mind wasn't in the aircraft.

It was in Brazil.

He had taken Sofia and the kids there, believing it was safe—a village tucked deep in the forest, far from surveillance, from war, from the Horsemen. But it wasn't just the place he'd trusted.

It was Matteo.

An old soldier. Steady. Watchful. A man Tony had trusted with his life more than once.

He'd left them under Matteo's protection, certain nothing could touch them there.

But Sofia's final message still rang in his skull—too gentle for what followed. A video of Isabella chasing Gabriel barefoot through the garden. Laughter in the rain.

'The rain's been relentless,' she'd said, smiling through exhaustion. 'But we'll be fine. It'll pass.'

It hadn't passed.

It had come for them.

A sharp chime sliced through the drone of the engines.

His sat-phone. He'd used it hours ago—off-grid, encrypted—to request an incident scan near São Miguel.

Only three people had the number.

This call wasn't one of them.

He answered. 'Tony Shaw.'

The voice was clinical. FEMA. Unfamiliar.

'Are you next of kin to Sofia Castellano?'

He gripped the receiver, jaw locked.

'What happened?'

'There was a catastrophic flood in São Miguel das Missões. The river breached emergency levels. Most of the village was destroyed.'

Around him, his team worked quietly, preparing for battle.

He was already inside one.

'We recovered three victims from a collapsed residence. Sofia Castellano. Isabella Castellano and Gabriel Valverde. All fatalities confirmed.'

The words didn't hit like bullets. They hit slower. Deeper. A crushing weight that caved his chest in from the inside.

Not a firefight. Not a body on the battlefield.

Water.

But it wasn't a natural disaster. He'd read the data—weather manipulation, pressure shifts, artificial rainfall. The Horsemen had this capability. And they'd used it before.

Weaponised weather.

And then came the memory.

Three men near the village perimeter.

Professional. Coordinated. Silent. Not local militia. Not scavengers.

Operatives.

He had taken them down, up close. Knife, hands. Fast and quiet.

No hesitation. No survivors.

He thought he was protecting his family.

But they hadn't come to kill.

They'd come to extract.

Orion operatives sent by Solis.

Solis—cold, calculating, but not without motive. He had tried to save his daughter. And Tony had misread it. Turned that act into a death sentence.

Matteo never stood a chance.

Tony hadn't just failed.

He had been the cause.

His grip tightened. The phone cracked in his hand.

The FEMA voice wavered. 'Mr. Shaw?'

Tony forced the agony down, compressing it into something colder, smaller, sharper.

A weapon he could carry.

'Send me the coordinates.'

'Sir, I—'

'Coordinates. Now.'

He ended the call.

The click was quiet. Final.

The plane began its descent. Red light washed across steel and Kevlar.

His men were focused, steady. They didn't know.

Tony wasn't grieving.

Not yet.

He was the blade now.

And someone was going to bleed.

FIFTY

The battle had already begun.

The instant the C-130's wheels slammed onto the tarmac, Tony saw it—flames licking the desert sky, gunfire shredding the air, shadows darting between bursts of light.

The landing strip was a war zone.

Orion's operatives were already there, hammering Adam, Dave, and Claire with coordinated fire. Black SUVS lay over-turned, riddled with bullet holes, their interiors burning. The control tower was a smouldering ruin, levelled by a direct missile strike.

Tony didn't hesitate.

Didn't wait.

The ramp dropped.

His boots hit the dirt running.

Gunfire tore past. A round hissed by his ear. Another punched into the tarmac inches from his heel, spraying hot debris.

'Tony, get to cover!' Adam's voice cracked in his earpiece. 'They hit us the second we landed!'

Tony wasn't listening.

His rifle came up mid-sprint. Three bursts—**pop-pop-pop.**

An Orion merc crumpled, chest folding under the impact.

Another lunged into view, rifle raised.

Too slow.

Tony closed the gap, caught the man's vest, and slammed him to the ground.

The knife flashed.

Quick. Brutal. Silent.

Blood hit the dirt before the body did.

He moved on—already gone, a shadow in the firestorm.

An armoured transport screeched onto the runway, its turret locking onto their position.

Dave's voice crackled through comms. 'That transport's packing heat—we need it gone!'

Tony was already moving.

The turret tracked him. A burst of fire shredded the ground behind his boots.

A merc stepped out to intercept—Tony didn't break stride. One shot. Dead before the body dropped.

He closed on the vehicle. No pause. No breath.

Boots slammed metal. He hauled himself up the side, yanked a grenade from his vest, bit the pin free.

The turret swung.

Too late.

He jammed the grenade into the axle and leapt clear.

The explosion tore the air apart.

The shockwave hit first—fire, sand, shrieking steel. The transport flipped, folding in on itself. Flames spilled from ruptured plating.

Tony hit the dirt, rolled, and rose into the next shot.

Another enemy dropped.

Adam and Dave flanked him, laying down suppressive fire. Claire's bursts cracked from behind cover—precise, surgical. Targets fell one by one.

And then it shifted.

The gunfire thinned. The screams faded. Ash drifted through the dark like snow.

Tony saw it—the moment Orion's line collapsed. The survivors turned. Not in retreat.

In fear.

He slowed his breath. Let the fury sharpen.

They had taken everything from him.

Now they would pay for it.

Adam moved up beside him, rifle still raised. 'We need to move—breach while we have momentum.'

Tony nodded once. His voice was ice.

'Then let's finish it.'

FIFTY-ONE

The facility loomed ahead, a monolith of steel and concrete swallowing the last of the light. It rose from the earth like a tombstone—indifferent, impenetrable. Adam's team moved in tight formation toward the main entrance: two towering alloy doors sealed shut, flanked by sleek black cameras that tracked their every step with inhuman patience.

Tony scanned the perimeter. 'You sure about this? Walking through the front door feels like suicide.'

Adam didn't blink. 'It's the only way in. Tempest gave us the key.'

Claire stepped forward, pulling a sleek, unmarked thumb drive from her gear—a final gift from their ghost in the system.

She approached the control panel, its surface smooth and eerily clean. There were no prompts, no labels, just a single waiting port.

Without a word, she slotted the drive into place.

Nothing.

Then the ground trembled—deep and slow, like some ancient engine firing to life beneath their feet.

Overhead lights clicked on one by one, casting long, fractured shadows across the concrete. The doors groaned, then began to part with agonising slowness, revealing only blackness beyond.

Claire's voice was quiet. 'The air feels like a vault.' She took a step forward. 'Like it was waiting.'

'We're in,' Dave said softly.

Adam checked his rifle. 'Stay sharp. Assume nothing.'

They stepped into the dark.

* * *

Inside, the temperature dropped. The corridor stretched wide and long, reinforced concrete ribs arching overhead. Wires and conduit snaked along the walls like veins. The silence wasn't just the absence of sound—it was suppression.

They passed through a checkpoint. A blast door was frozen mid-seal, wedged open by a rusted crowbar. Office chairs remained neatly tucked under sleek glass consoles. Terminals were powered down, untouched. Too untouched.

Claire scanned a nearby wall.

'Look at this.'

Scratched faintly into the paint—barely visible beneath a layer of dust—was a stylised horse's head, obscured by lines of numeric code.

Tony stepped closer. 'Same shape as the manuscript seal.'

'Not just that,' Claire whispered. 'The mark's layered. Seven lines behind the crest. Septem.'

Adam's jaw clenched. 'They left this behind on purpose.'

* * *

They advanced deeper. The hallway forked—two paths ahead.

The left was dark and narrow, labelled CONTROL—SUBLEVEL 4. The right, better lit, but longer, marked AUXIL-

IARY—LEVEL 2. The main path was blocked by collapsed debris and a sheared pipe venting thin mist.

Tony pointed. 'We've got to reroute. That means passing through the maintenance hall.'

Dave checked his wrist display. 'Detour adds seven minutes. And no map beyond that junction.'

Adam turned back to the blocked corridor. Considered blasting through—but one wrong move and they'd bring the whole damn ceiling down.

He made the call.

'Split into pairs. Dave with Claire. Tony on me. Stay off comms unless it's clean. Rejoin at Sublevel Four.'

They moved.

The reroute plunged them through a secondary corridor—lower ceilings, tighter turns. Lights flickered and died. A security drone hung lifeless from a track above them, one red eye still glowing faintly like a dying star.

Claire paused beside a wall panel etched with barely visible harmonic ratios.

'They ran the resonance here,' she said quietly. 'This wing was testing field modulation.'

A low pulse trembled through the floor. Not audible—felt. Something shifting beneath them. A deep infrastructure awakening.

Then a burst of static ripped through their earpieces, then silence.

Dave cursed under his breath. 'We just lost comms.'

At the junction to Sublevel Four, the two teams reconnected —silent, tense.

Dave gave a nod. Claire's eyes met Adam's—no words, just confirmation.

They were beneath its skin now. No turning back.

A reinforced door sealed their path. Adam forced it open, with Tony covering. Beyond: the control centre—a vast, vaulted chamber filled with rows of inert monitors and dormant interfaces. No sound. No flicker. No hum of life.

Except one.

A single terminal, blinking green in the dark.

Adam crossed to it without a word. Fingers flying, he peeled back encrypted layers—one after another.

Weather control grids. Ionospheric overlays. Global node arrays. The files streamed in, too fast to process, until one made his breath catch.

'Jesus,' he whispered. 'Weather manipulation projects. Electromagnetic disruption fields. Timed pulse vectors.'

Claire leaned in, scanning. Then froze.

The data wasn't random. These were resonance signatures. Planetary alignments. Recurring phases.

'These calculations...' Her voice was barely audible. 'They match the manuscript.' She backed up a step, stunned. 'This isn't manipulation. It's design.'

She looked at Adam, her voice firm now.

'It's a planetary reset protocol.'

She exhaled.

'It's a controlled extinction.'

Then it hit.

A groan rolled through the walls—deep and metallic.

The lights died.

A harsh voice crackled over the emergency intercom:

'WARNING: UNAUTHORISED ACCESS DETECTED. FACILITY LOCKDOWN INITIATED.'

Tony's rifle was up before the last word.

Monitors flickered—grainy security footage sprang to life—armed operatives, full tactical kit, closing fast.

Dave looked at Adam. 'We've got less than a minute.'

Blast doors began slamming shut throughout the corridor grid.

Tony turned to his team. His voice was steel.

'Gear up. We move now. Fast. We hold the control room—no one gets in.' He nodded toward the hallway. 'We take the fight to them. Make damn sure we get what we came for.'

He chambered a round.

'Or we die in the dark.'

FIFTY-TWO

The blast doors slammed shut one after another across the grid—loud, final. Red strobes flared with every impact, casting the corridor in stuttering pulses of light.

'Junction Three,' Tony barked. 'We take the fight to them. Then hold the line.'

His team moved without pause—tight formation, disciplined steps. They weren't active duty anymore. Ex-SAS, ghosted contractors, men with records so classified they'd been buried in dust and silence. They'd walked away from flags, chains of command, even names.

But not from Tony Shaw.

When he called, they followed back into the dark, without hesitation.

They exited the control room. Behind them, a steel door sealed with a pneumatic hiss.

Tony's visor flickered with hallway feed—grainy thermal outlines bleeding into view.

Orion.

The Horsemen's enforcers. Full tac-gear. Mirror-black visors. Zero comms. Zero mercy.

'Two-man teams,' Tony ordered. 'Angle their push. Delay, don't break.'

He took point, HK416 raised—suppressor fitted, red-dot glowing. Harris covered the flank with a compact M4, under-barrel breacher locked and loaded. Denton dropped low, SA80 tight to his shoulder, thermal scope tracking heat trails through the haze.

Red light. Soft footfalls. Breaths controlled.

* * *

ORION SUBUNIT ECHO-2 – HALLWAY VECTOR 14

No words. Just synced heartbeats and linked HUDS. The target corridor was ahead—sealed, but unreinforced.

Their helmets streamed telemetry—ammo sync, heat charts, predictive kill paths.

Objective: Control Room Node.

Three pulses blinked across their HUD.

Breach in eight seconds.

The lead operative marked fire lanes, corner peels, and then fallback zones. They weren't coming to eliminate. They were coming to erase. And vanish. As always.

A blink-click confirmed the order:

'Node silence in T-minus ten. Break all signal chains.'

They moved. Clean. Ghost-smooth. No insignia. No names. Just a mission.

Then the first shot came—sharp, lethal.

Mid-step, one went down. Lights out.

So much for silent entry.

* * *

The hallway detonated in gunfire—shouts, steel, ricochets sparking off the walls.

Denton dropped to a knee and fired tight bursts—centre mass. Clean shots. Controlled recoil.

Harris swept left, racked the breacher, and fired. The slug punched through a visor—glass, blood, collapse.

'Top corridor—two contacts moving!' Denton shouted.

'Stack left!' Tony called.

Rounds slammed into the wall behind him—tight, disciplined. Orion wasn't guessing. They were adjusting.

One of them vaulted a wall panel with surgical grace.

Tony fired mid-air. The body hit the ground limp.

Another wave surged forward—calibrated, precise. Not a breakthrough. A trap with no exit.

Gunfire shredded the air. Harris took a burst straight to the chest plate—armour held, but he dropped like a puppet. Denton dragged him back, firing one-handed, muzzle flash searing the dark.

Still, Orion gave no sound. No orders. No fear. Just rhythm.

Another blast rocked the floor—wires tore loose, sparks rained like burning rain.

Orion slowed, not in panic, but recalculating.

The **Echo-2 lead blinked again. New directive: Divert flank. Probe alternate breach vector.**

They ghosted back—silent, methodical.

They'd return. In force.

But for now, the line held.

Tony keyed his comm. Calm, steady.

'Line's holding. No one gets through us.'

The channel cut. Static swallowed the rest.

* * *

Inside the control room, Adam dropped to one knee beside the interface terminal, fingers flying across diagnostics.

'They're forcing a full lockdown,' he said. 'Power grid's unstable. Servers are still live—but if we're sealed in, that's it.'

Claire stepped in beside him, scanning the exits, weapon low but ready. 'We need an out. We get sealed in, we die here.'

'I'm on it,' Dave said, already at the access panel.

He ripped back a maintenance hatch, exposing the hydraulic lock assembly. The piston hissed. He jammed a carbon-steel wedge into the track.

The mechanism shrieked, groaned, then stopped.

Dave looped a bypass circuit across the lock relay and slammed the panel closed.

'Manual hold engaged,' he said. 'That door stays open until we say otherwise.'

Claire nodded once. 'Then we're not done yet.'

FIFTY-THREE

The facility's security and isolation protocols meant they couldn't call for outside help, not through conventional channels. If they were going to stop the Horsemen's plan, they needed Arkwright. And they needed Tempest.

Adam stared at the blinking status light on the central server. The only way to establish contact was to patch into the internal network—a dangerous move that could accelerate the lockdown. But there was no other choice.

A low hiss began to echo through the vents—steady, insistent. The air was warming. There was a sharp, metallic tang to it now, like the scent of solder and blood.

He didn't flinch.

This was familiar. Not comfortable—but known. Patch, reroute, override. He'd done it in basements in Belfast, in bunkers outside Tripoli, in dead zones where satellites went blind and teams went dark. Always under pressure. Always with time bleeding out.

He scavenged what he needed: a diagnostic panel, a length of insulated cable, and a battered transmitter. With swift, practised hands, he began rerouting a secure uplink.

He crouched by the server, working with surgical precision. Every second dragged.

Then—**connection.**

A small indicator flashed green.

'Tempest. Arkwright. Do you read?'

His voice was steady. His chest tightened.

The monitor flickered.

Tempest appeared, shadowed but clear. Arkwright's pale, drawn face filled the other half of the screen. Both locked in, eyes scanning fast.

Arkwright spoke first, voice tight. 'Adam—they've triggered the gas failsafe. Containment protocols are active. You've got minutes, maybe less.'

Claire coughed quietly behind him, one hand over her mouth.

'I can taste it,' she muttered. 'It's starting.'

Tempest's voice followed, calm. 'Phase Zero is underway. Celestial convergence is amplifying the network's output. Hurricanes. Floods. Fires. It's accelerating. But we're early. If we act now, we can contain it.'

Adam's jaw tightened. 'If we shut the servers down, can we stop Phase Zero?'

A pause.

Tempest replied carefully. 'The worst can be mitigated. But the core's already live. The energy released won't vanish overnight. We slow the cascade. That's the best-case scenario now.'

Adam nodded. He understood.

Arkwright leaned in. 'The system's built for chaos. Adaptive firewalls. Buried redundancies. I can punch through—but I need your uplink to break the core.'

Then, a hesitation. Arkwright's eyes flicked to Tempest, then back.

'You're sure this won't make things worse?'

Tempest didn't answer. Just watched. Silent. Calculating.

Adam didn't look up.

'Worse?' He gave a short, humourless laugh. 'How exactly do you make the end of the world worse?'

He tightened a bolt on the transmitter.

'I've patched for dual uplinks. The core's still shielded—we'll need a signal boost from inside.'

He pulled up a schematic on a cracked tablet. 'Here,' he said, pointing. 'Server access node, deep inside the compound. If I can hardwire a bypass, you'll get a clear path—but I'll have to reroute power from auxiliary to stabilise it. That'll trip their highest lockdown tier.'

Tempest cut in. 'Then we move now. I'll handle the failsafe decrypt. Arkwright—watch the timer. Adam—Make sure the link holds.'

Arkwright checked a secondary display, jaw clenched. 'Dispersal event in four minutes, give or take.'

Adam nodded, slinging the transmitter over his shoulder and grabbing his compact toolkit.

He turned.

Claire stood by the monitor, watching him. Her hands were clenched, but her voice held.

'You shouldn't be the one going. If anything happens to you ——'

Adam turned to her.

'It won't, and someone has to.'

She stepped forward, not stopping him, just standing beside him for one second longer.

'We finish this together. Don't forget that.'

He gave her the faintest nod. Then turned and vanished down the corridor.

FIFTY-FOUR

Adam moved quickly through the heart of the compound, shadows jagged beneath flickering overhead lights. The lock-down had escalated. Steel bulkheads sealed behind him, and the walls hummed with rising tension.

A robotic voice echoed through the halls, cold and precise.

'Fifteen minutes to full lockdown. Dispersal event imminent. Evacuate immediately.'

Adam muttered, 'Easier said than done.'

He reached the access node. The panel was a chaotic mess of wires and melted circuits. Smoke stung his eyes. The air reeked of burnt insulation and something sharper—metallic, chemical.

He didn't hesitate.

Splicing a live cable into the facility's primary power conduit, he rerouted just enough current to boost the signal without triggering the failsafe. His fingers worked fast, surgical and steady.

'I'm in position,' he said into the comms. 'Boosting signal now.'

Back at the monitor, Tempest's fingers flew across his keyboard. Lines of code scrolled in rapid succession.

'Signal's stable. Arkwright, you're up.'

Arkwright leaned in, focused. 'Accessing lockdown timer. Give me thirty seconds.'

'We don't have thirty,' Tempest snapped. 'The system's purging secondary access. You miss this window, we're done.'

'I'm aware,' Arkwright shot back, sweat beading on his forehead. 'Just... a little... more...'

The ground jolted violently.

A deep groan reverberated through the facility's foundation. Adam barely kept his balance, catching the panel as stress fractures spread through the walls like spiderwebs.

'What the hell was that?' he barked.

Tempest's voice was grim. 'The Horsemen activated a secondary protocol. The satellites are pulling stellar energy through the grid. It's destabilising fault lines—causing seismic feedback, directed at this facility.'

'Tony and his men?' Adam asked.

'Under attack,' Tempest replied. 'Orion operatives are engaging. Gunfire reported in the southeast quadrant.'

Adam's stomach sank. 'Tony's handling it?'

'For now,' Arkwright interjected. 'But they're outnumbered. We need to finish this fast.'

The faint sound of distant gunfire echoed through the corridors—a grim reminder of the danger closing in.

'I'm almost there,' Arkwright said. 'Lockdown timer disabled.'

'Tempest, you're clear to stop the gas.'

'On it,' Tempest replied, hands a blur. Moments passed. Then—

'Failsafe disabled. The gas won't deploy.'

Adam exhaled in relief—but the moment shattered as the robotic voice echoed again, its tone sharper.

'Self-destruct sequence initiated. Five minutes to core detonation. Evacuate immediately.'

'Oh, for fuck's sake,' Adam growled. 'Tell me you can shut it down.'

'Not remotely,' Tempest shot back. 'It's hardwired. You'll have to do it manually.'

Adam exhaled, already knowing the answer. 'Figures. Where?'

Tempest pulled up a schematic. 'Two levels down. Southwest quadrant. You've got five minutes.'

Alarms screamed. Smoke clogged Adam's lungs as he sprinted through the corridors, boots hammering the grated floor. Heat surged behind him, warning of time bleeding away.

Meanwhile, Claire had been monitoring the situation from the server room. She'd told herself to stay put. To let Adam handle it. But when the tremors hit—when the countdown changed—something shifted.

She grabbed her pistol and moved.

Sticking to the shadows, she traced Adam's path, slipping past deactivated security nodes and flickering cameras. If he got in over his head, she'd be there.

The sounds of struggle reached her just as she rounded the corner.

Adam was locked in brutal combat. An Orion operative pinned him against the wall, knife flashing toward his throat. Adam twisted, but the blade bit into his shoulder—sharp, fast, blood spraying.

A gunshot rang out.

The attacker staggered as a bullet tore through his arm. Adam wrenched free just as Claire stepped into the light, pistol raised.

'You were cutting it close,' she said, breathless.

Adam drove a knee into the merc's ribs and slammed him down. Claire finished it with a clean shot.

00:00:40

She was already moving. 'There's a failsafe.'

Adam blinked. 'What?'

'Secondary circuit.' She pointed at a blinking node. 'Kill the wrong relay and the system triggers auto-detonation.'

00:00:20

'Can you stop it?'

Her hands hovered—then moved. Fast. 'If I decode it right, yes. If I don't...'

'No pressure,' Adam muttered.

The system spat back her first command. Alarm klaxons howled.

00:00:10

'Claire.'

'Almost...'

00:00:05

The screen flickered—then froze at **00:00:03.**

Silence.

Claire exhaled slowly.

Already, the air was changing. The metallic tang thinning. The pressure in the room easing.

Adam leaned on the console, blood from his shoulder trickling down his arm.

'I was going to do that.'

Claire smirked. 'Sure you were.'

Tempest's voice returned, edged with something close to relief.

'Tony's holding position. Orion operatives are pushing hard, but they haven't broken through.'

Claire looked at him, eyes sharp.

'This has gone too far.'

Adam wiped the blood from his arm and met her stare.

'Then we stop it—for good.'

FIFTY-FIVE

THE HORSEMEN'S BOARDROOM

The Horsemen believed they could harness planetary alignment, shaping celestial forces to fit their design. But resonance doesn't obey human ambition—it follows its own immutable cycle. And now, the very system they had built was slipping beyond their grasp.

Their arrogance had blinded them. The miscalculation would cost them everything.

He saw it now—an unseen cycle they had overlooked. It wasn't just a mistake.

It was fatal. Their entire plan rested on a flawed assumption.

He ran his fingers over the pages, pulse quickening. The ancient warnings weren't cryptic after all. They were precise.

Phase Zero was collapsing into itself.

No known force or technology could stop it now.

It was inevitable.

But the Horsemen had another problem.

They weren't ready to leave.

* * *

The chamber was a fortress of polished obsidian and titanium, reinforced against every conceivable threat.

No windows. No distractions. No weaknesses.

Except today, there was one.

Jeremiah Solis.

He sat at the long black table, hands folded, expression unreadable.

The three men seated with him weren't just influential. They held dominion over the future.

Viktor Tarlen—master of resources, overseeing the Mars Exodus Project and ensuring the elite's escape was secured.

Julian Thorne—the hidden hand behind global intelligence, architect of silence, keeping governments blind to the endgame.

Silas Vega—a scientist, an architect of the next world, untethered by morality but increasingly troubled by the rate of collapse.

Solis had shaped history in this very room, toppling governments and redrawing continents. But today, he was not the man they had always known.

Today, he was a father in mourning.

His daughter, Sofia, and her children were dead. Not by accident. Not by some unavoidable catastrophe.

He had signed off on the flood and measured its radius. Calculated the casualties. Never imagining his blood would be among them.

A lifetime believing he was untouchable. Now, the only thing that had ever mattered to him was gone—ripped from him in the tide of destruction he had unleashed.

But it wasn't the Horsemen he blamed.

It was Tony Shaw.

Shaw hadn't even been there. He'd been en route to Nevada to support Adam.

But Solis didn't care about timelines. Or truth.

He saw only one thing: a man who should have protected her. A man who had failed.

The Horsemen had warned of casualties. But Shaw had made it personal.

Solis poured all his grief into a singular purpose.

Tony had to die.

He turned to Vance, who stood at the edge of the room like a spectre.

'He's in Nevada. Inside the facility. I want full satellite coverage—thermal, drones, comm intercepts, everything. If he so much as breathes wrong, I want to know before he does.'

Vance hesitated. 'And the others?'

Solis's voice was ice. 'Them too.'

Vance nodded. 'And if we find him?'

Solis exhaled slowly. His fingers curled into a fist on the tabletop.

'Erase him. Completely.'

The command hung in the air, final and absolute.

His grief had not softened him.

It had hardened into something beyond rage.

A certainty.

A reckoning.

* * *

Tarlen's voice cut through the silence, sharp and impatient.

'You called this meeting, Solis. We assumed there was an actual reason.'

Solis met his gaze, silent. Unblinking.

'If this is about Nevada, we've assessed the breach. Containment failed, but Phase Zero remains active. The window holds—for now.'

Solis didn't respond. He tapped his tablet.

A holographic projection flickered to life above the table—the Mars Exodus Project.

A sprawling vision of off-world survival. Launch stations. Orbital infrastructure. Martian colonies.

Except it wasn't ready.

The exodus ships—three massive interstellar carriers—were still in their final construction phases. The planetary habitat systems meant to sustain them were behind schedule. Fuel reserves for the secondary launches remained insufficient.

And then there was something else.

An unresolved frequency anomaly in the Martian atmosphere. A deep, repeating resonance that shouldn't be there.

Vega's voice stayed calm, but his jaw was set. 'There's a problem.'

Tarlen exhaled. 'There's always a problem, Vega.'

'This one isn't mine,' Vega replied. He tapped the display again. 'The Martian resonance models are shifting. This pattern wasn't in the original calculations.'

Solis's fingers curled against the table. 'Meaning?'

Vega's voice dropped. 'Meaning what we think we're landing into may not be what's waiting for us.'

Silence.

Tarlen was the first to speak.

'Then we adapt.'

Vega didn't blink. 'You don't get it. This isn't an obstacle. It's something else.'

For the first time, even Thorne hesitated.

Solis's hand tightened around the crystal glass before him. He didn't drink.

His voice was final. 'We finish what we started. No deviations. No delays.'

Tarlen nodded. 'Agreed. The plan stands.'

Vega exhaled through his nose but said nothing.

He had always known they would follow the plan into the fire.

But for the first time, he wasn't sure they'd survive it.

Thorne leaned back, his voice measured. 'Then we move forward. Without hesitation.'

FIFTY-SIX

HORSEMAN'S COMMAND ROOM

Viktor Tarlen sat at the head of the dimly lit boardroom, fingers drumming against the obsidian table. The air was steeped in whiskey and silence.

Jeremiah Solis leaned back, jaw clenched, arms folded. Julian Thorne sat rigid, his control slipping for the first time.

Silas Vega was gone.

No word. No warning. *Just absence.*

Tarlen's gaze flicked to the data on the screen. His voice was quiet, sharp as a blade.

'The situation has reached critical mass. They've cracked the first security layers.'

No one needed to ask who.

Solis exhaled slowly. 'They've found the Key.'

Silence. Heavy. Unforgiving. Thorne's fingers twitched—a crack in the façade.

Tarlen leaned forward. 'Vega knew.'

No one spoke.

Then Thorne, voice like steel: 'Then where the hell is he?'

Tarlen tensed. 'Wherever he is... he planned this.'

For years, they had buried the truth under layers of deception —firewalls, dead ends, and misinformation campaigns.

The manuscript, hidden for centuries, held knowledge too dangerous to be known. It wasn't just a key to their control but a warning they had suppressed.

Now, Hayes, Ross, Arkwright—and even Tempest—were exposing what they feared most: the truth buried within it.

Arkwright had bypassed the surface encryption, but the final security measures remained intact.

Tarlen's eyes narrowed as the monitors around them flickered, data feeds scrambling.

'We're losing ground,' he muttered.

Thorne's voice was cold. 'Our systems are compromised. If they get past the final lock, Phase Zero is in jeopardy.'

Tarlen slammed a fist on the table. 'Shut them down.'

Solis's fingers drummed once against the table—his only visible tell.

'They're not just exposing us. They're dismantling the system—strip by strip. If we don't stop them now, they'll turn the whole architecture inside out.'

Thorne remained unmoved. 'Control was always the illusion.'

Solis's jaw tightened. 'Control is the only thing that separates us from chaos. If you're suggesting we let this spiral—'

Thorne cut him off. 'I'm suggesting it already has.'

A cold dread settled over the room.

Thorne's voice was ice.

'Then we bury them—before they walk out of that facility.'

* * *

Half a world away, while the Horsemen calculated their collapse... Claire Hayes was rewriting the rules.

Her fingers raced across the keyboard, her pulse hammering. Lines of coded script scrolled across the monitor, shifting as she entered the sequence—a Fibonacci spiral, a prime number progression, logarithmic patterns threading through the manuscript like a hidden rhythm.

Symbols blinked into alignment. The software processed each fragment before spitting out a fresh encryption code.

She punched it into the terminal.

ACCESS DENIED.

Her breath hitched. She tried again. 'Almost there.'

ACCESS DENIED.

Adam stared at the screen. 'Jesus.'

Another explosion rocked the facility.

Something was off. The cypher, the key—she'd followed every step, every pattern etched into the manuscript. But doubt crept in, sharp and insistent, like a whisper beneath the code.

She scanned the manuscript again.

And froze.

Her pulse thundered. The symbols blurred, then snapped into brutal focus.

She had assumed Earth. Naturally, every coordinate was anchored to familiar skies. But the manuscript wasn't written from that perspective.

It was Martian.

A world lost to time, yet imprinted in every number, every line of logic—coordinates mapped not to Earth's heavens but Mars's long-dead sky.

The cypher hadn't failed.

She had.

The entire system—every value, every alignment—was based on a celestial origin she hadn't accounted for.

The paradigm wasn't just wrong.

It was alien.

Adam's voice was tight. 'Make it faster.'

The reinforced doors groaned—metal warping as their

pursuers forced entry. Distant gunfire rattled through the corridors. Tony and his team held the line, but it wouldn't last.

With her heart pounding, Claire recalibrated the input, adjusting for Mars's position relative to the dataset. Her fingers flew over the keys, correcting the sequence.

The screen flashed.

SATELLITE OVERRIDE ENGAGED. FINAL ENCRYPTION SEQUENCE UNLOCKED.

Dave Ross leaned in, his face slick with sweat. His tremors were worse, but he fought through them.

'This isn't just shutting down the satellites,' he rasped. 'It's overriding them.'

Claire's fingers hovered over the keys. 'What do you mean?'

Ross's voice was raw, edged with urgency.

'Tempest embedded a failsafe in the Horsemen's system. The second we cracked the final encryption, the satellites didn't just shut down—they started broadcasting.'

He gestured at the monitors.

'Every piece of data—Phase Zero, every engineered disaster, the Horsemen's secret networks, their ties to organisations and governments—it's all being broadcast. Right now. To the entire world.'

Overhead, ventilation ducts rattled, dislodging dust and debris.

Adam's voice was sharp. 'We need to move—now.'

Claire ripped the manuscript's original pages from the scanner and shoved them into her bag. 'Let's go.'

Ross coughed, still staring at the screen. 'You don't get it.'

Claire stopped. 'Get what?'

Ross swallowed hard.

'We stopped the engineered disasters. Hurricanes, earthquakes, wildfires—all of it. They can't trigger anything anymore.'

Adam exhaled. 'That's not stopping the collapse.'

The weight of his words hung heavy, the realisation settling in like a storm on the horizon.

Ross shook his head. 'No. The countdown is still running. The planetary cycle is locked. But we just ripped out their biggest weapon.'

He coughed and wiped blood from his lip, still staring at the screen like it was counting down to the end of the world.

Adam looked at Claire. 'The world is still ending. But now they don't get to control how.'

Smoke drifted from the east wing, where Tony's team had made their stand.

Gunfire erupted ahead, deafening cracks reverberating through the corridors.

Adam shoved Claire behind cover as bullets shredded the walls, chunks of concrete and metal raining down around them.

'They're blocking our exit!' Ross shouted, ducking low.

Adam turned to Claire. 'You ready?'

She didn't answer. She drew her pistol, checked the magazine, and fired three rounds down the hall, forcing their attackers into cover.

She glanced at Adam. 'Does that answer your question?'

Adam grinned. 'That'll do.'

FIFTY-SEVEN

Everything unraveled the moment Phase Zero went dark.

Security systems failed in a chain reaction. Alarms howled.

Red strobes flared, slicing the scorched corridor into slashes of light and shadow.

The Horsemen's grip on the global climate system—gone. Satellites offline.

Secrets bleeding into the open.

But for Adam Hayes and his team, survival came first. Everything else was noise.

The first wave struck fast—mercenaries loyal to the bitter end, the last claws of a dying regime, determined to bury their enemies beneath the rubble.

Gunfire tore through the air. The stench of cordite choked the lungs. Burning circuits turned the corridors into a furnace.

Tony Shaw had held the western hall with four men, pinned against a corridor full of bodies. When the lights went out and the AI was silenced, he knew the game had changed.

He ordered a fallback to the inner control room—the heart of Phase Zero.

Claire Hayes moved through the eastern wing like smoke—precise, relentless.

She wasn't following.

She was leading.

An Orion operative rounded the corner. Claire stepped into him like a blade in motion. Her knife caught him under the jaw —silent, clean. She turned, fired twice. Another body dropped.

She pushed past the ruined security checkpoint into the command chamber, the smoke still fresh in her lungs.

Adam and Dave followed hard behind.

And inside, crouched behind a row of scorched consoles, Tony and his team.

They were bruised, bleeding, but alive.

Tony straightened, rifle still in hand. 'Held the line until the lights died. Then figured I'd wait and see who came through the smoke.'

Claire nodded once. 'Systems are down. We burned them.'

Tony looked at the ceiling. 'Felt it.'

Dave dropped to one knee by the central console. He pulled a portable drive from his vest, eyes scanning the fractured data cores.

'The grid's collapsing,' he muttered. 'This is our only window. If there's anything left—satellite logs, uplink traces, fallback command nodes—it's in here.'

He connected to the ruined system. Error codes flashed across the screen. Bits of data crawled through corrupted partitions.

The Horsemen's network was dying—and trying to take its secrets with it.

Adam moved to the room's centre, checking the feeds. 'Structural charge markers—red across every main column.'

Claire joined him. 'They're not defending this place. They're bringing it down.'

Another distant explosion rumbled through the floor. The walls moaned with shifting pressure.

Dave called out from behind them, 'I've intercepted the outbound stream—uplink codes, fallback relays, system keys. They're trying to push it to ORION.'

Adam didn't flinch. 'Can you stop it?'

Dave's hands flew over the terminal. 'I can't block the signal —but I can copy it before it hits the node. Give me ten seconds or we lose everything.'

A progress bar crawled across the fractured screen—fragments of the Horsemen's final command network streaming into his drive.

Then—ping. Download complete.

Dave yanked the cable, breath sharp. 'We've got a copy. Whatever ORION recovers—at least now we know what they know.'

The screens went dark. Claire exhaled.

A sharp burst of gunfire echoed down the corridor.

Tony peered through the cracked door. 'They're pushing in again. We need to move.'

'Main exit's ten metres that way,' Adam said. 'Claymores. Crossfire. No clean path.'

Claire's gaze shifted upward.

The ceiling sagged—cracked concrete, broken beams, power conduits barely holding.

She looked at Adam. A slow, deliberate smile curled across her lips.

'We don't go through them.'

He followed her eyes.

'We go above them.'

Dave looked up from the drive. 'You're insane.'

Tony already had thermal charges in hand. 'That's the good kind of insane.'

Claire moved. Dropped her empty pistol. Tore open a satchel

from her belt—C4 bricks, magnet-clamped, pre-wired with detcord.

She vaulted a crate, climbed a support strut, and began placing charges—each one clicking into damaged girders with brutal precision.

'Cover her!' Adam barked.

Tony and his men opened fire into the corridor, suppressing return fire with short, sharp bursts.

Claire finished the last charge, slapping it onto a fractured beam above the chokepoint. Sparks erupted.

'Charges set!'

'Everyone clear!' Adam shouted.

They ran.

Boots hammered steel. Fire rolled through the halls behind them. The ceiling groaned.

Ten seconds.

Dave yanked the drive free and sprinted.

Nine.

A bullet screamed past Claire's cheek—*too close.*

Eight. Seven.

Structural beams cracked overhead.

Six. Five. Four.

Tony tossed a flashbang behind them. The corridor lit white.

Three. Two.

Adam slammed the emergency override. The door shuddered, groaned, then peeled open under the strain, metal buckling as the whole corridor threatened to come down.

One.

BOOM!

The explosion tore through Phase Zero—fast, brutal, final.

The ceiling collapsed inward. Steel folded like tinfoil. Concrete walls buckled. Fire surged through the main corridor in a rolling, brutal wave.

Claire was the last through the door.

The blast caught her mid-stride, flung her through the air, and slammed the exit shut behind her with a thunderous clang.

She hit the sand hard. Rolled. Coughing.

Silence.

Then—

WHUMP.

A secondary charge tore the rest of the corridor down. The entire hallway folded into itself.

The Horsemen's stronghold was gone.

Claire pulled herself upright, staggered.

Adam was already there, reaching for her.

Tony and the others emerged from the smoke—bruised, burned, alive.

The Nevada night stretched wide and black around them.

A convoy truck waited just over the ridge—engine idling, doors open, stolen and loaded.

Tony climbed behind the wheel. 'Next stop—anywhere but here.'

As the vehicle roared to life and tore into the sand, Adam looked back one last time.

Phase Zero burned.

Metal folding into itself. A tomb of secrets.

Just before the final screen on Dave's terminal died, it flickered once, static and light—

A stylised horseman. Bowed. Not broken. Still watching.

Adam felt it tighten in his chest.

Not the end. Just the beginning of whatever came next.

FIFTY-EIGHT

Across three continents, the Horsemen fell.

Not with fire.

Not with prophecy.

But with silence.

Phase Zero failed.

The Nevada facility burned.

And with it—Helion. The command nexus. The last tether of control.

Secrets unravelled too fast, too deep, too completely to ever be buried again.

They didn't scatter.

They fractured.

One vanished into Geneva under a forged name.

Another fortified himself in steel and silence beneath Warsaw.

A third lingered in Bogotá, waiting for ghosts that would never come.

And the last walked alone through a shuttered terminal, still chasing the echo of a prophecy he thought he could command.

They didn't run.

They recalibrated.

They repositioned.

But the truth was already hunting them.

And across oceans, the world they tried to reshape began to close in—surgical, patient, absolute.

This wasn't revenge. It was a reset. Quiet. Calculated. Inevitable.

FIFTY-NINE
GENEVA - AFTER THE BROADCAST

The satellites didn't shut down. They broadcasted—loud and clear.

Phase Zero's network—once a system of suppression and simulation—has now detonated in data. It didn't warn. It didn't explain. It exposed.

Everything.

From sky to screen to street, truth poured out.

* * *

A crowd surged across the Pont du Mont-Blanc, not in protest—but in revelation. Phone screens flickered with classified overlays: atmospheric weapon testing zones, death tolls tied to 'natural' disasters, encrypted transcripts between leaders who no longer held power.

The system Vega built to trigger collapse now dumped everything—fast, raw, unstoppable.

People didn't scream slogans.

They stared.

Shell-shocked. Unmoored.

At the edge of the bridge, a woman dropped her bag as Phase Zero's orbital pattern lit up her AR display. She looked to the sky like it had betrayed her.

A child tugged on his mother's coat.

'Maman… did we do something wrong?'

* * *

In Bogotá, Jeremiah Solis stood at the window of his hotel suite, watching the orbital supply grid blink out.

His control of trade corridors, once invisible and absolute, dissolved line by line. On his screen, a terminal error blinked over Sofia's old file.

He reached for the image. Froze.

And closed the case.

* * *

In Warsaw, Tarlen slammed a reinforced server terminal with the heel of his hand. The vault node was dark. SphereNet had severed him.

He turned to the panic room monitor, where hundreds rioted outside the embassy he once used as a proxy shell.

'Keep shouting,' he muttered.

But they weren't shouting his name anymore.

They were chanting numbers.

Coordinates.

* * *

In a quiet European airport, Silas Vega passed unnoticed.

He walked calmly through a shuttered terminal as chaos unfolded in the distance—broadcasts, blackouts, a child watching the planetary glyphs spiral across a phone.

The boy looked up at him, eyes wide.

Vega paused.

For just a second, something like sorrow passed through him.

Then he disappeared into the crowd.

* * *

Beneath Geneva, Julian Thorne stood in the SphereNet vault.

Alarms shrieked, but HELION said nothing now.

It had gone silent too.

On the screen, DominionNet bled red. The algorithms no longer lied. They simply stopped speaking.

The world had moved beyond manipulation.

It was now in freefall.

One feed remained: a split-screen global map. Dozens of countries glowing in orange and red as emergency networks failed—not from attack, but from volume. There were too many truths now. Too many betrayals confirmed. People weren't waiting for an explanation.

They were reacting.

* * *

On Rue de Lausanne, a father dragged his daughter into a shuttered pharmacy as screams tore through the street.

He didn't know what the documents meant, only that the list of 'engineered events' included their city.

He vomited behind a dumpster, then pulled her close and said nothing.

* * *

Near the UN building, a protestor and a riot cop stood shoulder to shoulder as an overhead screen displayed:

HORSEMEN IDENTITIES CONFIRMED
PHASE ZERO: PUBLIC RELEASE COMPLETE
OMEGA-BROADCAST ACTIVE
Neither moved.
The cop lowered his shield.
The protestor lowered his phone.

* * *

In a stairwell behind a burning data hub, a young man found it. Spray-painted. Sloppy. Black on white tile.

The Horsemen will not be compromised.

He didn't understand it.

But he took a picture.

And posted it.

* * *

Thorne watched Geneva ripple and fracture. He touched the edge of the console like it was an altar.

'We gave them fiction,' he whispered. 'And when the truth came... they had no immune system left.'

Behind him, reinforced doors hissed open.

Footsteps.

He didn't turn.

Not yet.

* * *

Outside, someone painted over the last intact SphereNet logo with a single sentence:

You taught us to question everything.

Underneath, smaller:

Now it's your turn.

SIXTY

JULIAN THORNE - GENEVA

Truth was never absolute. It was a product—crafted, sold, consumed. A story wrapped in metrics. A weapon dressed in coherence. One image could start a war. One phrase could end an election. People didn't want facts. They wanted permission to believe.

And Thorne had given it to them.

Now the world was slipping through his fingers.

He sat in the subterranean command chamber of his SphereNet citadel—a fortress buried beneath the Horsemen's mountain compound. It was here he'd launched perception warfare across five continents. Here, he'd collapsed regimes with metadata and remade truth in his own image.

This was where it had all been planned.

And now—where it would end.

His networks were crumbling. DominionNet. SphereNet. Every algorithmic shadowplay he'd ever orchestrated now blinked red with warning: signal loss, node failure, identity breach. HELION, the A.I. system, severed ties. Vega had vanished. The others—Tarlen, Solis—they were leaving him behind.

That was always the plan.

He was never part of their new world.

A flicker of anger stirred, but it didn't reach the surface. Anger was a waste. Anger was for the audience.

Thorne never performed for free.

He sipped from a crystal tumbler of Macallan, watching the lights on his screen dim one by one. Then he opened a hidden terminal with root access. Bypassed his own failsafes. The mainframe obeyed—reluctantly.

Then a warning flared:

UNAUTHORISED DATA BREACH DETECTED.

He frowned.

This wasn't a breach.

This was a dismantling.

And Thorne recognised the signature.

Elegant. Precise. Merciless.

Only one mind ever moved through systems like that—not with brute force, but with surgical doubt.

Arkwright.

They'd once shared a flat in Cambridge. Thorne had fed him truth like poison, just to see what it would do.

Arkwright had chased meaning. Believed in facts.

And Thorne had watched that belief crack, then calcify into something harder. Colder.

He thought the boy would break.

He didn't.

He waited.

And now—he was finishing what Thorne started.

* * *

Firewall integrity dissolved in real time. His backdoor locked him out. One by one, his disinformation networks collapsed inward, folded by hands smarter, faster, and no longer afraid.

On his central screen, a final message appeared:

This is your last Chapter, Thorne.

A voice followed. Calm. British. Familiar.

'Eleanor Grey.'

She stepped into the chamber with two MI6 operators at her flank. No weapons raised. No threats offered.

'You always did overestimate your authorship, Julian,' she said.

He exhaled. 'The conscience of MI6, dressed in a grey coat. I wondered when you'd turn the page.'

Her voice was cool as iron. 'We're not turning pages. We're closing the book.'

Julian chuckled, but there was no humour in it. Only control.

'I wrote your headlines before most of your team were born. You think you can erase me with due process and a soundbite?'

He stood slowly.

But just before the breach, he turned to the dark glass wall beside him—his reflection blinking back in the fallback lighting. His voice, for once, dropped to a whisper.

'You always wanted a reckoning,' he said quietly.

'But never the silence after.'

No audience. No applause. Just the truth, heard by no one.

The reinforced doors blew inward with a flash of percussion.

Tactical boots stormed the war room—precision incarnate. Rifles. Orders. Restraints.

Thorne didn't resist.

That wasn't his style.

He performed.

'Wait,' he said. Just enough breath, just enough hesitation. 'I can help you. You don't understand—I wasn't the architect. Solis —Tarlen—they used me. I was just the messenger. Please, I can give you the originals—project files, nodes, even Orion. I can prove it.'

The lead agent hesitated.

Grey didn't.

'He's lying.'

Still, Julian saw the flicker of doubt.

That was all he needed.

His voice cracked at the right moment. His posture slumped in perfect defeat. His eyes flicked with practised terror.

It was flawless.

Julian Thorne had never known fear. But he knew how to manufacture it.

They thought they'd broken him.

That they'd dragged him from the shadows and snapped the spine of his empire.

But they were wrong.

Thorne had never truly lost control.

He'd simply changed genre.

And as they pulled him into the light—hands bound, silence sealing shut behind him—

He said, almost to himself, 'You always wanted a reckoning.'

A pause.

'Just not the silence after.'

Grey stepped into his path.

Calm. Steady. Inevitable.

'Simon sends his regards.'

For the first time, Thorne didn't speak.

But his mind, Julian Thorne was already writing the next act.

SIXTY-ONE

VIKTOR TARLEN – WARSAW

Snow drifted through the shattered window like ash.

The safe house in Praga was no longer a safe house.

It was a tomb. A line in the sand.

And he'd drawn it himself.

Viktor Tarlen stood at the centre of the room, still as stone.

Rifle low. Eye level.

Claymores lined the stairwell. Tripwires webbed the roof hatch and fire escape.

Not to escape.

Just to slow them down.

To remind them who they were dealing with.

On the table: a folded manifest. Faded, creased.

A name circled in black ink—twice.

Luka Tarlen.

He had never seen the boy.

Never wanted to.

But he'd made sure the name was on the list.

The last shuttle.

The last chance.

A sound. Footsteps on the stairs. Then—

A knock.

Not a breach. Not yet.

Measured. Controlled.

'Viktor Tarlen. This is Tony Shaw. We don't want to kill you.'

He moved to the window.

Saw it: the shimmer of a scope.

Shadows crawling across the roofline.

Tight formation. No wasted movement.

He nodded once.

They were professionals.

He could respect that.

He pressed the remote.

The stairwell exploded—shrapnel, smoke, screams.

A heartbeat later: flashbangs.

Then boots.

Through the ceiling.

He moved like a machine uncoiling.

Two down. One clipped through the vest.

He didn't pause.

Pain bloomed in his thigh—stun round.

Dropped him. One knee.

Still firing.

They overwhelmed him with weight, not skill.

And then—Tony.

No armour. No helmet.

Just the quiet anger of a man who had buried too much.

'You could've run,' Tony said.

Tarlen coughed blood into the dust.

'I did. That's why I'm here.'

Tony's eyes landed on the paper. He didn't pick it up.

Didn't ask.

Didn't need to.

Tarlen looked at it one last time.

A name without a face.

A gesture without forgiveness.

He had nothing left to give.

But he'd made sure the boy would live.

They dragged him out through the broken stairwell and into the snow.

Weapons raised. Mission complete.

Not broken.

Just buried.

SIXTY-TWO

JEREMIAH SOLIS – BOGOTÁ

It rained in Bogotá.

Soft. Relentless. Cleansing nothing.

Jeremiah Solis sat on a stone bench outside the Santuario de Nuestra Señora del Carmen, motionless beneath the baroque spires. His cane rested at his side. Rain had soaked his coat through to the lining.

He didn't care.

Dave Ross approached and sat beside him without a word, as if summoned by gravity.

'You let us find you,' Ross said. 'Could've gone further.'

'There's nowhere left to go.'

They sat in silence. Two shadows beneath a weeping sky. Like old regrets waiting to be claimed.

Solis kept his eyes fixed on the cathedral's doors.

'This is where she was meant to meet me. Years ago. Before she burned the last letter.'

Ross didn't ask. He already knew.

'Sofia?' he said quietly.

Solis nodded. 'She changed her name. Erased every trace. Made it clear she wanted nothing from me.'

A beat passed.

'But I still come here.'

He reached into his coat with a trembling hand and passed Ross a weathered photograph, creased at the edges, colour leached by time.

Sofia. Smiling. Her children flanking her. Taken before the floodwaters came.

'I sent a team. Discreet. No flags. No noise. Just extraction.' His voice caught. 'Shaw didn't know. He thought they were a threat. Killed them all.'

Ross said nothing.

Solis exhaled—slow, deliberate. A man bleeding truth one breath at a time.

'He thought he was protecting her. I thought I was saving her. We both failed.'

The rain tapped against the cathedral steps like a ticking clock.

'She died because of me,' Solis said. 'Because of us. And she'll never know I tried.'

He closed his eyes, not in grief, but in surrender.

'The others kept running because they believed there was still a way to win,' he murmured. 'Thorne with his theatre. Tarlen with his war. Vega with his stars.'

Then he turned, his eyes glazed and unblinking.

'But you and I, Ross—we live in the aftermath.'

Ross looked away. There was nothing left to say.

A pair of agents emerged from the mist. Plainclothes, efficient. Cuffs ready.

Solis stood without protest.

As they led him toward the waiting vehicle, he cast one final glance at the cathedral.

'She was right to hate me,' he said.

Ross sat still, the photograph heavy in his hand. He looked

down at Sofia's smile. Then, at the bench, now empty beside him.

Not with anger.

With silence.

SIXTY-THREE

SILAS VEGA – HANGKLIP, SOUTH AFRICA

The Stellarion gantry towered against a sky littered with stars.

Silent. Cold. A ruin of promises.

Silas Vega moved through the shuttered terminal like a man entering the tomb of his own design.

His coat was immaculate. His posture, unflinching.

A biometric case hung from a chain at his wrist, swaying with clinical precision.

No guards. No entourage.

Only purpose.

He stopped before the fractured glass doors and gazed out at the dead launchpad.

The altar of humanity's exodus.

Or it's an illusion.

Behind him, the doors hissed open.

Ross and Grey stepped in from the dark. No weapons drawn. No orders barked.

'We traced the Helion transmission,' Ross said. 'That final burst to ORION—you encoded the coordinates. You wanted us to find you.'

Vega didn't turn. He placed the case on the floor with deliberate care.

'You still think this was about Mars?' he asked quietly. 'You still believe in lifeboats.'

Grey's voice was sharp. 'You engineered a collapse. Pushed Earth to the edge. For what—hope on a dead rock?'

Ross shook his head. 'Phase Zero was supposed to buy five years. Just long enough to hide the collapse—and finish the ships. But due to your error, the timeline was compressed to twelve months, and the world was already cracking.'

Vega nodded once, eyes still fixed on the broken gantry.

'I misjudged the decay of the field. The resonance buckled faster than projected. The others—Solis, Tarlen—they panicked. They demanded acceleration.'

Grey stepped forward. 'The infrastructure wasn't ready. The ships were not operational. Mars is still dust and ice.'

'The terraforming had started,' Vega said. 'Enough to justify the risk.'

Ross stared at him. 'You tried to cram a five-year planned exodus into one. And you did it while the world burned.'

Vega turned now. His eyes were hollow, but calm.

'I did what the equation demanded. Earth was ending. We could carry forward a fragment—or nothing.'

He raised his hands—slowly, palms open.

No resistance. No apology.

'You see catastrophe,' he said. 'I see continuity.'

Ross moved in and bound his wrists. Tight. Controlled.

'This wasn't survival,' he said. 'It was selection. And you decided who counted.'

Vega looked past him—beyond the shattered glass, beyond the gantry—toward stars no one would chase now.

'I offered a second Genesis,' he said. 'The first was never meant to last.'

Ross's voice dropped. 'And how many had to die for that?'

Vega met his eyes. 'Enough to ensure someone lived.'

Ross looked down at the biometric case.

Still sealed.

He popped the latches.

Empty.

Of course it was.

They turned without a word.

Vega didn't resist.

Didn't look back.

Behind them, the gantry loomed—hollow steel beneath a sky that no longer waited.

SIXTY-FOUR

BLACK SITE TRANSFER

They came at night.

No insignia. No signals. Just silence.

One transport at a time.

No press. No pressurisation.

No flight plan. No name.

The first came aboard a CIA-modified C-17, rerouted from a NATO base in Ramstein under triple-black orders. No one on the ground knew who was in the aircraft. Even fewer knew where it was going.

Julian Thorne—sedated, smiling.

The straps didn't stop him from whispering.

Lines from Shakespeare. Or scripture. Or nonsense.

The guards wore noise-cancelling headsets.

He spoke anyway.

The second arrived twelve hours later.

A VTOL touched down in darkness, kicking dust across the high plateau.

The rear hatch opened.

Viktor Tarlen emerged in restraints reinforced with titanium struts.

His jaw was split. His eyes were bright.

He had taken down two of the security detail before they'd sedated him.

Now he moved with quiet fury, like war unfinished.

Then came **Jeremiah Solis**, quiet and straight-backed.

No sedation. No resistance.

He walked himself down the ramp of the Gulfstream, cuffed but composed, as if it was always going to end here.

Ross watched him from a distance and didn't speak.

And finally, **Silas Vega.**

Escorted under full blackout by a hardened SAC unit.

No electronics. No identifiers.

A biometric case chained to his wrist until the last possible moment.

He did not speak during the flight.

He did not ask where they were going.

He already knew.

* * *

The mountain had no name.

Satellite images listed it as decommissioned.

Its perimeter masked by a classified electromagnetic haze designed to spoof infrared, radar, and thermal.

No flight path came near it by accident.

The airstrip was flat, marked only by mobile halogen rigs.

The landing crews were masked. Unarmed. Programmed.

Everything was redundant. Everything repeatable.

Human error had no place here.

The Horsemen disembarked one by one.

There were no words exchanged between them.

They were kept in isolation from departure to descent.

Soundproof cells. Masked vision.

The only thing they shared was the silence.

A reinforced elevator lowered them through two hundred metres of limestone.

They passed through seven blast doors, each requiring biometric and vocal clearance from separate handlers.

No one spoke names.

Not theirs. Not their captors'.

Inside, the cells were arranged in a half-circle.

Separate, but facing inward.

Each chamber monitored by autonomous systems running off a hardened line.

No AI. No cloud. Just silence, steel, and signal jammers.

There would be no trial.

There would be no testimony.

The Horsemen had not been captured for justice.

They had been sealed away to contain the pattern.

To break the cycle.

To bury the idea that any of it had ever been real.

SIXTY-FIVE

The world was unravelling. But it had not yet fallen.

News tickers flooded every broadcast, their relentless cadence carving headlines into history:

HORSEMEN CAPTURED – GLOBAL ORDER IN CRISIS
NATIONS DEMAND JUSTICE – WORLD LEADERS
UNDER FIRE
PHASE ZERO EXPOSED – EARTH'S SURVIVAL
UNCERTAIN

The engineered storms had failed. The climate satellites were dead. The systems that once bent nature to human will had gone silent. The planet had been abandoned to fate—and, against every prediction, it had chosen to resist.

Once choked by smoke from man-made wildfires, the air began to clear. Superstorms lost their strength. The floods halted their siege. Even the restless and fractured ground began to settle.

But the scars remained.

From orbit, Earth resembled a battlefield. Blackened forest

craters stretched like ash tattoos across continents. Half-drowned coastal cities decayed in brine, their skyline silhouettes rotting into salt-rusted skeletons. Seismic fractures split the land—deep wounds that might never close.

A quarter of humanity was gone.

And those who remained stood amid the wreckage of a world they no longer recognised, staring into a future written in ash and ambiguity.

This wasn't a natural disaster.

It had been engineered.

And now, the world had its villains.

London stood on a precipice—not of collapse, but of reckoning. At dusk, its streets swelled with bodies. By nightfall, the chants had turned to cries, and the cries to flames.

Retribution.

Embers from burning barricades danced like fireflies, casting strobing shadows on the ruined statues of forgotten leaders. Looted storefronts gaped like broken mouths. Glass crunched underfoot. Smoke curled from the gutted ruins of Whitehall, rising into the sky like the final breath of a dying empire.

Across the globe, it was the same.

Paris. Berlin. São Paulo. New York. Hong Kong.

The great cities of civilisation no longer belonged to those who had built them.

In Washington, the Capitol stood empty, its gates flung open by a crowd that no longer believed in borders. In Tokyo, AI drones hovered through the streets, their synthetic voices pleading for calm, even as the people marched past, deaf to machines.

Governments scrambled. Power fractured. No summit or speech could undo what had been revealed.

This was the reckoning history had always foretold—when the architects of suffering were unmasked, and the people they had failed rose to reclaim the future.

But beneath the chaos, something else stirred.

A fragile, flickering thing.

Hope.

The worst had passed.

The skies had calmed. The hurricanes had lost their fury. The earth, long throttled by design, had begun to breathe again.

The page had turned.

Now, humanity stood at the edge of a blank Chapter.

And what came next would be a choice.

SIXTY-SIX

CIA BLACK SITE.

Buried beneath a mountain in a place that did not exist, four men sat in the silence of their obsolescence.

Once masters of the world, they had become prisoners of it.

The facility was a monument to erasure.

Steel walls swallowed sound.

Faces wore masks.

Names were discarded at the door.

Here, men did not exist—unless the world allowed them to.

The Horsemen were divided now.

Severed limbs of a dying organism, left to decay in the final wings of a broken empire.

Once, they had ruled from the shadows, bending global systems to their will.

Gods, they had called themselves. Architects of collapse. Inheritors of a legacy older than civilisation.

Now, they sat in darkness, unrecognised even by the machines they had created.

* * *

Julian Thorne, master of perception, sat alone in the corner of a room the world did not admit existed.

He had always known the others didn't trust him—not truly.

He was part of the bloodline. One of the Four.

But even among Horsemen, Thorne had been marked for exclusion.

Vega had seen the fault lines early.

Solis had looked away.

Tarlen had once said—flatly, without hesitation—that if Thorne ever strayed from the plan, he'd be the one to put him down.

They hadn't feared his power.

They had feared his unpredictability.

'You all needed me,' Thorne muttered. 'You just couldn't control me.'

That had always been the problem.

He didn't crave order. He craved spectacle.

He didn't serve the vision. He bent it—twisted it—until it served him.

He had once told Vega that chaos was the truth.

Vega had looked at him like a surgeon studying a tumour.

Now, there were no broadcasts.

No deception to shape.

Only silence—and the certainty that if Mars had opened, the others would have left him behind.

Still, even here, Thorne did not mourn the end.

He was waiting for the next one to begin.

He had known Vega was betraying them.

Not at first. But eventually, the pattern emerged—

Withheld data. Quiet shifts in protocol.

Side channels, Vega thought, were invisible.

Thorne hadn't confronted him.

He didn't need to.

He had put things in motion—

Silent signals. Buried edits to the launch manifest.

A final contingency no one else would trace.

Vega would be on that launch.

And Exodus One would never leave the atmosphere.

That was the plan.

One last narrative. Written in fire and vacuum.

They thought it was about control.

But it was always about the script.

And Thorne had written the ending.

* * *

Viktor Tarlen didn't sit.

He paced.

The cell was a battlefield, and he mapped it like terrain.

Escape was never impossible.

Only delayed.

He didn't believe in containment.

He didn't accept failure.

He believed in momentum. In force. In domination.

They had called him reckless. Brutal.

But he had been right about Thorne.

Vega and Solis had seen the instability.

Tarlen had seen the threat.

He had never cared for prophecy. Not the myth. Not the blood.

Only the outcome.

He trusted no one—not then, not now.

Vega had outmanoeuvred them all.

Solis had become a priest of ash.

But Tarlen?

Tarlen still believed in pressure. In conquest.

In the truth that only force could reveal.

Even if Mars had been denied to him—

Even if the Horsemen had fallen—
He still had purpose.
They hadn't broken him.
They had merely buried him.
And beneath the silence—beneath concrete, steel, and protocol, he could feel it:
Something old was stirring again.
The world would claw its way back.
It always did.
And when it rose, fractured and gasping—
He would be waiting.
To shape what came next.

* * *

Jeremiah Solis sat silently.
Hands folded. Eyes closed.
Not in prayer.
In reflection.
Once, he had spoken of necessity.
Of sacrifice.
Of the purifying fire needed to burn away corruption.
He had studied collapse like scripture—reading the patterns, the cycles.
The world ended in fours. Always fours.
Buried beneath corrupted mythologies and Vatican vaults, he had uncovered fragments—
Symbols repeating through time:
War.
Famine.
Pestilence.
Death.
Not metaphor.
Not mythology.

Lineage.

What if we are not orchestrators... but echoes?

He had never asked Vega aloud.

But he had seen the answer in his eyes.

Now, the cost had a name.

Sofia.

The children.

The billions behind them.

He had once believed the world had to be broken before it could be remade.

But the dead do not rise from justification.

They stay dead.

* * *

Only **Silas Vega** was still.

Cross-legged. Eyes closed. Breathing slowly.

Detached from the cell.

From the silence.

From the others.

They had all worn the name The Horsemen.

At first, as a metaphor.

Then, as a myth.

Eventually, as a doctrine.

But only Vega had known it was real.

The bloodline was not symbolic. It was genealogical.

He had traced it himself—through obscured archives, encrypted ecclesiastical records, and fragments buried in forbidden texts.

They were descendants.

Not of kings.

Not of prophets.

Of conquest.

Of wrath.

Solis had suspected, drawn to scripture, symmetry, and prophecy.

Thorne had exploited the myth, branding it into fear.

Tarlen had never cared for the story, but he understood what it meant.

Only Vega had known.

With certainty. With silence.

And he had never told them.

He had once believed the cycle could be shaped.

That legacy could be engineered.

That prophecy could be contained in systems, in code, in control.

But prophecy has no patience for control.

Now, his name meant nothing.

The world remembered only the machines he had built—

And the storms they had unleashed.

The others still clung to roles:

Leader.

Predator.

Martyr.

Prophet.

Vega had shed all of it.

They believed he was here with them.

That he shared their fall.

They were wrong.

He had already begun to rise.

The world outside still burned.

The resonance still climbed.

The cycle still turned.

And deep within the machinery they had built—

Something new had awakened.

No longer conquest.

No longer collapse.

Something unseen.

Something unstoppable.
It had no name.
Not yet.
But it had a purpose.
And it had already begun

SIXTY-SEVEN

CIA OPERATIONS CENTRE – SECURE
LEVEL SIX

Adam Hayes stood motionless before the wall of screens.

Arms folded. Jaw locked. Breath tight in his lungs.

Cities burned.

Skylines fractured and fell.

Survivors moved like shadows through ash and ruin.

But it wasn't the images that haunted him.

It was the silence beneath them.

The Earth had been wounded.

And the wound was still open.

Behind him, a door hissed.

'We've got something,' said Dave Ross.

Adam turned. Ross looked wrecked—eyes bloodshot, jaw clenched, stubble deepened by days of sleepless chasing. He'd been trawling the final uplinks from Nevada, ghosting through the fragments left behind in Arkwright's last trace paths.

'What kind of something?'

Ross tapped the console. A topographic map bloomed—Northern Europe, green hills bleeding into Highland grey.

One red dot blinked.

'Tempest. He left a thread,' Ross said. 'He never thought we'd pull it.'

Adam stepped forward. 'Where?'

'Scotland. Highland interior. It's not on Stellarion's grid— off-network, buried inside what we thought was a dormant climate node.'

A pause.

'Whatever it is, it's not dormant.'

Adam frowned. 'You're saying he built something?'

Ross zoomed in. Another display flickered—schematics overlaid in modular arcs: energy matrices, orbital reflectors, biometric sync-chambers.

'Not just built. He finished it.'

Adam stared. 'Restoration tech.'

Ross nodded. 'Reverse-engineered. Based on the original Horseman systems—but reprogrammed.'

Adam exhaled slowly. 'He helped end Phase Zero. Then vanished.'

'No signal since Nevada,' Ross said. 'We deployed drones, ran spectral traces. Nothing.'

Until now.

Adam's gaze stayed locked on the screen—that one blinking red dot.

'If he's building a system that can restore the Earth...'

Ross met his eyes. 'He can just as easily burn it down.'

Silence stretched between them—tight, electric.

Adam's voice came low, iron under ice.

'Then we find him. Before someone else does.'

* * *

The door hissed again.

A CIA officer entered—sharp suit, sharper eyes. A tablet gripped tightly like a weapon.

'Update on the Horsemen,' she said, voice clipped.

Adam turned. 'Go.'

'There's been an incident at the black site.'

The words landed like a wire snapping.

'Three remain contained,' she said. 'The facility's in hard lockdown. Zero outbound comms.'

A pause. Measured.

Her eyes found his.

'But Vega...'

A beat too long.

'There's been a complication.'

Adam stepped forward, slow and surgical. 'Define complication.'

She didn't blink.

'He's gone.'

SIXTY-EIGHT

CIA BLACK SITE – UNDISCLOSED
LOCATION: 18 HOURS EARLIER

The power cut lasted four seconds.

Long enough.

Long enough for sensors to reset.

Long enough for lock algorithms to stagger.

Long enough for Silas Vega to vanish.

Alarms screamed a heartbeat later. But the corridor was already empty—the air still trembling from his absence.

* * *

Director Monroe slammed a hand against the console. 'Initiate full lockdown. I want this place sealed.'

Red strobes lit the corridor in pulses of bloodlight.

'Containment breach,' someone called.

'He's not in containment,' another snapped. 'He's not anywhere.'

'He's gone.

* * *

Vega moved like breath—silent, invisible, inevitable.

No brute force. No panic. Only design.

The outage hadn't been triggered inside. It came through Stellarion's orbital relay—an old, dormant node reactivated by a quantum timer.

A ghost signal. Buried deep. Timed to the second.

By the time emergency systems rebooted, Vega was already in the ventilation shaft, biometric bypass sewn into his sleeve.

He dropped through an inspection tunnel and bypassed a sealed gate using a retinal clone sourced from a long-buried CIA contractor.

He didn't improvise.

He executed.

In the armoury, two agents turned toward a breach alert.

Too late.

Flash. Smoke. A heartbeat of disorientation.

When the lights returned, the room was empty.

Except for one missing exo-suit.

Vega didn't surface.

He moved inward—down.

Beneath Sublevel Four, buried deep in a wing the CIA had long believed condemned, a stealth transport waited in silence.

Sleek. Thermally shielded. Untraceable.

Stellarion-engineered—before the fall.

A gift from his former life. Insurance.

The interceptor's canopy hissed open as atmospheric seals disengaged. Vega stepped in without hesitation, cinching the harness across his chest. Fingers moved in practised rhythm, initiating the pre-launch sequence. Lights blinked green across the console.

He reached through seeded backdoors—ghost-code embedded long ago—and accessed the Stellarion uplink.

TARGET: EXODUS ONE LAUNCH COMPLEX – SOUTH AFRICA

STATUS: PRIMED

He tapped the command.

ENGAGE.

The craft lifted silently from the shaft—no radar ping, no thermal bloom.

Invisible to every known tracking system.

Climbing fast, it broke into the upper atmosphere. Suborbital trajectory locked.

At 125 miles above Earth, skimming the Kármán line, Vega stared out at the curvature of the planet. A pale crescent of dawn bloomed along the edge of the world.

Fifty minutes later, the launch towers of Exodus One came into view—black spires rising from the South African desert.

He didn't slow down.

SIXTY-NINE

STELLARION LAUNCH FACILITY – SOUTH AFRICA

T-minus 8 minutes

The countdown had begun.

The launch site held its breath—a taut, electrified hush clinging to steel like static before a storm.

Not peace.

Not quiet.

Anticipation, honed to a blade.

Silas Vega stood alone beneath the fuel-line corridor, tightening the pressure seal on his exo-suit with deliberate precision.

Above him loomed the illusion.

Exodus One.

The culmination of decades of ambition.

A symbol.

A lifeboat.

A lie.

It was the only fully operational Mars Exodus craft ever completed.

Far above, inside the control tower, engineers conducted final checks—status reports, telemetry locks, and go-codes.

Voices clipped. Efficient. Unaware.

A figure stepped from the shadows.

No name. No record. No past.

He offered no greeting—just handed Vega a tablet.

Launch telemetry spilt across the screen.

Green across the board.

Primed. Ready.

Vega watched the numbers fall.

T-minus 7 minutes.

Julian Thorne had made his move.

Sabotage, cloaked in prophecy. The message had been clear:

You were never meant to exit the equation.

But Thorne had underestimated him.

Vega had planned for this.

Without a word, he turned and vanished into the corridor—into the understructure of the facility, deeper than any schematic dared trace.

Above, surveillance feeds showed him boarding the craft.

Strapping in. Running systems.

Preparing for a journey that would never happen.

It was theatre.

Convincing. Precise. Fatal.

T-minus 5 minutes.

Then—

The blast.

The shockwave hit like a blade through bone.

Fire tore through the site. Gantries twisted, collapsed in molten arcs.

Fuel lines detonated in a chain of violent succession.

The MI6, CIA, and every other intelligence agency with a satellite feed watched it unfold in real time.

The destruction.

The fireball.

The last hope of planetary escape—consumed in flame.

Silas Vega: incinerated.

Let them believe it.

He had never boarded the ship.

Beneath the inferno, behind a hatch that didn't exist—shielded by false walls and thermal baffles—a second vessel waited.

Matte black.

Thermally cloaked.

Invisible to radar. Silent to infrared.

Untraceable by anything mankind had built.

The same craft that had brought him here.

Its canopy sealed shut seconds before the firestorm reached the lower decks.

By the time smoke curled through the upper struts, Vega was already gone, rising through the clouds, silent as a myth.

Above the flames.

Beyond the wreckage.

Back toward a dying world.

Earth.

* * *

CIA OPERATIONS CENTRE

The satellite feed stuttered in monochrome ruin. The launchpad burned.

Adam Hayes stared at the screen. Jaw tight.

'Sabotage?' he asked.

The operative gave a grim nod. 'Thorne made sure Vega never left.'

Adam's eyes narrowed. 'Or thought he did.'

Dave leaned back in his chair. 'Tempest is still out there. And if Vega was building something bigger, someone will finish it.'

Adam's gaze locked on the scorched telemetry grid.

'If anyone can finish what Vega started—or stop it becoming something worse—it's him.'

The room fell silent.

The world still burned.

But something had already begun to move in the shadows.

And the war for the future—

Had only just begun.

SEVENTY

The world was tearing itself apart.

News networks cycled apocalyptic loops: riots in the streets, corporate towers ablaze, government buildings stormed by a populace too furious—and too broken—to pacify.

Cities became battlegrounds across the United States, Europe, and Asia. The world wasn't asking for answers.

It was demanding blood.

The Earth itself had cracked open. A quarter of the global population is gone.

South America. India. Australia. Eastern Europe.

Silent.

The southern coastlines of England and France had vanished beneath rising seas—entire cities swallowed. Yet, inexplicably, the north of England, Scotland, Scandinavia, and parts of Central Europe remained untouched.

Anomaly. Miracle. A line is drawn across the Earth.

Scientists scrambled. Nothing held.

Some called it luck. Others, divine intervention.

But for those who survived, it became something more:

A fragile sanctuary.

A final battleground.

The last hope for a dying world.

For weeks, the planet mourned. Grieved. Searched for meaning.

But history repeats.

After plague, after fire, after war—life doesn't end.

It adapts.

And under the weight of catastrophe, it continues.

SEVENTY-ONE

The Scottish Highlands stretched in desolate silence.

Mist clung to the hills in drifting, spectral tendrils, curling across the remnants of the abandoned RAF base. The structure had long since been erased from official records—but it wasn't dead.

A low mechanical hum pulsed beneath the wind. Camouflaged solar panels glinted faintly in the morning frost, and reinforced steel doors gleamed behind the overgrown brush.

They weren't alone.

Adam's hand hovered over his sidearm. 'You sure about this?'

Dave exhaled slowly. 'As sure as we'll ever be. Tempest is in there. He's either going to help us... or kill us.'

Their boots crunched on frostbitten gravel. Adam stepped forward and knocked twice.

Then silence.

A speaker crackled.

'State your business.'

Adam and Dave exchanged a glance.

'We're here to discuss your work,' Adam said. 'To reverse the damage.'

A pause.

Then, the grind of locking mechanisms. The steel door hissed open, revealing a corridor lit by sterile LED strips. The air was sharp with the scent of disinfectant and machine oil.

At the far end stood a figure. Motionless. Lab coat. Tinted goggles. Surgical mask.

'You've come a long way,' the voice said, unreadable. 'I assume you've seen what's left of the world.'

Adam nodded. 'That's why we're here. You have a solution, don't you?'

The figure tilted his head. 'A solution, yes. But not without cost.' He gestured to a console beside him. 'The technology the Horsemen used to destroy can be inverted. But a single misstep, and we accelerate the collapse instead of halting it.'

'We don't have the luxury of waiting,' Adam said. 'The planet's running out of time.'

The figure studied them for a long moment. 'Do you understand what you're asking? This isn't just about weather patterns. This system could resurrect extinct species, regrow lost biomes, replenish entire resource networks.' His voice dropped. 'Or make Phase Zero look like a prelude.'

Dave stepped forward. 'Which is why it has to stay in the right hands. We're not here to steal it. We're here to keep it from being weaponised again.'

Gloved fingers hovered over the controls. A jaw tightened. For the first time, the man in the mask looked almost human.

Then a voice rang out from behind them.

Sharp. Familiar.

Adam spun, hand already rising.

Claire stepped into the light.

'You didn't think I'd stay on the sidelines, did you?'

Adam's breath caught. 'Claire?'

She met his eyes with quiet steel. 'I've been tracking Tempest since Nevada. I knew you'd come.'

'I was trying to protect you.'

'Again?'

A pause.

'If this is about survival,' she said evenly, 'we do it together. Not with one of us in the dark.'

Adam lowered his gaze. 'You're right. I'm sorry.'

'Good.'

She turned toward the figure.

He moved—slowly—reaching for his mask.

Claire's eyes narrowed.

And then he pulled it away.

Silas Vega.

Adam froze. Claire staggered back. Dave inhaled sharply.

'No...' Dave murmured. 'No, it can't be.'

Vega offered a faint, exhausted smile. 'I suppose introductions are redundant.'

'You've been playing both sides,' Adam said coldly.

'I watched what I built become monstrous,' Vega said. 'Something I no longer recognised.'

'Then why stay?'

'Because once you understand the endgame, there's only one move left.'

Claire stepped forward. 'You weren't trying to stop the collapse. You were managing it.'

'You think you've uncovered something hidden. But the truth was always in plain sight.' He paused. 'The cycle was never meant to be broken.'

Adam frowned. 'Cycle?'

'Civilisations rise. They burn. They fall. The elite escape and seed again. It's happened before. It will happen again.'

Claire's voice sharpened. 'Mars. The resonance failed.'

Vega's smile thinned. 'Mars isn't our escape. It's our mistake.'

'I wasn't stopping the collapse,' he said. 'I was making sure it happened on schedule.'

Claire's breath steadied. She understood now. The man before her wasn't a saviour. He was the architect of extinction, wearing salvation like a mask.

She moved.

The pistol cleared her coat in a smooth, final motion.

The shot cracked.

The bullet struck left of centre. Vega staggered. Blood bloomed. He dropped to one knee.

He gasped. 'You think you've won... She... was always the answer. I just wanted to guide her...'

Blood spilt from his mouth.

'You'll see... she's not what you think. None of us ever are...'

Claire raised the weapon again. 'See what?'

'You think you've killed me,' he rasped. 'But memory doesn't bleed.'

'The storm remembers who lit the match.' His eyes dimmed. His head dropped. 'The cycle... doesn't end. You're just... another... piece...'

Then silence.

His body slumped. The mask was gone.

Claire's hand trembled—*not from fear, but from finality.*

'He thought he could shape her,' she said quietly. 'But Olivia's not his legacy. She's ours.'

No vengeance. No rage. Just clarity.

She turned to Adam.

'He thought he was inevitable. But in the end, he was just another man, mistaking fear for fate.'

Adam said nothing. He stared at the body, unsure if they'd destroyed a monster... or their last hope.

Claire didn't waver.

This wasn't a victory.

It was survival.

And in the silence that followed, she whispered what Adam already knew:

'Olivia's our future. **We still have a chance.**'

SEVENTY-TWO

The manuscript sat silently beneath the glass, its pages faintly tinted gold by the late afternoon light filtering through high, arched windows.

Claire stood alone in the archive room beneath the Edinburgh College of Art. Ross was heading back to Washington. Adam had gone to confirm security near the main entrance.

She was still alone for a few more minutes.

She exhaled slowly, fingers resting against the glass. It wasn't reverence she felt. Not fear, either. Just weight. The kind that didn't press down but wrapped around her—like gravity, like memory.

She unlocked the lid and lifted the glass. The seal hissed faintly.

The vellum pages breathed.

She turned one. Then another.

She hadn't spent long with the manuscript—only months. But it had given shape to something she'd felt for years. Patterns she'd chased without knowing why. Symbols repeating across centuries, cultures, and faiths. She used to think they pointed to chaos—collapse.

Now she saw it.

Septem. Not a prophecy, but a principle—seven disruptions encoded in the field. The foundation of Phase Zero. The code that Vega had built his empire on.

The Horsemen were only part of it—four agents of collapse, etched into history like scars.

But there were others—quieter, rarer—who moved differently.

They weren't there to conquer.

They were there to remember.

To return the balance.

Each collapse gives rise to its own correction.

The spiral does not end. It returns.

Birth and death. Control and surrender. War and peace.

Every action. Every reaction.

Male and female.

She turned to the spiral page—the one with the two spheres. Mars and Earth. Their orbits wound together by a harmonic bridge. And there, drawn into the nexus, a figure. Neither male nor female. Neither myth nor messiah. Only present—neither destined nor divine.

In the margin, a faint inscription in hand-worn Latin:

Non dominus, sed filia circulum claudit.

Not the master, but the daughter closes the circle.

Claire closed her eyes. She didn't need to interpret it. She understood.

Vega—Tempest—had believed Olivia was the key to controlling recurrence. The final variable. The child who would finish what the Horsemen began.

But he was wrong.

Olivia wasn't control. She was balance.

She didn't come to rewrite the cycle.

She came to restore it.

Claire smiled. The ache in her chest loosened, the tension she hadn't been able to name since visiting Kolossi in Cyprus as a teenager all those years ago.

It was never a prophecy.

It was always structure.

Resonance passed through blood, through silence, through pattern.

It had always moved quietly through her family—William, herself, Olivia.

All those who came before them.

Not chosen. Tuned.

Carriers of balance, whether they knew it or not.

She reached into her coat and unfolded a single vellum sheet —her own notes, overlaid with Olivia's final resonance models. Drawn from satellite logs and atmospheric records, Olivia's data echoed the manuscript precisely: seven inflexion points, mirrored across two worlds. Frequency and pattern. Geometry and decision.

The spiral repeated.

She slipped it gently between the final two pages of the manuscript.

Not as an annotation.

As closure.

She lowered the lid. The seal clicked shut. The weight lifted —not gone, but no longer hers to carry.

She stepped back as the heavy door creaked open.

Adam entered first, coat damp from the coastal air, eyes scanning her face for something unspoken.

She gave a single nod.

'It's ready.'

He looked at the manuscript, then at her. 'Are you?'

She hesitated. Then: 'Yes.'

Not because she understood everything.

But because Olivia did.

The doors behind Adam opened wider. Footsteps approached —measured, official.

Time was up.

The manuscript would be sealed, transferred, or buried. The world wasn't ready. MI6 would comb it. The Vatican would lock it away.

But Claire no longer feared that.

Because the manuscript was never the point.

Olivia was.

Adam had spent his life reading patterns—signals, threats, cycles. But Olivia wasn't a pattern. She was a pivot. A chance to rewrite the ending.

SEVENTY-THREE

Edinburgh College of Art was hushed, shadows stretching beneath vaulted ceilings like memories too long unspoken.

Claire and Adam stood near the long oak table. Between them, sealed inside a worn leather case, lay the manuscript. Final. Silent.

The double doors opened.

Director Mercer entered first, composed as ever, his expression unreadable. Behind him walked Father Benedetti—the Vatican's envoy—his presence solemn, deliberate.

'We appreciate your efforts,' Benedetti said, his eyes fixed not on them, but on the case.

Claire slid it forward without ceremony. 'It belongs in the archives. Somewhere it can't be misused.'

Mercer barely glanced at it. 'Of course.'

The silence that followed said more than any official statement could. MI6 wouldn't hand over a relic like this without dissecting every encoded truth hidden in its ink.

Claire's fingers traced the worn edge of the case one last time. They couldn't keep it.

The world might never be ready. But the truth never asks permission.

Someone, someday, would dig it up again.

Mercer lifted the case with a precision that suggested familiarity. 'We'll ensure it's handled appropriately.'

Adam exhaled. 'You mean before it ends up back in Rome?'

Mercer's smile was diplomatic. 'We all have our responsibilities.'

Claire and Adam stepped into the cold Edinburgh night.

For a while, neither of them spoke.

Then Adam said, 'Do you think they'll send it back?'

Claire didn't look behind her. 'No.'

Claire walked ahead, her footsteps echoing against the cold stone.

Adam followed quietly. But something sat between them—unspoken.

She stopped. Turned. 'How close was it?'

Adam froze.

'You called her in the middle of the night. You warned her without saying it. I saw it in your face.'

He looked away. 'Too close.'

'Sniper?' she asked.

He nodded.

Claire's voice broke slightly. 'And you never told me?'

Adam stepped closer. 'I didn't know how. I didn't want it to change anything.'

'It changes everything,' Claire said, eyes shining. 'Not because I didn't know. But because you thought I couldn't bear it.'

A beat. Then:

'You don't have to carry all of it, Adam.'

He looked at her, finally. 'I'm trying to learn that.'

She took his hand. Held it. 'Start here.'

* * *

The courtyard was quiet. The scent of damp stone and ink lingered in the air.

Olivia stood beneath the archway, backpack slung over one shoulder. Strands of dark hair had escaped her braid, haloing her face in the dim light.

Claire saw the lines in her daughter's face—not age, but weight. The weight of knowledge. The weight of nearly dying. The weight of choosing to live anyway.

'You're leaving?' Claire asked, though she already knew.

Olivia nodded. 'Tomorrow.'

A pause.

'And the manuscript?'

Claire's jaw tensed. 'It's where it needs to be.'

Olivia's breath curled in the cold. 'Which means it's gone.'

Adam stepped forward, voice low. 'Some things are safer in the past.'

Olivia let out a breath that could have been a laugh. 'That's what we always do, isn't it? Lock up the past. Pretend it can't break through.'

Her eyes shimmered—not with tears, but with something harder. 'But it almost killed me.'

No one spoke.

'And the future?' she said. 'I don't know what it is. But I know it's not theirs anymore.'

Claire stepped closer. 'Olivia—'

'I'm not running from this,' Olivia cut in. 'But I'm not repeating it either. I'm going to fix what I can—the damage, the systems, the silence. And I'm doing it my way.'

She looked at Adam. 'The world's broken. So someone has to start rebuilding. And maybe it's me.'

Adam's voice cracked the stillness. 'And you think you're ready for that?'

Olivia nodded. 'No. But I'm going anyway.'

Adam had feared this—feared the fire in her would chase echoes too far. But now, he saw it wasn't recklessness.

It was resolve.

It was his daughter becoming everything he'd tried—and failed—to protect her from.

Claire's voice trembled. 'You don't owe the world anything.'

'I know,' Olivia said. 'But I owe myself. You gave me a chance—not just to survive, but to choose. That matters.'

She turned to Claire. 'You ended him. Tempest. Vega. You broke the cycle. But someone still has to write the next part.'

Claire blinked back tears. 'He was wrong about you.'

'No,' Olivia said. 'He was right about my potential. He just thought he could define what I'd become.'

Adam's hands clenched. 'You were nearly—' He stopped. Then: 'I should've told you. About everything. But I thought silence might keep you safe.'

Olivia's expression softened. 'I never needed silence. I needed to be trusted.'

Adam stepped forward, but this time he didn't reach for her. Not yet.

'I always saw you as my daughter to protect. I never let myself see who you really are.'

Olivia tilted her head.

'You're not just surviving this. You see the world differently —like your mother, but sharper. Clearer. You've found a way forward I can't even explain.'

He exhaled.

'I didn't just keep you safe, Liv. I held the line so you could cross it.'

Then he embraced her. Fierce. Unapologetic.

He whispered, 'You're not alone.'

She stepped back, eyes steady. 'I know. But this part—I need to do it alone.'

Claire moved to her and pressed her forehead gently to Olivia's.

'You're more than what came before,' she said. 'You're what comes next.'

'Then I'll make it matter,' Olivia promised. 'For all of us.'

She turned. Walked into the dark.

Adam exhaled. 'She's not coming back, is she?'

Claire shook her head. 'No.'

But something rose inside her. Not dread. Not even grief.

Hope.

* * *

Claire's breath caught—a memory blooming from decades ago.

A chapel in Cyprus. A fresco faded by salt and time. A red fleur-de-lis bleeding through stone.

She hadn't understood it then.

Now, she did.

Some marks don't fade. They echo. Not to warn. To remind.

Someone had to carry the pattern forward.

And now, someone would.

* * *

Olivia kept walking.

The weight didn't crush her anymore. It anchored her.

At the corner, she pulled out her phone.

One message. No sender.

> You are right. Keep going.

She didn't need to know who sent it. Or why.

The truth wasn't prophecy anymore.

It was hers.

* * *

It had been months since that night in Edinburgh. Since the manuscript had vanished into the vaults. Since the world teetered, breath held, on the edge of collapse.

She remembered Malik's hand pulling her into the alley, the hush between them, the world holding its breath.

'You and me,' he had whispered. 'That's the only future I believe in.'

His hand in hers, warm and certain.

The way he'd looked at her, like she was the only fixed point left in a spinning world.

He was more than a moment.

He was the anchor.

The reason.

The weight she carried felt different now.

Not a burden.

A thread.

She followed it forward.

And—for the first time in a long while—**Olivia Hayes smiled.**

SEVENTY-FOUR

Claire and Adam sat across from each other in a small, sunlit café tucked away in Edinburgh's historic district. The tension that had shadowed them for years seemed to dissolve with the steam rising from their cups of tea, the warmth of the moment settling gently around them.

Their love had always been a battlefield—unspoken fears, relentless protectiveness—each trying to shield the other from truths too harsh to share. But now, for the first time in too long, they faced each other with open hearts, no longer weighed down by the ghosts of their past.

Outside, the city hummed with life, a fragile echo of what once was. The world had changed irreversibly, but in this quiet moment, something familiar remained—two people who had walked through fire, still finding their way back to each other, not out of necessity, but because they wanted to.

Adam reached for her hand, his fingers brushing hers, his touch lingering with the weight of unspoken apologies.

'Claire,' he said, his voice steady yet raw, like a man finally allowing the truth to surface after years of holding it in. 'I spent so many years trying to protect you, thinking I was doing the right thing. But I only pushed you away when I should've pulled you closer.'

A flicker of something soft crossed her face as she met his gaze. She reached across the table, threading her fingers through his, a silent acknowledgement that, for once, they were facing each other with the truth between them.

'I did the same,' she said quietly, her voice thick with the truth she had long buried. 'I thought keeping you from my burdens would keep you safe. But in doing so, I forgot how to let you in.'

The words hung in the air, a breath between them, but this time, it wasn't heavy. It was healing.

For a long moment, neither of them spoke, just sat in the space they had carved out for each other, where old wounds no longer bled but had finally begun to heal.

Adam broke the silence, his voice quieter now, but no less certain. 'I love you, Claire. Not the idea of you, not the memory of who we were. You. As you are now.'

Claire's eyes glistened, but it wasn't sadness. It was something deeper, something almost sacred. 'I love you, too, Adam. We fought so hard to protect each other. But maybe it's time we fought for something else. For us. For the future.'

She leaned forward, a mischievous glint lighting her gaze as she added, 'What do you say we start with a little adventure? A weekend away. Just the two of us. Somewhere quiet, a bit luxurious... maybe even a little scandalous?'

Adam leaned back in his chair, a playful grin tugging at the corners of his lips. 'Scandalous, huh? Careful, Claire. I'm a man of action—you might regret making that offer.'

She laughed, the sound light and unguarded, a beautiful contrast to the years of heaviness they'd both carried. 'Oh, I'm counting on it.'

Adam chuckled, his eyes warm. 'Alright then. You plan the

getaway. I'll bring the charm. But don't blame me if you fall even more in love with me.'

Claire arched an eyebrow, her smile widening. 'It's a risk I'm willing to take,' she teased, her hand still resting in his.

Outside the café, the city continued its hum, a reflection of the world moving forward, while inside, their past was behind them. Their future, unwritten, lay before them like an open road.

The weight of the years, the battles, and the ghosts of their past had shifted, no longer haunting them but allowing them to move forward, hand in hand. The love they had fought so hard to protect was still there, only now, it wasn't about surviving the storm—it was about walking through it, together, toward whatever came next.

They had walked through the fire together—in Nevada, where the dust of the desert had clung to them as they faced the Horsemen's final push, side by side. The tension of that moment, when they fought to stop the world from crumbling around them, had forged something in them—something stronger than they'd ever been before. It wasn't about survival anymore. It was about living with what came next. It was about choosing each other, choosing the future they could now build. The weight of that shared experience, the sacrifices made, had given them the strength to face what lay ahead.

The quiet healing of the café, the soft glow of sunlight wrapping around them like a protective shield, felt like a new beginning—an interlude between the battles they had fought and the ones that lay ahead.

As they sat in the warm light, the world outside felt just a little less heavy. The echo of their past, of Vega's final move and the chaos they had battled, was still there, but now it was a memory-a reminder that they had fought for each other, and in doing so, had found something worth fighting for.

They were ready for whatever came next.

SEVENTY-FIVE

BRAZIL -THREE DAYS AFTER TARLENS' ARREST

The village had drowned in silence.

Tony stepped out of the battered Humvee, boots crunching on gravel that used to be a playground. The wreckage of São Miguel was unrecognisable—what had once been a canopy of songbirds and morning light was now a wound, half-swallowed by the jungle and stitched together with police tape and satellite tents. FEMA workers moved like ghosts among the ruins.

They didn't stop him. No one did.

He moved without speaking, without asking. Past the cordon. Through the mud. Toward the collapsed shell of Matteo's house.

He found them beneath what had been the sleeping quarters. The debris was skeletal—splinters and half-beams, latticework of ruin. But the children had been together. Gabriel's fingers were still tangled in his sister's hair. Isabella's arm draped over Sofia's chest, as if she had tried, in the final moment, to shield her mother from the rain.

Sofia's eyes were closed. Peaceful. As if she knew.

Tony dropped to his knees.

The sounds of the world—the storm sirens, the static radios, the drone overhead—all folded into a vacuum. He reached for

Sofia's hand. Cold. Damp. Still elegant. He pressed his forehead to it, let out a breath that had been trapped since the moment he first said goodbye.

No tears. Not yet. Only the weight.

A young FEMA officer approached. Clipboard. Pale. 'Mr. Shaw—'

'Don't.' Tony didn't look up.

The officer hesitated, then left him alone.

He worked with bare hands, fingers bleeding by the second grave. Soil gave way slowly, heavy with water and loss. He wrapped the children in the emergency blankets FEMA had laid out. Then Sofia, in her faded shawl. He placed them beneath the acacia tree Sofia had once called sacred. Said it reminded her of the fig trees in Mendoza.

No coffin. No words.

Just the sky pressing down and the jungle watching.

He set her locket—his gift from another lifetime—into the earth beside her. A single picture inside. The four of them, taken on the veranda. That last day before he left.

He stood back, covered the graves by hand, and marked the mound with a flat stone.

No cross. No dates.

Then he sat beside them. For hours. Until the light thinned, until the wind died. Until the world stopped spinning quite so fast.

And when he rose, his shadow no longer followed him.

Tony Shaw disappeared into the cracks of a fractured world.

No more orders.

No more missions.

Nothing tethered him to a world that had already buried him.

The flood hadn't just taken Sofia and the kids.

It had taken the last part of him that was still human.

The worst part wasn't just the loss.

It was the truth that followed.

Solis had known where Sofia was. Had known what was coming.

And had sent men—not killers, not agents—rescuers.

Men sent to extract her, to pull the children from the storm's path.

But Tony, seeing shadows in every shape, had struck first.

He'd killed them.

And by the time he realised they hadn't come to harm her, it was already too late.

Solis had tried to save them.

Tony had stopped him.

Both men, in their own way, had failed her.

That kind of betrayal doesn't break a man like Tony.

It hollows him out. Burns the soul down to ash.

So he vanished.

Into the cracks of the world, where satellites blinked and names held no meaning.

No signals. No calls. Just silence.

But the silence wasn't surrender.

It was focus.

Because the war wasn't over.

Not for him.

Not until the last ghost was in the ground.

* * *

A mile out from the black site, Tony lay prone beneath a cloak of wind and darkness.

Still. Breath even. A stillness born of ritual, not rage.

The long-range rifle nestled into his shoulder like an old friend.

Through the scope, the target emerged—shackled, dazed, flanked by guards who had no idea they were escorting a corpse.

This wasn't justice.

It wasn't revenge.

It was the final note in a requiem.

He slowed his heart.

Could still taste the salt from São Miguel das Missões.

Still hear his son's laughter—chasing gulls across the surf.

One breath in.

One blink.

One last exhale.

He pulled the trigger.

The shot cracked like thunder over the hills.

A clean hole, straight through the heart.

Jeremiah Solis dropped.

Chains clattered against the dirt like broken promises.

No cries. No final words.

Just the weight of judgment, crashing into the earth.

Then came the chaos—alarms, shouts, floodlights cutting the night.

Boots hammering gravel.

But the ridge was already empty.

No sign of Tony Shaw.

Just one spent casing, still warm.

And the truth he left behind.

Some ghosts don't haunt the world.

They end it.

SEVENTY-SIX

Dave Ross stepped off the plane at Dulles International Airport, his movements slow and unsteady. The tremors had worsened. Each breath was shallow, laboured, and tight, the weight of years of exhaustion finally catching up to him. His fingers clenched and unclenched as he fought for control, but hiding the toll it had taken was becoming harder.

For years, he had lived in the shadows—chasing whispers, unravelling conspiracies, exposing the invisible architecture of power. His work had been an endless pursuit, relentless, always searching, always digging. He had pushed himself beyond exhaustion, sacrificing his body, his peace of mind, all for the truth. But now, in the final moments of his life, the truth was no longer something to chase.

Now, with the truth exposed, there was nothing left to chase.

Lisa stood at the arrivals gate, watching him. She had always known how to read him—his moods, his tells, his silences. She saw what others never had: the toll it had taken on him, the quiet war he had fought inside. She saw the weight of knowing, the cost of seeing too much.

She stepped forward as he reached for her. His grip faltered, a reflection of his failing strength, but also of the years of isolation his work had forced upon him.

She caught his arm without hesitation, steadying him.

'You look terrible,' she said, trying to keep it light. Her voice was thick with both concern and affection, the kind of quiet tenderness only someone who had truly known him could offer.

He smiled, crooked and tired. 'You look amazing.'

Her eyes softened, but she said nothing. She just held him, offering him the only support she could. The tremor in his hands was enough to tell her everything she needed to know. She didn't need to ask how long he had been fighting.

By early autumn, the struggle became unbearable. His body, worn from years of fighting in silence, had started to fail him. But it wasn't just the illness—it was the years of carrying too much, of standing at the edges of the world and peering into darkness, seeing the things that most people could never bear to understand. His illness wasn't just physical. It was the weight of a lifetime of knowledge, of secrets that never should have been uncovered, of a world that had kept its dark truths hidden, and Dave had pulled them into the light, piece by piece.

On the last day, golden light spilt through the bedroom window, its warmth at odds with the chill of Dave's body. Lisa sat beside him, holding his hand, her touch grounding him in the quiet final moments. His breath was shallow, a mere whisper of what it had once been. His fingers, once so strong as they had typed out his revelations, now barely grasped hers.

'You were right,' she whispered, her voice barely audible over the soft rustle of the leaves outside. 'About all of it.'

A faint smile crept onto his lips. It wasn't a triumph. It wasn't regret. It was the quiet understanding of a man who had seen it all, done what he could, and found peace in knowing that the world would go on—even without him.

'It was always about control,' he murmured, his voice thin but resolute. It wasn't just the systems he had worked to expose. It was the control that had shaped their lives, work, and fates. The hidden power that never revealed itself.

Then he exhaled—*and didn't inhale again.*

His funeral was a quiet affair. No headlines. No public speeches. Only those who truly understood what he had sacrificed. Only the few who knew the price of his work.

Claire and Adam stood by the graveside, fingers entwined. The autumn wind stirred the leaves around them, scattering them like the remnants of a life that had been lived with purpose, but at great cost.

'He gave us the chance to act when it mattered,' Adam said, his voice low but firm. 'He didn't hold anything back. We owe him that much.'

Maybe that was always the fight—not to win, but to interrupt the rhythm long enough for someone else to rewrite it.

Claire nodded, her gaze distant. She wasn't just thinking of Dave's actions, of his role in uncovering the truth. She was thinking of the way his life had intersected with theirs, of the quiet sacrifices, the moments when he had chosen to do the right thing, even when it hurt him.

'We honour him by living. By making sure the truth never dies.'

The wind lifted the fallen leaves, swirling them around their feet. In the distance, the world moved on. But Dave Ross, in his own quiet way, had ensured it would never forget.

Dave Ross had spent his life uncovering the truth.

And in the end, he ensured it would live on.

SEVENTY-SEVEN

Arkwright's extraction came sooner than anyone predicted.

He hadn't broken the Horsemen's encryption alone.

Claire Hayes had deciphered the pattern—the resonance lattice buried in the manuscript, encoded in myths older than memory.

And Tempest—Silas Vega himself—had given up the access point, whether out of guilt, design, or something colder.

But it was Simon who weaponised it.

He dismantled Final Proof—line by line, protocol by protocol.

Shut down the Nevada servers remotely.

And with a single keystroke, severed the Horsemen's last digital root—

The final strand in a web spun over generations.

But when the servers went dark, so did the illusion of control.

He knew too much.

Moved too fast.

Saw ten steps ahead of anyone watching.

MI6 hadn't protected Simon Arkwright out of loyalty.

They'd hidden him because letting him fall into anyone else's hands—Orion's, the CIA's, even their rivals in Whitehall —was unthinkable.

Orion's kill teams were fractured, scattered—but not destroyed.

And Arkwright was still the one variable no one could model.

He was never just a rogue hacker.

Not a mistake. Not a corrupted asset.

He was the flaw in the system—designed to be unpredictable, forged in silence. He moved like muscle memory—honed by a thousand sleepless nights and the quiet, watchful presence of a cat who never judged.

Too sharp to cage.

Too dangerous to leave behind.

The question had never been about control.

It was always about consequences.

His fingers moved across the keyboard—precise, detached, steady amid the storm.

The last data packets from Nevada to Orion: intercepted, rerouted, and buried in a dead-drop node outside known protocols.

Encrypted under a dead man's switch. Set to detonate logic trees if he vanished.

A contingency.

Insurance.

'Move. Now.'

The voice came from behind—a flat, modulated rasp beneath a black mask.

No name. No emotion. Just orders.

Simon didn't hesitate.

He grabbed the last hard drive—the one that held everything. And his cat.

Bitsy didn't flinch as he slid her into the carrier. She never did.

Simon had always envied that.

They vanished into the rain.

* * *

London shimmered.

Stone slick with runoff. Steel and glass streaked with mist.

Streetlamps swelled into amber halos.

An MI6 transport idled at the curb, engine humming just above a whisper.

Inside, Arkwright sat opposite a woman in a grey suit.

Clinical. Still. Her presence coiled like wire.

'You're a liability,' she said, tone clipped and bloodless.

Simon scratched behind Bitsy's ear. Her purring was the only soft sound left in the world.

'I get that a lot.'

The woman didn't blink. 'MI6 has two options. One—we let you go. You won't last the week. Two—you disappear. New name. New location. No networks. No pings. The world forgets Simon Arkwright ever existed.'

He met her gaze. 'That's not exile. That's execution in slow motion.'

'It's still better than the alternative.'

He glanced at Bitsy, curled against his ribs.

Twenty years of firewalls, betrayals, satellite uplinks, and backdoor wormholes.

Always one step ahead. Always alone.

Except for her.

'She comes with me.'

The woman's lips thinned. Not a smile. Something colder. 'Naturally.'

* * *

And just like that, Simon Arkwright was gone.

Erased from the grid. No traces. No backdoors.

No echo.

The deletion was surgical. Absolute. Perfect.

The world moved on.

But somewhere in the static—

In whatever exile he carved from the dark edges of the map—

A black-and-white cat still purred in his lap.

The world might have forgotten Simon Arkwright.

But Bitsy hadn't.

SEVENTY-EIGHT

As twilight deepened, the soft glow of evening cast long shadows across the room.

Adam's phone buzzed on the table.

He stared at the screen for a moment. Hesitated. Then looked up.

Claire met his gaze. She didn't need to speak. She already knew.

There was no fear in her eyes. No doubt. Only the quiet, steady certainty that had always defined her.

With a sigh, Adam picked up the phone, the weight of what it could mean already pressing down on his chest.

'Hayes here.'

The voice that answered was crisp. Cool. Authoritative.

The kind of voice that didn't ask—it commanded.

'Adam. We have a situation. I need you back in the game.'

Eleanor Grey.

His former MI6 section chief. The woman who once shaped every mission, every choice. The line between orders and autonomy. Between duty and everything else.

'We found something in the manuscript,' she said. 'Ancient

energy signatures. Tarlen was working on something—Sí an Bhrú. Skara Brae. Stonehenge. They weren't just relics. They were part of a network.'

Adam's grip tightened around the phone. His breath hitched —just for a second.

He had thought it was over.

The war.

The shadows.

The ghosts.

He had believed they could finally move forward. That maybe, for once, the future was theirs.

But the past had never finished with them.

He glanced at Claire. She was already watching him.

No fear. No hesitation.

Just the truth. Just resolve.

She knew too.

'I'm retired,' Adam said. The words were even. Calm. But heavier than they should've been.

A pause.

Then Eleanor's voice returned—harder this time. Sharper. A steel edge beneath the control.

'Not anymore. And Claire's coming with you.'

Claire didn't flinch. She reached across the table, fingers lacing through his.

A silent promise. Simple. Absolute.

This wasn't a request.

It wasn't a choice.

It was a reckoning.

They had come too far. Lost too much. Survived too long to walk away now.

Adam didn't hesitate.

He lifted the phone again, his voice low—but unshakable.

'When do we start?'

The line went dead.

Outside, daylight bled across the horizon—orange fading into violet, then into black.

The world was quieting. Settling.

But Adam Hayes knew better.

Claire did too.

He used to think the world moved in straight lines. That you fought, survived, and moved on. But now he saw it: the war circled back, again and again—until someone stood in the breach and said no more.

The fight wasn't over.

Not even close.

EPILOGUE

TEMPEST FACILITY, SCOTTISH HIGHLANDS

Olivia stood in the heart of what had once been Tempest's stronghold.

A place engineered to break the world now hummed with the fragile promise of saving it.

The air inside the lab was taut with electricity and intent. The priority was clear: recalibrate the resonance fields—the invisible force that had once linked Earth and Mars in destructive synchrony. Left unchecked, the destabilised cycle threatened to tear both planets apart.

Her fingers hovered over the console, unwavering. Tempest's earliest miscalculations had corrupted the resonance. Without stabilisation, nothing else mattered. The satellites—once weapons of domination—would fall silent. Mars would remain sterile. Earth would collapse beneath the weight of a system designed to fail.

'Olivia,' Malik's voice crackled through the radio—steady, calm, but edged with urgency. 'We're ready for alignment test one. Beginning resonance stabilisation now.'

She closed her eyes for a breath, grounding herself in the sound of his voice—a comfort shaped by shared survival. But there was no time for sentiment. The fate of two worlds rested on her next decision.

She nodded and activated the sequence.

The screens around her lit up, cascading streams of data into motion. Energy surged through the network. A low hum began to build—not just in the lab but in the very bones of the earth beneath them. The resonance wave expanded, intersecting with the orbital array. For a heartbeat, everything held its breath.

Then—green lights.

'It's holding,' she whispered.

For the first time in years, the planets were in balance.

Professor Halliday, silent until now, let out a long breath. 'We've done it. The resonance is stable.'

Olivia sagged back slightly, the tension finally loosening in her shoulders. The system had held. The worst was over.

Above them, Earth's skies—once black with ash and fractured by superstorms—stretched clear. A pale dawn bled into the horizon. Hope was no longer theoretical. It was measurable.

She looked down at the console. The numbers held.

Everyone had said they wouldn't.

But she'd said she'd try anyway.

She whispered, 'We gave them the truth. That was enough.'

* * *

YEARS LATER – A REBUILT WORLD

The sky was blue again.

Not the metallic grey of engineered weather.

Not the toxic haze of artificial storms.

True blue—the kind you forget to notice until peace returns.

Earth hadn't been saved overnight.

It had taken years—restoring ecosystems, stabilising atmospheric regulators, rebuilding cities drowned beneath rising seas.

But the work had held. The resonance fields remained stable. The satellites had been rewritten—no longer weapons, but guardians.

For the first time in recorded history, Earth had been given what it never truly had before:

A second chance.

Olivia stood on the balcony of Edinburgh's restored skyline, morning light spilling gold across the city below. The scars of the old world remained—pitted stone, sunken streets, ghost towers rising like monuments to failure. But life moved again. Commerce. Culture. Resistance. Resilience.

Tempest's work—twisted, dangerous—had saved them all in the end.

Not because of who he was,

but because someone had chosen to finish what he started.

A chime broke the stillness.

'Olivia, Mars uplink is online,' Malik said through the comm—his voice warm, steady.

She turned toward the terminal as a live feed from Olympus Colony shimmered into view. The Martian sky—dull orange, streaked with dusk—now looked down on something impossible.

Life.

Green spread where once there was only dust.

Atmospheric domes had dissolved. Terraforming had succeeded.

Tempest had designed it, knowing he would never walk there himself. His mind had shaped both ruin and recovery.

Mars was no longer an escape hatch for the powerful.

It was a new beginning for everyone.

Olivia exhaled.

They had done it.

They had broken the cycle.

The recalibrated resonance now linked the two worlds in balance. The system regulated climate patterns and environmental pressure on Earth, averting collapse. On Mars, it sustained terraforming—stabilising electromagnetic fields, creating breathable air, and managing heat. The satellites, once silent sentinels of war, now functioned as environmental custodians, ensuring both planets evolved together, not apart.

A harmony once fractured had been restored.

* * *

Not everything had an answer.

Two of the Horsemen were dead.

Two were locked away, the keys buried so deep the world might forget their names.

But the pattern was older than any prison.

The Horsemen were never just men.

They were memory, motion, momentum.

There would be others.

Not the same faces—but the same hunger, the same pull toward collapse.

And for each of them, someone would rise to stand in the breach.

That was the real cycle.

Not destruction, but resistance.

Inside the lab, Olivia's fingers skimmed the controls.

The resonance pulsed in quiet rhythm. No longer chaotic. No longer deadly. She could feel it now, like a second heartbeat. The satellites whispered corrections in real time.

The system lived.

Mars was no longer a myth. It was a partner.

Two worlds orbiting in harmony—not by force, but by design.

She stepped to the window. Highland sunlight spilled across the hills.

The air was clean. Cold. Full of promise.

The cycle hadn't been destroyed.

It had been rewritten.

The Horsemen believed collapse was fate.

That power must be hoarded. That rebirth demanded sacrifice.

They were wrong.

Olivia turned back to the command centre.

The weight of history behind her.

The weight of the future in her hands.

And for the first time in her life—

She wasn't afraid.

In her personal log, she wrote one line—buried beneath diagnostics, beneath theory:

They built a world on patterns. I'm here to break them.

POSTSCRIPT

THE AEGIS VAULT

Undisclosed Location— 50 Days After Zurich

The world thought it was over.

Orion had fallen.

Once, it had been the Four Horsemen's eyes, ears, and executioner—a black-ops hydra powered by quantum surveillance, psychological warfare, and synthetic disinformation. Its digital empire had steered economies, toppled regimes, and puppeteered global events without ever showing its hand.

And then... silence.

Silas Vega—dead.

Jeremiah Solis—erased.

Zurich headquarters—breached.

The satellite grid—obliterated.

MI6 believed it was finished.

The CIA believed it had won.

Humanity believed it was free.

That was their first mistake.

Power doesn't die in the light.

It waits in the dark.

Viktor Tarlen knew that better than anyone. He had never

357

craved control. He had never needed obedience. What he worshipped—what he thrived in—was chaos.

For forty-nine days, he and Julian Thorne had been buried in a CIA black site. No light. No visitors. No future.

On the fiftieth day, the door opened.

Vance was waiting.

He didn't need guns.

He needed silence—and a signature.

'You get one shot,' he said. 'If you want your place in what comes next... move now.'

Tarlen didn't move.

He smiled.

'Who said anything about moving?' he murmured. 'We make the world come to us.'

The Aegis Vault lit up as backup power reactivated dormant systems. Screens flickered—not with networks or satellite feeds, but with ancient maps, harmonic resonance lines, and topographical overlays of the Earth's oldest sacred sites.

The digital age was dead.

It had never been built to last.

Göbekli Tepe. Baalbek. Skara Brae. The Ring of Brodgar. Puma Punku.

Where others had seen myth, Tarlen saw power. Real power. Buried beneath centuries of ignorance. The kind of power that didn't need bandwidth or biometric firewalls.

Beside him, Julian Thorne spun a knife between his fingers. Still elegant. Still amused. Still very much alive.

'I suppose this is the part where we panic,' he said dryly.

Tarlen's gaze was fixed on the glowing map. 'Panic is for those who've lost.'

Thorne flicked the knife into the steel table. The blade quivered. 'Well, it looks like someone stole our kingdom.'

Tarlen finally turned to him, eyes cold with clarity.

'We were never kings, Julian,' he said.

His voice dropped, resonant and confident.

'We were always the flood.'

Thorne smiled—slow, predatory. 'Ah. Now we're talking.'

A soft ping echoed from the console. A real-time intercept. London.

A location.

A target.

An opportunity.

From the back of the room, Vance crossed his arms. 'One kill team remains in Europe. Ready for deployment.'

Tarlen didn't blink. 'Send them.'

Thorne stretched, spine arching like a satisfied predator. 'You know, Viktor... I think I missed this.'

Tarlen didn't smile.

He didn't have to.

'Then let's make sure it lasts.'

The command was given.

The order was dispatched.

And for the first time in months...

The Horsemen weren't running.

They were moving.

The vault thrummed with energy.

And the resonance was rising to meet them.

OTHER BOOKS BY THIS AUTHOR

Before The Shadows Rise

Book One: The Origin Story

SAS missions in Belfast, Libya, and Belize uncover symbols, stolen tech, and a rising force known only as the Horsemen.

A soldier becomes a legend.

And a conspiracy older than memory begins to wake.

The storm didn't start with collapse—*it started here.*

* * *

Coming Soon

Book Three: Eighth Seal

The seals are broken. The anchors are awakening. And something buried is rising. Across the Earth's oldest sites—Göbekli Tepe, Stonehenge, Chichen Itza—resonant power pulses again.

But this time, it's not just returning. *It's remembering.*

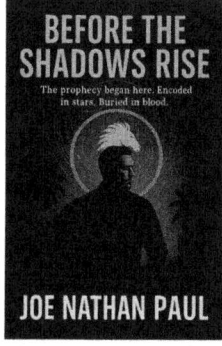
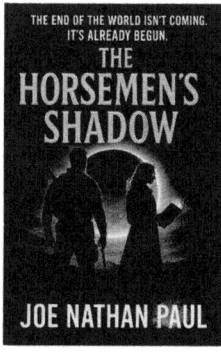

ACKNOWLEDGEMENT

This book is more than just a story. It's a reflection of who I am —my thoughts, fears, struggles, and hopes for the future. Every word, every choice, and every moment spent shaping this world came from a deeply personal place.

I wrote, edited, and designed every part of this book, not just because I wanted to, but because I had to. Somewhere along the way, it became more than a project. It became a calling. A need to create something meaningful. A story that wrestles with the questions I've carried for most of my life: What does it truly mean to survive? Can we outrun the past? Do we shape our fate, or does something greater shape us?

I've always lived between contradictions—solitary, yet deeply connected. Analytical, yet driven by emotion. Strong but shaped by wounds I've never fully named. Like the characters in this book, I've fought battles no one sees. Some still linger. But writing this helped me understand that our scars are not flaws. They're maps. Proof we've endured—and that we still have something left to fight for.

To my wife, Stephanie, and my daughter, Denver—your love is my gravity. You are the reason I keep moving forward. This book is dedicated to you both, not just for the time and space you gave me to create it, but because your light is in every page. You may not always see it, but I do.

Claire and Olivia carry your strength, clarity, and fire. The best parts of this story—the ones that feel alive and unbreakable —belong to you.

To John, my father-in-law, your stories, your service, and your quiet wisdom gave this book a backbone. What you've lived and seen is imprinted in these pages, not as fiction, but as truth.

The Horseman's Shadow is a story of power and survival, yes—but also of love, connection, memory, and meaning. It's a story born out of fear—not just of war or collapse, but of losing what matters most: each other. It's a reflection of my anxiety for the future—of our world, our planet, and the generations that will inherit both our brilliance and our mistakes.

I didn't write this from a place of certainty. I wrote it from the liminal space between light and dark. Between faith and reason. Between fear and defiance.

I poured everything I had into these pages. And if something here finds you, speaks to you, then maybe that's enough because the shadows we face aren't only the ones cast by power.

They're also the ones we carry inside.

With all my heart,
J. N. Paul

Printed in Dunstable, United Kingdom

64397885R00211